Going Blue

A Lost Key Mystery

Book 2

Jeff Hutcheson

Pneumanaut LLC
Gainesville, GA

ISBN: 978-1-7365683-3-0 (Paperback)
ISBN: 978-1-7365683-4-7 (eBook)

Cover Art: Corazon Guzman-Thornton, Artist
Cover Design: Lieve Maas, Bright Light Graphics
Interior Design: Amit Dey

Names: Hutcheson, Jeff, author.
Title: Going blue / Jeff Hutcheson.
Description: Gainesville, GA : Pneumanaut LLC, [2023] | Series: A Lost Key mystery ; book 2
Identifiers: ISBN: 978-1-7365683-3-0 (paperback) | 978-1-7365683-4-7 (ebook)
Subjects: LCSH: Women marine biologists--Gulf Coast (U.S.)--Fiction. | Medals--Fiction. | Treasure troves--Gulf Coast (U.S.)--Fiction. | Best friends--Fiction. | Rescues--Fiction. | LCGFT: Detective and mystery fiction. | BISAC: FICTION / African American & Black / Mystery & Detective.
Classification: LCC: PS3608.U8587 G64 2023 | DDC: 813/.6--dc23

Dedication

To Sherri, my wife, my soulmate, my muse.

Table of Contents

CHAPTER 1

Rescuing Buddy

Cutting the engine to her personal watercraft, Dr. Keri Macintosh glided to the dock of her houseboat nestled in an inlet just off Perdido Bay. Swiftly and efficiently securing the craft, she grabbed her life vest and work bag, then climbed the short stairs to a generous deck composed of plank boards covered with artificial turf. Two extra comfy, all-weather lounge chairs, a small table, and a six-foot, plastic palm tree wrapped with dozens of tiny white lights gave the space a cozy feel. Despite the cool vibe, living here hadn't been part of her plan.

Tossing the gear in the corner, she pulled off her navy blue NOAA work cap, shaking her shoulder-length sandy blonde hair. The music of Bruce Springsteen welcomed her from an old radio attached to the outside wall of the houseboat. A small, square answering machine flashed from inside the kitchen. She grabbed a pitcher of margaritas from the fridge, filled a tall glass, took several gulps, and pressed the play button.

"Hey Keri, you there?" The woman's voice belonged to her best friend, Bailey. "You're starting to piss me off, girlfriend. You better not still be working in the marsh. It's getting dark." Keri took another gulp of her salty nectar as the message continued. "You're already home, aren't you? Put down that 'rita and call me!" The reprimand ended with a click.

Keri sighed. "Yes, mother."

She refilled the glass and headed outside to a small table covered with an indigo-colored silk cloth. An old wooden box served as the centerpiece—its lid open, pictures and mementos spilled onto the tabletop. A large, round, blue candle sat on the right side, and a Mexican sugar skull adorned the left. Keri set her drink down, gently picked up an old ring attached to a silver chain necklace from the keepsakes, and fastened it around her neck. She retrieved a wooden matchstick from a half-empty box and struck it along the grainy strip, igniting the flame, and then lit the blue candle, giving a long glassy look at the photos of her and a young man. In many of the shots, the two were smiling and laughing. She gently brushed her hand across one of the larger prints, longing to feel her fiancé's stubbled cheek or run her fingers through his thick, black hair.

"Talk to me, Tony," Keri whispered.

A plink startled her as a small, thick, wet piece of rope landed on the deck beside the lazy lounge. One end had been wrapped in thick yellow tape. Then Keri heard a splash near the dock, followed by several whistles and clicks. She spotted the culprit—a bottlenose dolphin bobbing in the channel. She walked over to the deck railing to get a better look and recognized the gray markings.

"Well, hello, Ben. Good toss. What are you doing here?"

The mammal swam back and forth erratically. He jumped and splashed, then clicked at Keri. She hurried to the dock and knelt to greet her marine friend. She had begun her career in Marine biology studying dolphins, but she never imagined the connection she'd make with these intelligent creatures.

"What's the matter, boy?

Ben made several chirps, clearly trying to communicate.

"Where's Buddy?" Keri asked. "He usually comes with you."

The dolphin jumped at Buddy's name, flopping sideways with a big splash before swimming toward the bay. He stopped abruptly and looked back at Keri.

"Oh no, has something happened to Buddy?"

Ben whistled louder.

"Okay, okay…" Keri froze as a blue glow appeared in the water about ten yards ahead of the dolphin. *What the…?*

Ben jumped and clicked. She'd never seen him so agitated.

Keri grabbed a life vest and bounded onto her personal watercraft, which she had long ago dubbed the B&B in honor of Buddy and Ben. "Let's go."

She cranked the engine, and the craft immediately sped forward, the throttle stuck in the open position as usual. Barely managing to keep one hand on the steering, Keri steadied herself on the worn seat cushion. Regaining her balance, she whacked the handle to release the throttle and adjusted the speed to match Ben's. As she followed the dolphin, each arch of his back left a blue trail in the water. Keri checked the wake from her craft—all dark. *That's odd,* the biologist thought. She fixed her eyes on her gray friend, who led the way.

Soon the mouth of the Perdido Bay spat her out into the Gulf of Mexico. Ben swam swiftly toward the horizon's faint, fading gray line. Keri followed about five yards behind. Her anticipation grew to a fevered pitch. Speeding onward, her heart raced as fast as her watercraft. Keri's stomach twisted in knots as her anticipation grew with each passing second, like a gathering tsunami. *Where the hell are you taking me, Ben?* The wild thought crossed her mind that maybe this had something to do with Tony. Perhaps the dolphins had found him and were leading her to his location. She missed Tony and longed to see him, hold him again, and feel his arms around her. She knew this unexpected excursion probably had nothing to do with her missing beloved. Still, a dreadful feeling settled in her gut.

Keri glanced at the gas gauge. The needle registered just above the red warning line, barely enough fuel to return home. Ben stopped abruptly and the B&B shot past. She circled back and turned off the engine, clicked a flashlight, and scanned the water. A gray mass wrapped in thick brownish webbing floated a few yards away. Buddy had been caught in an old fishing net.

"No, no! Please, no," Keri exclaimed as she removed the life vest to give her more maneuverability for this rescue. She grabbed a knife from her supply compartment and dove into the water.

When she reached the dolphin, she heard a hiss of air from its blowhole. *Thank God you're still alive.*

"Oh, Buddy, what happened to you?" Keri said, cradling the netted mass.

Buddy whined, and his eyes opened. The net had torn a cut on the right side of his head, probably from when he had tried to break free.

"That might leave a scar, my friend." She patted him gently. "Hang tight. I'm gonna get you out of here."

Several ends of the rope had been capped with yellow tape. *Ben must have chewed off a piece.* Keri cut sections of the thick mesh, careful not to nick Buddy. He wiggled out of the confines and circled about. Ben joined him. The dolphins squealed loudly, celebrating Buddy's new freedom. They glided over to Keri and nuzzled her gratefully.

"You're welcome," Keri replied.

She turned to swim back to the B&B. Only it was gone. The watercraft had floated about twenty-five yards away from her and the current had continued to push it farther out into the Gulf and on a southwestward course. Buddy's head surfaced on Keri's left side as she began to paddle toward her ride. He moved closer, and she gripped his dorsal fin and held tight. As if part of a show at a sea aquarium, the dolphin towed Keri back to her watercraft.

She climbed on board and smiled at her ocean friend. "Thanks, Buddy."

The dolphin clicked and whistled as if to say you're welcome, then Ben joined him, and they swam off. Though Buddy was injured, Keri knew that he would heal more naturally and probably quicker among his own kind than with a human vet. She'd learned from her studies that dolphins were very good at caring for their own.

The sun had set, and the stars twinkled as the evening transformed into night. Keri estimated she had about fifteen minutes of daylight left. She sat quietly, enjoying these final moments of the fading day. As Keri stared at the last rays of light, she felt the strangest urge to chase the sun. The thought of disappearing over the horizon felt comforting. Of course, this idea made no logical sense and would be extremely dangerous. Still, the light beckoned.

Keri looked back toward the shore. The Florida panhandle had receded even more now, and the opening of the Perdido Pass had shifted farther east. Retrieving a small spyglass from an equipment pouch, she opened it to full length and peered into the device. The dark silhouette of an abandoned oil rig perched on the horizon. A buoy floated to the right. Keri panned the small telescope searching for the glowing water she had seen earlier, but found nothing. Finally, she collapsed the looking device. The breeze felt chilly now. She stared at the horizon as the sunlight took its final bow.

Time to go home. Just as Keri cranked the engine, a bluish glow in the water appeared about twenty yards to her left. In the corner of her eye, she thought she saw a man floating on a surfboard, but the image vanished as soon as she turned to look. As before, the watercraft lurched forward, throttle wide open. Distracted by the strange sighting, the sudden movement threw Keri off the back and into the Gulf.

CHAPTER 2

Matilda

"Oh, come on!" Keri yelled, treading water. She could only watch as the B&B headed farther into the Gulf, the life vest flapping behind. One of the straps must have gotten caught in the seat.

Why didn't I put that on before I cranked the stupid thing? The scientist slapped the water. *Rookie move, Keri. Steady, breathe,* she told herself. *Assess the situation, then act.* The B&B, barely visible now, continued its course to nowhere. Swimming for the shore was her only option. Keri lay flat on her back, kicking and paddling toward the beach. After several minutes, she stopped to assess her progress. The shoreline had withdrawn. *Not good.* The current had pulled her outward. *I could use a dolphin ride about now.* "Ben! Hey Buddy!" she called, but her marine friends were gone.

At least the sun had warmed the ocean to near bath temperature. Hypothermia wouldn't be an issue. The challenge would be to conserve energy and find a path out of the current and back to shore. Keri leaned back and swam east. The stars above twinkled, and Keri took comfort that the heavens were watching. Although an excellent swimmer, her arms and legs began to ache. She stopped and checked her progress again. The ocean had pulled her farther out.

"Crap!"

Her heart thumped rapidly. She tried to stay calm. Panic wouldn't help and might even make things worse. She continued her swim east, sometimes just kicking to allow her arms to rest. Scanning the distant shoreline, she spotted a tiny glow of light coming from a beach house. That would be her new point of reference. Keri began kicking and paddling again, pushing past the pain in her muscles this time. When she stopped, she barely had enough strength to tread water. After floating on her back for a few minutes, Keri took a deep breath, then allowed herself to sink. The water enveloped her with a loud rush in her ears, followed by peaceful quiet. Her spine tingled as if she'd just stepped into a soothing balm.

The ocean seemed inviting, like it held the secrets she longed to know. Weightless and warm, and with a lungful of air, she rested and slowly floated down. For the first time in months, Keri felt some peace. She had cried enough these last few months to fill the Gulf. But why did she sense relief here, suspended in the murky sea? A strange but disturbing thought crossed her mind. Wouldn't it be nice if she could breathe while underwater? What if she could inhale this liquid comfort? Maybe it would feel like being in the womb. She let the Gulf seep into her mouth and tasted the saltiness. She opened her eyes and felt the sting of the saltwater, but she quickly adjusted. She couldn't see far into the blackness but felt surprisingly safe. A faint blue glow appeared a few yards away. At first, Keri assumed it was the bioluminescence, but it seemed softer, almost ethereal, and it occurred underwater. Then she felt *his* presence as if her beloved was here.

Please, show me a sign. I'll come to you.

A loud horn roared deafeningly above her. When she looked up, the surface glowed brightly. Keri swam to the top and breathed in the fresh air. She raised one hand to shield her eyes from a spotlight now trained on her. Two more blasts screeched as the approaching craft slowed and came alongside. Long wooden beams stretched outward on both sides of the vessel, thin nets tightly wound around them. A tall, robust woman stood at the stern, hands curled into fists on her hips. As the boat bobbed in the waves, her silhouette remained as fixed and sturdy as the central mast. Thick, flaming red hair danced in the wind across her broad shoulders. Strength, beauty, and intellect blended into a rugged sensuality, as if she could haul in those nets without the help of pulleys, while at the same time enchanting any would-be suitor. Her five ex-husbands were living testaments that both were true.

"Cut the engines! Person overboard!" she bellowed, peering over the side. "Keri, what in the world are ya doin' out here, hon?"

"Matilda!" Keri replied. "Oh, thank you, God."

A crewman threw an orange, doughnut-shaped lifesaver to Keri. She wriggled into the center of it and paddled to the back of the boat. They assisted her onboard.

"I'm so glad to see you," Keri said, completely exhausted, leaning with her elbows on her knees. "I don't know how much longer I could have lasted."

The captain's face wrinkled in strong concern. "What happened?"

"Ben showed up at my houseboat—never seen him so upset. I followed him out here. It turns out Buddy had gotten tangled in an old fishing net."

Matilda scoffed. "Those damn irresponsible amateurs."

"Buddy's fine. I cut him free."

"That's good."

Keri looked over the side, then back at the captain. "Did you see any… glowing water?"

The furrow in Matilda's brow deepened. "No, not lately anyway. Why?"

Keri averted her eyes. "No reason, just thought I saw some bioluminescence earlier."

The captain squinted her eyes at Keri. "You okay, hon?"

Keri forced a smile as a wellspring of grief began to spill through her eyes. "I miss him."

The shrimp boat captain nodded understandingly, then said, "I know it hurts, hon. But he ain't in that water, and you ain't no fish. You're a marine biologist, Keri. Don't be gettin' any crazy ideas again. Ya, hear me?"

Keri chuckled at Matilda's metaphors. "I hear you."

"Don't make me catch you with my nets," Matilda threatened, staring at Keri. "You know I will."

"Yes, you will," Keri answered, touched by the shrimper's loving threat. Suddenly it seemed like three years ago. Keri could feel the pull of those shrimp nets surrounding her, saving her from a grief-stricken decision to disappear into the ocean.

"How did you find me?" Keri asked.

"We were heading in for the day when that thang you call a boat came roaring by. I recognized it as yours, only no one was at the helm. I see you haven't fixed the throttle yet."

"Been meaning to get around to it."

"Mm-hmm," the shrimper replied with a rebuking tone. "And you just happened to fall off the B&B?"

"I got distracted. Like I said, I thought I saw someone… I mean some glowing algae."

Matilda squinted skeptically. "You about gave me a heart attack, young lady."

"Sorry about that."

"We're damn lucky I found you."

Keri gave Matilda a long, grateful look. "Thank you!"

"No thanks necessary," the captain replied. "I'm just glad you're safe." Then she looked up. "Take us home, boys!"

The horizon blended into a solid wall of darkness now. Not far from where Keri had been rescued, unseen by her or the shrimp boat captain, the water glowed blue, then faded again.

CHAPTER 3

October 17th

When the shrimp boat reached the Perdido pass, the trawler slowed, turned right at Walker Island, and headed inland toward Keri's home. The moon reflected a shimmering path through the dark waters and backlit several lingering clouds like giant suspended nightlights in the sky.

"Cut the engines," Captain Matilda ordered as a small fishing boat approached.

A slender man sat in the back of the small craft, one hand on the stick throttle of the single motor. This evening, as with most days, he sported an old, stained fishing vest, the kind with multiple pockets, and an equally "broken-in" camo-colored ball cap with 'I'd Rather Be Fishin' ' stitched across the front.

"Cricket!" Keri exclaimed.

"Hey, Keri," he replied.

Cricket wasn't his real name, but it might as well have been. He worked at the local car wash but acquired his nickname because of his love for fishing and a certain kind of bait.

Matilda joined Keri at the starboard side. "Cricket's gonna take you the rest of the way home," the captain said. "I need to get my catch off this boat before it gets to smellin'."

Keri hugged her sea-faring friend. "Thanks. You saved me."

"I got your back, hon. But you be more careful."

"I will, and may you have fair winds and following seas," Keri said. Then she climbed down to the bass boat and sat on the middle bench.

The fisherman removed his cap and bowed his head. "Captain, it's good to see ya."

Matilda barely nodded, then barked, "Take us home boys."

"She's something else, ain't she," Cricket said, donning his cap.

Keri smiled. "You sweet on Matilda?"

"Naw, I just admire her, that's all," the fisherman answered, still staring toward the shrimp boat.

"Well, I'm sure she's looking to expand her shrimping business."

"What are you talkin' about?"

"Guess who are the captains of her fleet?"

Cricket shrugged.

"Her five ex-husbands."

"Is that right? Well, I'll be darned. Hmmm," Cricket commented as if he were pondering the possibility of becoming number six.

"Besides, I thought you were secretly crushing on Bailey."

The fisherman adjusted his position. "I don't know what y'er talkin' about."

Keri smiled. "Sure you don't."

Cricket opened the throttle and steered toward Lost Key. Even though the small craft had no running lights, Keri felt safe. The local fisherman always bragged that he could navigate these waters in his sleep. He'd proven his prowess the night he saved Mark and Bailey from a couple of thugs back on Dauphin Island. Keri imagined how terrifying it must have been riding in this small boat while someone shot at them. Fortunately, Cricket knew a secret way through the brush, and they had escaped.

"I see you got the bullet holes patched," Keri said.

Cricket nodded confidently. "This ole gal's tough," he boasted. "She's still got some life in 'er."

Keri smiled, appreciating the fisherman's loyalty to his old boat.

"So, how's your dolphin buddy?" Cricket asked.

"He's gonna be alright, thankfully."

"You know, normal people don't have fish for friends."

"Dolphins are mammals, not fish," the biologist stated.

"No offense intended. It's just amazing how close you are to them."

"I used to study dolphins. That's how I met Ben and Buddy's pod. One day I accidentally dropped a yellow swim cap in the water and one of them brought it back to me. I tossed it back to them just to see what would happen, and they retrieved it again."

"No kidding, wow."

"At first, I thought it had something to do with the color yellow, but after a while they'd bring back anything I pitched to them. I figured they just needed to get to know me better. These are wild animals. You don't just swim over and pet them. They may look like they're smiling all the time, but they could hurt you if they felt threatened. Besides, the oils on our human hands aren't good for them. Anyway, my relationship with them grew over time, especially with Ben and Buddy."

"Well that there is just plum amazing, Doctor Keri."

The marine biologist smiled. "Yeah, it is."

A few miles later, Keri saw the glow from the windows of her houseboat. She'd never turned the inside lights on when she had suddenly departed, so that could only mean one thing.

As Cricket pulled alongside the dock, a voice greeted her. "About time you got home," said a young woman near Keri's age, scowling from the top of the deck stairs. She stood with one hand on her hip and wore dark blue shorts and white boat shoes. Her shiny black hair brushed the shoulders of a faded gray sweatshirt, ragged at the ends.

"Hey, Bailey," Keri said, smiling slightly. Then she turned to her chauffeur. "Come on up and have a margarita."

Cricket glanced at their fuming friend. "Take a rain check on that, I got to go catch a fish."

"Right now?"

Cricket looked at Bailey again, whose scowl had intensified. "Umm, yep, now is the best time."

Keri smiled as she read Cricket's hat. "I don't blame you. I'd rather be fishin', too." Climbing out of the boat she said, "Thanks for the ride."

"Anytime." He shot Bailey a final look. "Good luck."

The fisherman glided away, and Keri ascended the steps to the main deck of her houseboat.

Bailey held up a hand and blocked the entrance.

"What?" Keri asked, feigning ignorance.

"You know damn well what!" Bailey fired back.

Keri avoided her friend's piercing stare.

Bailey stepped closer and said, "I've been trying to reach you for days. You don't answer my calls. You're never here when I come by these past few weeks."

"I've been working!" Keri said sharply.

"Then today, of all days, you decide to take another swim in the middle of the Gulf!"

The comment surprised Keri. "Matilda contacted you."

"She's worried about you. So am I."

"Look, I was rescuing Buddy."

Bailey gave her a skeptical glare. "I heard all about your dolphin tale."

"It's true. I saved Buddy," Keri said, slightly annoyed. "He would've drowned if I hadn't cut him loose. He'll have a scar to prove it."

"Okay, I believe that part of your story. But you, falling off the B&B? Really?"

"Serious, serious," Keri said, maintaining eye contact.

Bailey scrunched her brow and squinted her eyes. "Don't say that unless you mean it."

"I know the rule, girlfriend." Then she repeated, "Serious, serious."

Bailey's expression softened, and her shoulders relaxed. She seemed more hurt than angry.

"I'm sorry," Keri said. "But at least I'm not running off chasing crooks like you did."

Bailey's nostrils flared, and her jaw clenched. She held her reprimanding posture for a minute longer, then wrapped her arms around Keri in a loving hug.

Keri hugged her back, leaning her head on Bailey's shoulder, as her grief spilled down her cheeks again.

Bailey squeezed her friend tight, saying, "Don't disappear on me like that. You hear me?" Then she looked Keri in the eye. "I'm concerned about you."

Keri took a breath. "It's just been tough lately."

"This time of year, always is," Bailey said and hugged her again. "We'll get through it."

Keri pursed her lips and nodded. Her mind knew she'd get through it, but her heart believed the pain would never end.

Bailey put one arm around Keri and escorted her onto the deck. Pushing aside several open books featuring various pirates and the treasure history of Lost Key, they sank into the two lazy lounges. Each grabbed a freshly made margarita Bailey had prepared and listened to the beach music serenade them over the old radio.

Bailey smoothed her sweatshirt with her free hand, pulling at a thread on her frayed garment. She rolled her eyes, set her drink down, and snapped the string away. It unraveled more.

"Comin' undone there?" Keri teased.

"It would seem so." Bailey grabbed her glass and raised it toward the small memorial table that Keri had set up before her unexpected excursion. The round blue candle still flickered to one side, illuminating several pictures of Keri and her beloved. A larger one had been taped to the underside of the keepsake box lid. The photo captured the couple in a side hug and smiling at the camera.

"To Antonio," Bailey said, lifting her glass.

"To Tony," Keri said, breathy and tearful. She took several gulps of her drink and noticed Bailey staring at her.

"What?" Keri asked.

Bailey shook her head and sipped her drink.

"Look, don't hassle me right now." Keri looked at Bailey and downed the rest of her salty nectar. "You got a problem with that?"

"Maybe," Bailey said.

Keri's face flushed in anger. She considered a few choice words but suddenly realized she wasn't mad at her best friend. The last thing she ever wanted to do was hurt Bailey.

"Sorry. I don't know what's wrong with me," Keri said solemnly.

"I do," Bailey replied, looking concerned. "It's October seventeenth, the anniversary of the day the love of your life went missing."

Keri stared vacantly at the memorabilia. "I can't believe it's another year already."

"Nineteen ninety-two, three years since… that day."

"Feels like it happened only hours ago."

"November first is not far away," Bailey said. "The Day of the Dead."

Keri nodded. "Día de los Muertos," she said with a slight Spanish accent, mixed with a southern drawl.

"Isn't the Day of the Dead supposed to be a celebration?" Bailey asked.

"Oh yeah, you should see the shindig Antonio's family throws," Keri answered, pouring herself another drink. "It's quite a party."

"Are you going? You know they miss you."

Keri shook her head and adjusted her posture again as if the deck chair had suddenly become uncomfortable. "No. It's just too painful. I love the idea that he would somehow come to visit me on that day. But instead, I feel his absence even more intensely. After three years, I thought the pain would get better, but it gets worse."

"Grief works by its own schedule," Bailey said, taking another sip.

"If I could just find some closure, some answer as to what happened."

"There may not be one."

"There has to be!" Keri said more loudly than she intended.

"You may have to accept what you can't find."

Keri's eyes fixed on her friend as the hard truth of that statement fully landed. "How do I do that?"

Bailey grabbed her friend's hand. "Not by yourself. We'll find a way together."

Keri patted her friend's arm. "I don't know what I'd do without you."

"Well, you're never gonna have to find out." Bailey's face gave a playful expression. "I brought you a gift just to ensure that very thing."

She reached into her pocket and pulled out two bracelets made of dark brown leather with weavings and beads of yellow. Keri perked up, touched by this thoughtfulness.

"You make these?" she asked.

"Yep. No other two like these anywhere," Bailey said with a smile. "They're friendship bracelets."

Though grateful for the gesture, Keri said, "Aren't those for high schoolers?"

"They're for friends," Bailey retorted. "Stretch out your arm."

Keri smiled as Bailey tied the bracelet around her wrist.

"Now, make a wish."

Keri closed her eyes, then said, "Done."

"Never take this off. Got it? You wear it until it falls off naturally, and your wish comes true." Bailey smiled, very satisfied with herself. "Your turn. Tie one on my wrist."

Keri tied the other bracelet around Bailey's arm.

"Remember, there are people who love you on this side of life, too," Bailey said in a reprimanding tone after she had made her wish.

Keri smiled and held up her arm with the new wristlet attached. Bailey lifted hers as well. They clicked bracelets and simultaneously said, "Friends forever."

CHAPTER 4

A Piece of Eight

The next evening Keri stood ankle-deep in the marsh she loved and protected. Black rubber wading boots kept her feet dry and shielded her from any dangerous creatures lurking below. Her sandy blonde hair had been pulled into a ponytail through the opening in the back of her navy blue ball cap with the letters NOAA stitched across the front. A clipboard dangled to one side from a leather strap around her neck. She cradled a long camera lens in one hand, her fingers adjusting the focus. Her other hand wrapped about the base with one finger poised above the shutter button. When she got the sharpness just right, she took a photo of a budding plant, another of a tadpole, and several more of various species of wildlife that made this marsh their home.

Keri paused and smiled. She felt grateful not to be shackled to a tiny cubicle bogged down in some mind-numbing tasks while the fluorescent lights sucked the life from her spirit. Keri's office consisted of miles of sugar-white seashore, protected wetlands, and state parks between Pensacola, Florida, and Orange Beach, Alabama. Nature's office brimmed with life.

The fading sun painted the sky with rich reddish blues heading toward the black of night. The chorus of night creatures would soon join the sounds of the wind and the waves as they prepared their song. As she relished the twilight, a fish flipped in the air and made a small splash nearby. Another minor disturbance off to the right drew her attention. Though in love with this swampy stretch, Keri remained ever alert. She squinted toward the wavelet, her eyes adjusting to the dimming light. The more dangerous creatures never make much noise. Even a ripple in the water could be an approaching snake or, worse, the stealth wake of a gator. A small head peeked above the water, followed by a grayish-green shell trailing behind. A turtle had come to visit. She could see the familiar heart-shaped discoloration on top of its back. This reptile wasn't just any sea turtle. She and Bailey had rescued it one day from the side of the road and released it back into its natural habitat. Since then, the marine creature had thrived and frequently appeared when they were near. Like a grateful pet, it often arrived carrying something in its mouth, as if presenting a gift for saving its life.

"Snaps! It's you!" Keri said. She splashed over toward her marine friend. She raised her camera and clicked a shot. It turned left, then right, then stopped. "It's okay, Snaps. It's just me. Smile."

The tortoise cradled a shiny object in its mouth. Snaps' gifts usually amounted to nothing more than an old beer can, a pop-top, or just plain trash. The fact that Snaps brought the items made them priceless. Keri also valued these for another reason. Determined to protect these marshlands, the marine biologist had been building an inventory of all the crud that didn't belong and sharing that information whenever she could. She loved opportunities to showcase the beauty and wildlife of these wetlands. If people could see the majesty of the bayous, then they'd stop using them as their personal garbage dump. She presented beautiful pictures and films of nature at its best and then highlight all the stuff discarded there. Her talks ended with a big reveal when she would say, "Don't take my word for it; the wildlife brought me this trash."

"What did you bring me today?"

She squatted down for a closer look. Instinctively, the sea creature retreated into its shell, dropping its gift into the water. She quickly grabbed the object before it hit bottom.

"What have you found, Snaps?" She turned it over in her hand, studying it carefully. She held a gold-looking coin, somewhat dulled from age and being underwater. She ran one finger around the uneven edges, tracing the roundish shape. It looked homemade or banged up. A cross had been embossed on one side, surrounded by the words "Libertad." Carved on the flip side, she saw the face of a lady who looked to be wearing a crown as if she were royalty and a date that read 1785.

Keri gasped. She blinked several times, pressing the medallion hard between her fingers, half expecting this to be a fluke sand dollar. But it held firm. It was indeed an old coin.

"Snaps, where did you get this?" Keri asked.

Her turtle friend looked left, then right, paddled a couple of feet, and stopped.

Keri's mind raced as feelings swirled inside her like someone had unlocked a keepsake of memories of her beloved Tony, telling tall tales of shipwrecks and treasure.

She rubbed the object with a dry spot on her navy-colored NOAA pullover. Once the dirt had been wiped clean, the gold color shined. It looked like an old Spanish dollar, "a piece of eight," as they're called. If that were true, what would this be worth?

"Snaps, if this proves authentic, you've just ruined my presentation," she said.

The turtle floated. Its head turned toward her as if it could understand what she said.

Keri feared word would get out that there might be Spanish gold here. Then the marshland would be overrun with treasure hunters and opportunists, searching and digging, with little regard for protecting this delicate ecosystem.

"Come here, boy. You deserve the credit for this find," Keri said. She gently placed one hand under the turtle's belly to steady the creature. He protested at first, kicking his webbed feet as if in danger, then relaxed and turned his greenish head toward her. Next, Keri laid the coin atop Snap's shell. "Hold still," she said. Grabbing the camera hanging around her neck with her free hand, she aimed the lens for the shot.

As she depressed the button, the sound of another click startled her. Whirling around, Keri's foot caught on something under the water, causing her to lose her balance. The marine biologist fell sideways into the marsh. Instinctively she let go of Snaps as she tried to brace herself with one hand and hold the work camera high in the air with the other. Keri caught a glimpse of someone at the edge of the shoreline, retreating behind the brush.

"Who's there?" Keri called. "The park's closed."

No one answered; the hazy figure had disappeared.

Keri maneuvered to her feet and sloshed a couple of steps in the shin-deep water toward the sighting.

"Hey, wait!" she yelled.

A car door thudded shut. Then an engine started, followed by the crunching of tires gripping the gravel-dirt road. The sounds quickly faded into the twilight.

Keri turned to check on her turtle companion, but he too had disappeared.

"Snaps? Where are you?" Keri said, scanning any possible hiding places the reptile might have fled.

She didn't see Snaps anywhere, and the fading light of day made spotting him even more challenging.

The marine biologist splashed back to her truck, slung her equipment bag on the front seat, and grabbed a flashlight. She fanned the beam across the area, carefully looking for that grayish-green shell or the glimmer of a gold coin, but nothing. Snaps and the medallion had vanished into the night.

Keri walked toward where she had seen the stranger. She discovered some tire tracks a few yards ahead and knelt to get a closer look.

Were these here before?

Keri slowly waded back into the water, panning the light in a semi-circular path. She carefully searched the area where she had fallen, but no sign of the medallion. Despite the balmy evening, a chill swept through her. These wetlands had become Keri's private sanctuary over the years, but tonight she felt unsafe.

She returned to the truck, laid an old towel on the driver's seat, and scooted behind the wheel. As Keri started the engine, she noticed a small card underneath the windshield wiper. She pulled it from under the blade. In the dim light of the cab she saw the image of her beloved. Keri gasped as her heart leapt to her throat. The photo, worn and cracked, had captured Tony radiant and smiling, sitting on the back of his boat, hair wet as if he'd just come up from a dive. His cheerful expression looked like a kid giddy with infatuation. She shivered at the handwritten note on the back.

Tony would have loved what you found.

CHAPTER 5

The Visitor

Keri drove, eyes fixed forward. Emotions churned inside. Her stomach felt as twisted as the winding roads leading home. The mysterious stranger in the park had set her on edge. Yet Keri felt even more disturbed by the photo left on her windshield. She'd never seen it before. Had the mystery person taken it?

Soon, the familiar dolphin-shaped mailbox greeted her with a smile; the lucky number 117 tacked down the post. Keri turned into the dirt driveway and pulled up to a small white picket fence and homemade wooden welcome sign that read, 'Come sit a spell.'

Still feeling jittery and annoyed, she climbed out of the truck and ambled to the gate leading to the deck of her houseboat. Keri kicked off her shoes, scrunched her toes in the plastic turf, and took several full, slow breaths trying to soothe her nerves. The old outdoor radio welcomed her with a beach song. This deck had become her favorite cozy outdoor space. Strings of tiny glowing clear and blue bulbs adorned the fence, the deck railing, and even some windows. Keri loved lights, especially the blue ones.

She'd constructed this mini oasis to flow seamlessly into the old houseboat. Next, she gave the aged craft a makeover with new plank siding, a blue tin roof, and more lights. However, tonight the place felt as artificial as those lights strung around it.

Despite appearances, Keri didn't live alone. Like a houseguest who had overstayed their welcome, grief had appeared the night her fiancé had vanished and never left. Work cooled the prolonged pain by taking her mind off the reality of Tony's disappearance. Studying treasures and pirates provided similar solace. She had loved listening to Tony spin tales of ancient marauders and lost gold, and how he got all boyish as he told them. For Keri, the greatest treasure, now a fading memory, was their time together.

She tossed her keys onto the kitchen counter, then pushed the flashing button on her message machine.

"Hey, it's me," Bailey said. "You working late again? It's Sunday, a day of rest. You've heard of rest, right? Hurry up and call me. Time to take a break and play."

"Jeez, girl," Keri answered while reaching for a pitcher of margaritas in the fridge. "Just give me a minute."

Keri took her drink outside and sat it on the round table between the two lounges. Then she opened the memorial box and propped the new picture against the lid. Lighting the candle, she settled onto one of the lazy chairs. She poured herself a tall one, raised a glass to her departed, and took several big gulps. As far as shrines go, this one wouldn't win any awards, but then awards weren't the purpose of such memorials. The intent was to make the departed loved one feel welcomed when they came for a visit. Keri had learned about this Day of the Dead ritual from Tony's family. She had been setting up her ofrenda ever since that awful night. Though it helped ease her suffering, he never visited, at least as far as she knew. Of course, the Day of the Dead officially occurs November first, but Keri figured the departed don't worry about calendars like the living do. She'd welcome a visit from her love anytime.

Sighing, she guzzled down the rest of the salty lime-green indulgence, let her head fall back, and stared at the new photo. *Why does Tony look so happy?*

Melancholy enveloped her as she fondled the old ring hanging from her leather strap necklace. Looking at a string of numbers engraved inside, Keri shook her head and smiled. Only Tony would inscribe a betrothal gift with some kind of secret code. A heaviness returned. Now she'd never know what these numbers meant.

It's gonna be one of those nights.

She gazed dreamlike at the dull, graying gift her beloved had given her. No jeweler would have put this on display, full of dents and imperfections on the surface, and scratches on the inside. The gift comforted her. No other engagement ring could match this one. Tony hadn't bought this at any jewelry store. He'd found this special gift on an ocean-floor dive.

"Keep this close, and I'll always be near," he had said.

A warm breeze caressed her, carrying a pleasant, familiar aroma. She held the ring tightly, closed her eyes, and drifted. Memories played in her mind of her and Tony laughing. Like the night she couldn't take her eyes off him as he lay propped up on one elbow, waiting for her, covered from the waist down under a thin sheet. The pale moonlight spilled through the windows, bathing his smooth, tan skin and toned muscles with a radiant glow. She had put on the shirt he'd worn that day. Propping one knee on the foot of the bed, she slowly unfastened the buttons one at a time, preparing to join her lover.

Keri sat up with a start, no longer in that bedroom bliss but back on the deck. She realized why the aroma of the breeze comforted her. It smelled just like Tony! She crossed her arms, trying to hold the memory around her. A tingling sensation caused her to shiver. That's when she heard the whisper.

"Go blue," a very faint voice said.

Keri gasped and listened intensely. "Who's there?" she asked for the second time that day.

She turned her head one way, then another, but saw nothing. The wind gusted. She sat motionless, her eyes drawn to every sound, tracking even the tiniest movement. A loud thud echoed from the living room, followed by what sounded like the rustling of pages.

Keri's heart pounded. She thought of running next door and getting Clem to check things out. Instead, she stood motionless, focused on the doorway.

Oddly enough, she didn't feel in danger. Tony's comforting sweet smell and the whisper in the wind were somehow disarming. The mysterious rustling had to point to something other than an intruder. Could it be true?

Oh, please, let it be him. Keri's mind vividly imagined him sitting on the couch, ready to regale her with another treasure tale and a plausible explanation of where he'd been for the past three years.

Curiosity overwhelmed her hesitation; she rushed to the door and peeked inside. "Hello? Anybody there?"

The chimes jingled in the wind. Adrenaline flowing, senses fully alert, Keri scrutinized the room and located the source of the odd disturbance. A book had fallen off the shelf and lay open on the floor. Relief at finding no intruder gave way to disappointment at seeing an empty sofa. Frustration and grief swelled like a storm surge inside her. She picked up the sugar skull from the small ofrenda table and flung it into the channel.

"Stupid superstition!" she yelled. Leaning against the doorframe, she slid down and cried.

Composing herself, Keri moved to pick up the hardback. She paused, then squatted. The book had opened to a page with a picture of an ancient coin with rough, uneven edges. She stared at the imprint. "No way."

The picture looked just like the artifact Snaps had brought her. A board creaked just outside the door, and Keri glimpsed movement in her peripheral vision.

Keri gasped, turned, and said, "Tony?"

A tall, broad-shouldered man completely blocked the doorway.

He smiled. In a brusque voice, he said, "Hey, Keri."

CHAPTER 6

Clem

Putting her hand over her heart, Keri gasped. "Oh, Clem, it's you."

Clem remained in better shape at fifty-eight than most men half his age. He'd traded the uniform for shorts and flip-flops when he retired from the Navy. The homemade tank top, which looked like Clem had cut off the sleeves with dull scissors, revealed his still fit and muscular arms. His balding head might have been the only sign of aging, except he kept that hidden most of the time with a bandanna. Tonight's covering looked like a mini-American flag.

"Didn't mean to startle you," he said in a robust, gravelly voice.

Keri smiled. "Always good to see you, my friend."

Clem reached to help her from the floor. "Tough night?"

"Yeah. Worse than usual."

As Keri took his hand, nostalgia came over her. She remembered the night this gentle, strong guardian had appeared like an angel amid her despair. Keri had been lying flat in the bottom of a small boat attached to a dock in a remote cove off the bay. She remembered gazing up at the night sky as the skiff gently rocked in the waterway. A million stars twinkled and sometimes even arranged themselves into shapes. Water had seeped through a tiny hidden leak and pooled underneath her up to the back of her ear. Her legs and arms felt heavy and detached from her body, like water-soaked sandbags. Her emotional gas tank depleted, she'd lost the will even to shift positions. Keri didn't care if she sank. She had no control over these moods. They came and went as they pleased.

"Hey, you gonna move into that dinghy?" a voice asked over the noise of the night creatures.

Keri's heart skipped. She lifted her head, surprised by how much effort it took, and could only make out a tall, broad, shadowy figure. The man took another step, and she noticed he walked with a slight limp.

"Clem, is that you?" she asked. Though she'd only met him once or twice around town, she knew the most important thing she needed to know when encountering a strange man in the dark of night. He was safe. But shouldn't she have felt more afraid?

"Yep, it's me," he replied, raising an eyebrow as he surveyed Keri's situation. "What happened to your house?"

"Nothing. I just can't seem to stay inside," Keri said, letting her head fall back and splash into the rising water.

"So, you decided to sleep out here alone and in a sinking boat? Hmm."

Keri didn't answer. Suddenly, the stars swayed back and forth. Clem grabbed the mooring and pulled the boat next to the dock. He bent down and stretched his hand to help her out of the skiff. She grabbed his arm, and he pulled her effortlessly onto the small pier.

"It's time to go home, young lady," he said in a gentle, yet firm, voice.

"I'm not leaving him," she protested, despite her backside being soaked.

Clem didn't argue. He didn't try to explain how illogical her statement sounded, nor offer empty platitudes of comfort. Instead, he looked at her with compassion. The old Navy vet seemed to understand that while lying in a sinking boat would not help Keri find her missing fiancé, she needed to wait at the spot where Tony had last been seen, where the authorities had recovered his empty truck.

"I've got a proposal for you," Clem had said. "I've got a houseboat that needs some attention. You're welcome to stay there. Instead of paying rent, you fix up the place."

The offer had felt like a gift from God. Over time, their friendship became an anchor in Keri's life. She could always count on Clem. Here she stood, tonight, aware that he had helped her to her feet again.

"So, what did ya find there?" Clem asked.

"Oh, this? Ah, nothin', just research," Keri answered, closing the resource.

Clem glanced at the book lying on the floor and raised an eyebrow. "Looking for lost treasure?"

"Nah, you know me better than that. Treasure hunting's not my thing. Although they say there's lost gold in these waters."

Clem nodded. "Hmmm, well, if you find something, you might better turn that over to the authorities ASAP. Word of treasure attracts all sorts of strange characters."

"Ain't that the truth," Keri replied. She thought of the coin sitting atop Snaps' back. Then she looked at Clem. "Tony dreamed of finding lost treasure," she said softly, unwittingly echoing the message on the back of the mystery photograph. "Sometimes, it seems like he's here."

"He is. The departed are always with us."

He spoke with such certainty, and there wasn't a hint of doubt in his expression.

"I want to believe that," she said.

"He's with you. I know it."

Keri choked with emotion.

"Is that what's got you upset tonight?" Clem asked.

Keri wrinkled her brow, puzzled at first, then said, "The sugar skull."

"Most folks I know don't toss their memorials into the bay."

"Nothing gets by you, does it?"

"Not on my watch."

Keri peered at him with a pleading expression. "Does it get any easier?"

Clem stepped into the room and gently put one arm around her shoulder.

"No," he said softly. "But you can learn to live with it. You have to, or it will eat you alive."

Keri sighed heavily, her shoulders slumping. Clem embraced her in a grandfatherly hug.

"I don't know if I'll ever be okay with him being gone," Keri said, sniffling.

"Of course you won't. It's not about getting over it. But you will have to accept what happened."

Keri shook her head. "How? How can I possibly learn to live with this?"

"One day at a time, young lady." Then he looked at her with a commanding stare. "Lean on those who care about you."

Keri nodded. Clem patted her on the shoulder and stepped back onto the deck.

As he opened the gate to go home, he turned and said, "Might be a good idea to reach out to Bailey. You know how she worries about you."

Keri summoned the suggestion of a smile. "She's already left me a message. I'll call her."

Keri watched her strong protector limp toward his house. The warm breeze played a pleasant harmony as it blew through the chimes. Mixed in the melody, Keri thought she heard a soft voice again say, "Go blue."

CHAPTER 7

Smells & Visions

Lost Key Realty had slowly transformed since the new company, Thomason Brothers from Mobile, had taken ownership. The office remained in its original spot on the corner of Gulf Beach highway and Sorrento Road, but most of the building had been refurbished inside and out. The old oyster-shell parking lot had been paved with smooth concrete decorated with colorful renditions of local wildlife, including sea turtles, dolphins, and pelicans, another of Pensacola's celebrated creatures. The old real estate office sign had been replaced by a brand-new one reading 'Welcome to Lost Key.' Now, you weren't just welcomed to a business, but to a new emerging community. Lush greenery surrounded several freshly planted palm trees, creating a tropical landscape adorning the new entrance.

Stunning, Keri thought to herself.

Keri spotted Margaret Jane, the former owner of Lost Key Realty, loading boxes into a minivan, and parked next to the office. Margaret's short blonde hair shined, her eyes less puffy than last time Keri had seen the broker. Retirement seemed to agree with her.

"Hey, MJ," Keri said, climbing out of the old pickup.

"Keri! How are you?" MJ welcomed her with a big smile and a warm hug. "How's the marshland?"

"Much better without anyone dumping their crud into it." Keri could hardly believe that just a few months before, Martin, a crook posing as a developer, had poured homemade fake oil into the protected lands to drive the market down. She still wondered about the lasting effects of that pollution.

"I can't believe I fell for his scheme," MJ said.

"Well, how many pseudo-pirate, fake developer, mentally ill people do you run across? He fooled a lot of people."

"Bailey knew something was off about him from the beginning."

"That gal is in a league of her own with her psychic intuition."

"Ain't that the truth," MJ agreed.

"You look like you're feeling well," Keri stated.

Margaret Jane had been suffering from an elusive disease that had exhausted her energy and left her hurting. Even the doctors continued to be baffled as to the cause. But at least she seemed to be standing straighter and moving more easily.

"I feel better than I have in a long time," MJ said. "Especially since Thomason Brothers took ownership and I handed the reins to Bailey. I'm staying on in a consulting role to help Bailey get settled."

"You're leaving your legacy in good hands."

"The best," MJ said with a wink. "I'm so grateful the company will continue." She surveyed the renovations and seemed pleased. "This old place has been in my family for three generations. I can let go knowing it will have new life."

"Speaking of your protégé, where is my Bailey gal?" Keri asked.

MJ tilted her head toward the back door. "She's in my… I mean *her* office."

Keri stepped through the back door into the broker's entrance. She found Bailey standing behind the desk sorting papers.

"Hey!" Bailey exclaimed. Her face lit up at the sight of her friend. The new broker breathed a sigh of relief, and then her expression changed to an annoyed look. She crossed her arms and stared at Keri. "You didn't return my call yesterday."

Keri made an 'okay' sign with one thumb and forefinger. "Message received," she said.

Bailey relaxed her arms and nodded.

Keri looked around and smiled. "The new digs look good on you."

"It's coming along," Bailey said.

Keri sniffed. "It still smells like the old dive! Even after all the renovations."

Bailey shrugged. "Yep, afraid so," she answered, opening a window.

"Does it always stink like this in here?"

"No, not always. Sometimes the odor travels to another room."

"What? Seriously?"

"Serious, serious," Bailey answered.

"Y'all have a ghost roaming around?" Keri asked.

"Maybe," Bailey replied, then she looked up and said, "Hey, the bar's closed. Go home."

"Yeah, I'm sure you scared it off."

Bailey gazed at Keri and wrinkled her brow. "I know that look. What's up?"

Keri handed her friend the mysterious photo from the night before.

Bailey gasped. "Great pic of Tony!"

"Yes, it is. But I've never seen it before."

Bailey raised one eyebrow. "What? Where did you find it?"

"I found it tucked under a wiper blade on my truck."

Bailey scrunched her forehead. "I'm surprised they snuck past Clem."

"They didn't. I found it as I headed home from work last night."

"One of your students?"

Keri glanced away before answering. "No, the field team had already left."

Bailey glared. "You stayed in the marsh by yourself?"

"Bad move, I know," Keri said. "Listen to me. As I finished cataloging for the day, I saw someone."

Bailey looked at Keri, eyes wide with concern.

"I only caught a glimpse of this person before she took off," Keri said.

"So, this stranger was a woman."

"Yeah, at least I think so."

"And she's the one who left that photo and note for you."

"It would seem so," Keri concluded.

Bailey stared at the image again. "That's creepy. Why would she have a picture of Tony?"

Keri shrugged, then looked into Bailey's eyes. "Later, when I got home, I sensed his presence."

"Tony?"

Keri nodded.

Bailey raised her eyebrows and nodded. "You've thought you spotted him many times before. Remember, the doc said that's a normal reaction when we lose a loved one."

"No, this was different."

"Did you lose any sense of time? Or not remember how you got somewhere?" Bailey asked, concern etched on her face.

"You sound like my therapist," Keri said.

"I'm not your therapist. I'm your friend, and you didn't answer my question."

Keri let out a sigh. "No," she replied. "I know what you're thinking, but I'm not… disassociating or whatever the shrink called it."

"Did you tell the doc?"

Keri looked away and swallowed hard.

"When's the last time you saw her?"

Keri shrugged. "I don't know, a couple of months, maybe."

"I can't believe you! Don't you want to feel better?"

"What good does talking do? She can't bring him back. Hell, she can't even help me get any closure. Talking with her is a waste of time and money."

Bailey huffed; her face flushed. "This is killing you, my friend. You've got to let him go."

"Never!" Keri fired back as tears pooled in her eyes.

Bailey held up the photo. "Maybe this triggered memories of Tony," Bailey said.

"I wasn't just remembering. He was there last night on my houseboat!" Keri said, her hands shaking slightly.

She stared at her friend pleadingly and clutched the engagement ring around her neck. *Not now, Bailey, please.*

Bailey seemed to grasp the unspoken plea. She leaned forward and said, "I just can't stand to see you in so much pain." Her expression softened.

Keri nodded, warmed by the love of their friendship.

"Tell me more about what you experienced," Bailey said.

Keri breathed a sigh of relief and continued. "Later, I swore I felt his breath on my neck as he whispered in my ear.

Bailey raised an eyebrow. "Wow, that's intense."

"That's what I'm saying. This time was different." Keri's eyes tracked every nuance of expression on Bailey's face. As far as she could tell, her friend believed her.

"What did you hear?"

"Something that Tony used to say—*Go Blue*," Keri whispered the last two words.

Bailey's mouth opened and she rubbed her forearms. "You're giving me chills, girl."

Keri leaned closer. "I could smell him," she said softly. "I'm telling you, Tony came to visit last night."

They sat quietly for a few moments. Keri felt sure Bailey understood. After all, her best friend had not only seen a ghost before, but had talked to one. The elegant lady spirit had helped Bailey sell the house no one could sell to the only family meant to live in it. Those supernatural events led to Thomason Brothers buying out Lost Key Realty and starting the exciting new local development.

"You had tea with the long-deceased Ms. Worthington. Remember?" Keri said.

"Of course I do. I'll never forget it."

Bailey gently clasped Keri's hand, the one holding onto the ring. "I believe you…" Then Bailey gasped, and her expression took on the dreamy state Keri had come to know so well.

"What are you seeing?" Keri asked.

Sometimes Bailey experienced visions—another secret they shared. During these episodes, Bailey saw images of things that had happened or events that would occur. Keri had come to trust Bailey's otherworldly insights. These premonitions had led her friend to the old house in Mobile that night, where she'd met the regal ghost who owned it.

"I see a gold coin," Bailey said. Then she tilted her head. "Tony is standing in a graveyard." Her face contorted into a foreboding look. "A struggle with… someone, I can't see who. It's a woman. You both fall… A blue light underwater." Bailey stared, looking at nothing, then focused on Keri. "That's all."

A tingling sensation like an electrical current traveled up Keri's arms.

"Mean anything to you?" Bailey asked.

Keri didn't know what to make of Tony standing in a graveyard or the blue lights underwater, but she'd already found the coin. That confirmed that these other insights would occur. Yet the last part, about the struggle and falling, filled her with foreboding.

"Are you seeing my death?" Keri asked.

"Oh Lord, I hope not."

"What else could it mean? You saw me falling, then blue lights underwater. Maybe it's the light people speak of when death is near."

Bailey paused before responding. "I don't know," she answered. "I didn't see you dying, just falling."

Keri scanned the night sky, contemplating what Bailey had told her. "Well, one thing seems certain, a storm's comin'."

"Look, I don't know what my visions mean. I'm not even sure they are real until they happen."

Keri stared at her gifted friend and pointed to the note on the back of the picture.

"What?" Bailey asked.

"I already found a coin."

CHAPTER 8

Photos

Later that evening, Keri sat on the stage of the medium-size auditorium located in the Marine Aquatic Center at the University of Pensacola. Instead of her usual navy-colored NOAA pullover, she wore a blue and green colored knit shirt, with a white conch shell logo. She fiddled with the keyboard and small mouse, adjusting an image on the computer. A projector had been attached to a laptop which shined the image onto a larger screen at the back of the main stage.

"Hey, Doctor Keri!" a voice called from the back of the room.

"Hey, Bailey. Come on in. I'm just getting ready for my presentation tonight."

"Cool," Bailey said, as she began making her way down the steps. "I love your talks. Nobody defends the Gulf Coast like you do."

When Bailey reached the bottom, Keri gave her a high-five. "Have a seat."

"Never seen that shirt on you before," Bailey remarked.

"University colors, and the insignia of the marine biology department."

"Gotcha, professor. So, you ready?"

"Almost. I'm just making sure I know how to use this new Picture Point program."

"That's neat. So, it works like a slideshow, only the slides are on the computer."

"Yep, that's right," Keri answered, fiddling with another photo. "The software for this program takes six floppy disks. Jade installed it on the computer for me. I have to arrange them in the Picture Point."

"How is our goth friend doing?" Bailey asked.

"Jade's great, and back on the job. They've almost completely restored the Dauphin Island Marine Center since what happened a few months ago."

"From the way that fire was raging, they're lucky the whole thing didn't burn down." Bailey stared vacantly as if watching a replay of the harrowing event.

Keri pointed to a small cardboard holder. "Those are the actual prints back from the office," she said. "Go ahead and take a look. I haven't even seen all of them yet."

Bailey opened the package and pulled out the freshly printed photos.

Atop the stack sat the shot of Snaps with a dull gold medallion on his back.

Bailey's eyes filled with excitement. "Well, look at that. So, this is the coin you found?"

"Yeah. Snaps brought it to me." Keri scanned the auditorium to ensure they were still alone, then pulled a copy of *Ancient Treasures* from her backpack. "Last night, when Tony visited, this book had fallen off the shelf and lay open to this exact page."

Bailey compared the photo Keri had taken to the one in the reference book. They looked identical. "Wow! Incredible!"

"The stranger startled me as I took that picture."

Bailey looked as if she'd eaten something rotten. "I've got a bad feeling about that."

"It spooked me too. I reported the incident to the office."

"What happened to the coin?"

"Snaps and the medallion disappeared during the commotion."

"Maybe the coin fell off his back," Bailey wondered.

"I searched as best I could last night and again this morning."

"What about using your dad's undersea camera?"

"Already tried that. It wasn't much help in the murky water. I even did a little magnet fishing to find that piece of eight."

"Magnet fishing?"

"Learned it from Cricket," Keri said. "It's simple. You take a good-size magnet, tie a strong cord on it, and cast it in the water."

Bailey smiled. "Hmmm, magnet fishing. Tools of the modern scientist."

"Hey, you'd be surprised what you can pick up."

"Will a medallion stick to a magnet?"

"Not if it's pure gold. But if it's only gold-plated, covering another metal underneath, then the magnet would grab it. Anyway, no luck."

"This pic is not part of your presentation, is it?"

"Oh, no way. Don't need any amateur treasure hunters mucking up my marsh."

Bailey leafed through more photos. "You got some beautiful shots here."

"God is the master artist. I just capture it on film."

Bailey paused at the following picture. She tilted her head and rotated it slowly, trying to make sense of the greenish, blackish blur. "What's this one?"

Keri scrunched her brow. "I'm not sure; I don't remember taking it."

A couple of more shots followed, similarly out of focus.

Keri gasped at the next photograph. Though hazy and unclear, the image appeared to be a woman with long hair, face, and body turned sideways, as the camera had caught her running. Her lead arm seemed to push a branch of scrub brush out of the way. She held a dark object in her other hand, but the lens was too out of focus to capture it.

Keri clicked the computer mouse until the picture point brought up the corresponding slide projecting the image on the larger screen. They both studied the magnified picture.

"This is the stranger I saw last night!" Keri exclaimed.

"She looks like a ghost."

"The camera is moving, and so is she. That's why several of the photos are out of focus. My work camera is digital. If you hold the button down, it will keep taking photos. When I tripped, I must have accidentally depressed the shutter release as I held on to the camera to keep it from falling into the water."

Bailey scrutinized the image, then inhaled sharply. "This is the same woman I saw in my vision."

"Are you sure?"

"I mean, the photo is fuzzier, but the feeling is the same." Bailey stared blankly at nothing momentarily, then turned wide-eyed to her friend.

"What?" Keri asked.

"She looks familiar, like I've seen her before."

Keri felt a chill. "Where?"

Bailey touched Keri's arm. "Where's that drawing you showed a few months ago of a female pirate. Remember?"

Keri thought for a moment, then recalled. "You mean Jaquolette?"

"Yes! That's the one. Get that book."

Keri grabbed *The Pirates of Lost Key* from her pack.

"You carry that with you?" Bailey asked.

"This was one of Tony's favorites," Keri answered, as she flipped through the reference, stopping at the page she'd shown Bailey months ago.

They looked again at the artist's rendering of a lady pirate with fiery red hair, full cheekbones, and ocean-blue eyes—a stunning portrait.

Bailey held the photo of the mystery woman next to it. "Hmmm."

Keri read the caption below the photo in the book. "Jaquolette Delahaye was believed to be one of the most infamous and irresistibly beautiful female pirates. She had a reputation for being ruthless in acquiring her spoils and quick to punish those who had wronged her. She earned the nickname 'Back from the Dead Red' when she faked her death to evade her pursuers."

"Yep, that's it," Bailey said.

"A few months ago, you were certain the woman in your vision was the legendary pirate lady who died long ago."

"Correct."

Keri pointed to the recent photo. Her gut tightened. "Now, you think this is a picture of Jaquolette?"

"Well, it's the same feeling anyway." Bailey studied both pictures intensely. "What if you caught a ghost on camera?"

Keri shivered at first but quickly dismissed that notion. "No, she's not a ghost. I heard a car door close and an engine start. The tires crunched on the gravel road as they drove away."

"But you didn't see the car?"

"No, but I did find fresh tire marks."

"Well, ghosts don't usually drive cars, unless…"

"Please, you don't really think she is that notorious raider returned from the grave?"

"Of course not," Bailey replied. Just for an instant, her expression changed as if she wondered if it could be true.

"Bailey," Keri said. "Our mystery woman is *not* a 300-year-old buccaneer come back from the dead."

"Yes, I know," Bailey said. "Besides, I couldn't handle it if that were true. I know we've both seen spirits, but if she is some resurrected dead pirate, I'm outta here."

"Oh, and you're just gonna leave me to deal with her?"

"Well, you'll come with me, of course. After all, we ain't ghostbusters."

Keri chuckled.

"It's good to see you laugh."

Keri grinned. Her best friend could always cheer her up.

Bailey's smile faded. "It's just that I get the same foreboding when I look at both of these pictures."

"Then they must be connected somehow," Keri said, as possibilities churned in her mind.

Keri began to pace back and forth on the stage. "What's the link between her and the legendary pirate from the past?"

"Maybe there isn't one."

"There's gotta be," Keri said. "Everything is connected; all life, all events are interwoven with others."

Finding interconnections was Keri's gift. Cataloging wildlife wasn't only a job, but more like her passion. She believed her meticulous observations would eventually create a map revealing the interrelatedness of all the diverse life in the bayou.

"That's so cool how you see life as a delicate tapestry."

"That's what it is," Keri said with absolute certainty. "If people could see that we are all bound together, then folks might treat the environment and each other as rare and precious."

"Yeah, but all we got to go on are these flashes in my mind."

"I trust your visions, Bailey, so the question is not whether these two women are connected, but how."

"Since when did my visions become part of your deductive process?"

"Since you going barefoot, that's when. A scientist observes what is real, whether she understands it or not."

Bailey smiled. "So, what's next, detective, scientist, Doctor Keri?"

Keri mused momentarily, then said, "Start with the gold. I know that's real. I held it in my hand."

"Maybe the university can tell us more about the medallion."

"I'd rather word didn't get out about possible treasure in the marsh. That place would be crawling with all kinds looking for their fortune and holding little regard for nature's real bounty."

"Gotcha," Bailey replied. "So, we need someone knowledgeable about this area and lost treasure and who would be discreet."

Simultaneously both women said, "Max!"

"Sounds like a plan," Bailey said.

Keri glanced at the clock as students began entering the auditorium. "It's almost time for my seminar." She quickly shut off the projector. "I've got to get ready."

"Meet me for breakfast tomorrow," Bailey said.

"Sure, what time?"

Bailey gave her friend a look that said, 'Really?'

"Of course," Keri said. "Your usual time."

Bailey winked. "See you then, my friend."

CHAPTER 9

Tropical Palm

The Tropical Palm, a local favorite, sat on a small finger of ground jutting into Perdido Bay, which made it accessible by land or water. Keri often traveled there via the B&B, stopping on the way to her outdoor office. Although a local fisherman had recovered her runaway watercraft, today, she drove her old pickup.

Keri spotted Bailey's yellow Jeep parked next to the door and steered the truck into an adjacent space.

The breakfast crowd was in full swing. The place hummed with conversations and all the sounds of satisfied customers eating a hearty meal.

Keri spotted Bailey sitting at the counter.

"Well, look at this. We got both of the dynamic duo today," a lady behind the counter quipped.

Bailey swiveled her seat toward Keri and waved her over. The voice belonged to Mary. She and Max owned and operated the diner and made an effective husband-wife team. They'd built their home around the back, so the restaurant felt like an extension of their kitchen. Mary walked around the counter and gave Keri a big hug.

"Good to see you," Keri said.

"I'm glad you found your way back here again, Keri. Been missing ya."

"Missed you too," Keri replied as she scooted into an empty seat beside Bailey.

Mary poured another cup of coffee and slid it in front of Keri.

"You're late," Bailey said.

"Only about ten minutes," Keri stated.

"Thirteen. I always come here at seven fifty-seven."

"Give me a break. I haven't had my first cup of coffee yet."

"I'm just messin' with ya," Bailey said.

Mary squinted at the two women. The corners of her mouth turned upward slyly. "So, what are you gals up to?"

Keri and Bailey exchanged glances.

"Breakfast," Bailey said, sipping her coffee.

"Mmm hmmm," Mary replied.

"We also want Max to look at a picture," Keri said.

"Picture of what?" Mary's slight smile turned downward.

"Snaps and… an artifact," Keri answered.

Mary set the coffee pot back in its warmer, then addressed the dynamic duo sternly. "Don't go gettin' him all worked up about lost treasure. Ya hear?"

Bailey and Keri nodded.

"I don't need him spending days on end searching for gold that just ain't there."

"Understood," Bailey said.

Then Keri added, "We just need him to look at a picture I took the other day."

Mary gave them both a stern glare of warning. "I'll let him know you're here."

Keri spotted a copy of the *Mullet Wrapper,* the local paper, lying next to an empty plate, obviously left behind by a previous patron. The headline grabbed her attention—*De Luna Shipwreck Discovered!* A dark, grainy picture accompanied the headline. The underwater photo showed an object poking out from the sandy bottom.

She slid the paper between her and Bailey. "Did you see this?"

"See what?"

Keri read silently for a minute before answering. "Looks like the university found a shipwreck believed to have been part of Don Tristán de Luna's fleet."

"You mean like THE Don Tristán de Luna? The one who founded Pensacola?"

"Yep!" Keri answered. "Says here, they discovered the wreck off Emmanuel Point in the Pensacola Bay, in about twelve feet of water."

"Wow! That's exciting."

"I wish Tony could see this," Keri said softly, studying the front-page photo.

"Me too," a deep crusty voice answered.

The comment belonged to a six-foot-tall man wearing an apron and a stained chef's hat. The wrinkles on his aged weather-worn face and the tattoo of anchors on his arm conveyed that he was no stranger to hard work, or hard times.

"Hey, Max," Keri said.

The old cook's face beamed like he'd seen two rays of sunshine. Max greeted the women and placed two piping hot plates of shrimp and grits, Bailey's favorite, in front of them. This particular meal had become known as the Bailey special and continued to be one of the most popular items on the menu.

"I ordered for both of us right before you arrived," Bailey said. "I also asked Max to throw in a side of pancakes."

"Looks yummy," Keri said.

"Did they find any gold on that shipwreck?" Bailey asked.

Keri scanned the article further. "It doesn't say, but I bet they will."

"Maybe," Max said.

"I thought all those old ships carried riches on board," Keri said.

"Many did," Max answered. His anchor tattoo rippled on his forearm as he wiped his hands with a dishtowel. He flung the rag over one shoulder and continued. "The de Luna expedition was one of the most well-funded undertakings of its time. So, they probably carried some gold with them. However, when it comes to finding real loot, I'd lay odds with the pirates, especially that Billy Rogers fella. He became famous for stealing from other ships. There's a lot of his fortune still missing."

Bailey looked at Keri and silently mouthed, "Billy Rogers?"

"Later," Keri whispered.

No one knew more than Max about the possible hidden treasures in Lost Key. When he wasn't cooking for the diner, the retired Navy vet had a passion for treasure hunting.

"Yeah, but didn't most of those exploits happen near Santa Rosa Island?" Keri asked.

"That pirate stashed stolen loot all over this panhandle, not just in Fort Walton," Max stated. "Some believe he even hid some coins in the Perdido River."

Keri chewed the next bite more slowly. The Perdido River merged into the marshland where she was cataloging the wildlife. *Hmm,* she thought. Her inquisitive mind started to ponder the connections.

"There's more treasure right here than they ever found down at Sebastian," Max stated.

"Where's Sebastian?" Bailey inquired.

"It's on the Atlantic, below Melbourne," Max said. "They are ready to open a museum to showcase their discoveries. I can't wait to see that."

Bailey glanced at a large map hanging on the wall above them. "Maybe you oughta put that in the museum for safekeeping."

Max looked up at the framed parchment hanging on the wall above them. "Never thought I'd see that one again."

"Something happened to it?" Keri asked.

"Martin, I mean Thomas, took it when he claimed possession of this property," Bailey explained.

"That's so weird that his real name is Thomas. He just assumed the name Martin as part of his fake persona," Keri said.

"Yeah, and it's so wild that he's Mark's childhood friend," Bailey said.

Mary appeared behind them with a fresh pot of coffee. "And how is that boyfriend of yours, Bailey?"

"He's great." Bailey smiled as she answered, her cheeks glowing. "Mark is having so much fun redesigning the Lost Key office, and his work looks so cool."

"It does," Keri agreed.

"You haven't even seen around back. You're gonna love the pool. It's so awesome."

Keri swung the conversation back to their original focus. "Why was Thomas so interested in your map?"

Mary topped off the coffee and tended to other customers. Max glanced in his wife's direction, then said, "She don't like me talkin' about lost treasure too much. She's afraid I'll get lost in another hunt."

Mary turned toward them as if she'd overheard what her husband had said. Max winked and smiled playfully. Mary only gave a steely stare in return.

"Because this map is the real deal," the cook stated, pointing to the picture. "This ain't no tourist copy. In fact, there's supposedly another similar map older than this one, which contains the exact markings of lost pirate loot."

"So, Thomas dug up your parking lot looking for buried treasure?" Keri asked.

"Well, he claimed to be looking for some old keepsakes he and his grandfather buried."

Keri scrunched her brow and stared at the ancient rendering of Lost Key. "What if Thomas was looking for something more than his grandfather's chest of mementos?"

"Or what if that box contains something more valuable than just keepsakes," Max added.

"That would explain his elaborate plot to take control of the Tropical Palm and surrounding marshland," Bailey said. "Otherwise, why go to all that trouble?"

Max agreed. "Martin's grandfather, the old hermit as folks 'round here called him, was a bona fide treasure hunter."

"What if there's a fortune buried right under our noses?" Bailey seemed only half serious with her comment, though her eyes sparkled.

Max raised an eyebrow. "Well, y'all know what I think."

Keri gave him a skeptical look. "This is the Gulf Coast, Max, not the Gold Coast."

"The folks in Sebastian call it the treasure coast," he replied.

"You know what I mean."

Keri smiled. She loved Max's childlike wonder when discussing pirates and their past adventures.

Keri noticed Mary staring at her from across the room. "I don't want to get you in trouble, Max."

"It's alright, Keri." He smiled at Mary who only glared in return. "I was part of the salvage and rescue team for the Navy. So, when I go looking for lost things, I tend to get obsessed."

"I just assumed you were a cook when you were in the service because you're so good at it," Bailey said.

Max smiled. "Thank you. I also cook."

"Who has time for treasure hunting anyway?" Keri raised her voice slightly as she spoke. She turned her attention to her flap jacks, carved a perfect triangle bite, and pushed it through a pool of syrup. The morsel melted in her mouth.

"So, you gals have a picture you want me to look at?"

Keri nodded, her mouth still full of pancakes. She fetched the photo from the stack and handed it to the cook/treasure hunter.

Max's expression turned somber.

"What?" Keri asked in a muffled voice.

"Not here," he said, his tone more serious and commanding. The old vet's eyes scanned the diner before looking at the two women with an unfamiliar and chilling aspect. "Y'all finish eating, then meet me out back."

He handed back the photo, set his dish towel on the serving window, and whispered something to Mary. Whatever he said, she put her hands on her hips and pursed her lips. She clearly didn't approve. Then he disappeared through the kitchen door.

CHAPTER 10

Treasures & Tattoos

They met Max around the back of the restaurant at a rustic wooden shack that the old vet had clearly fixed up, making a few adjustments of his own. While some of the sidings had been replaced, he seemed intent on preserving as much of the original wood as possible. Keri supposed that replacing the rusting tin roof would be next. The newer, more prominent home where Max and Mary lived sat not twenty feet away.

"This used to be the only building out here on the point," Max said, fumbling with a key chain. "Local legend says this was the home of a recluse hermit."

"Thomas' grandfather?" Bailey asked.

"Yep, I believe so," Max answered. "A sudden storm popped up one day, capsized his boat, and killed him."

"We read about that hermit," Keri said.

Max found the key he was looking for, unlocked the door, and stepped through the entrance of his hideaway, waving them inside. Except for two windows, the only light came from a dim bulb hanging from a long wire. A large wooden table dominated the center of the room, with renderings of Lost Key spread out before them. A variety of maps of the area covered the inside like wallpaper. Some looked new and modern, and others seemed more like ancient parchment from a ship long vanished. Several photos depicted Max in his younger Navy days, wearing scuba tanks, and standing on the ships alongside members of his salvage team.

"Welcome to my man cave," Max said proudly.

"This is amazing," Bailey said.

Keri noticed a picture of an astronaut, wearing a space suit, helmet to one side, with a fake celestial background.

"Is that Jim Lovell?" Keri asked.

Max smiled broadly. "Yes. One of my heroes."

"Wow, that is so cool," Bailey said.

"You know Mr. Lovell was a Navy pilot," Max said.

"I had no idea," Keri answered.

"Trained right here at Naval Air Station Pensacola, before he became an astronaut. He was my inspiration to join the Navy."

"That's really awesome," Bailey added.

"He's quite a man. Everyone knows about his missions to the moon, but have y'all heard about his miraculous night-landing on an aircraft carrier?"

The ladies shook their heads.

"It happened on a mission out in the Pacific. He was flying his F2H Banshee aircraft in the Sea of Japan returning to the USS Shangri-La. Since it was combat conditions, there weren't the usual landing lights on the carrier. To make matters worse, his homing beacon was being jammed so he had been flying in the wrong direction. Jim turned on his map light to get his bearing when his when the plane's electrical system shorted out, leaving him in the dark. Those landings have to be precise. Come in too low and you'll crash into the ship, too high and you might overshoot the landing hook designed to stop you from flying right off the edge of the landing deck."

"What did he do?" Bailey asked with an awestruck look on her face.

"He was flying completely blind," Keri added.

Max nodded. "That's when he saw a green, bluish glow in the water."

Keri gasped. "Bioluminescence!"

"Exactly," Max said. "The large propellers of the ship had stirred up the algae and left a long trail in its wake, creating Jim's landing lights."

"That's unbelievable!" Bailey said.

"Oh, it really happened alright. Jim said he never would have seen the glow if the cockpit lights hadn't shorted." Max paused thoughtfully. "I guess you never know what events will lead you home."

Scanning the maps and photos covering the walls, Keri said, "Max, this must have taken quite a bit of work."

"This is a few years of study, but I love it. There's a treasure right around here in this bay." He focused on Keri. "I'm even more convinced of it now."

Keri smiled and gave him the photo of the coin.

"Where did you take this?" he asked. His tone raised the hairs on Keri's arms.

"Out near the bayou. I've been cataloging the wild-life. Snaps brought it to me."

Max grinned and shook his head.

Keri shrugged her shoulders. "He brings me stuff now and then. This time he found that."

"I've been searching these waters for years," Max said. "I got a brand-new magnetometer, state-of-the-art underwater metal detectors, plus the best cartography anywhere. Who knew that all I needed was a turtle."

Both women laughed.

"Do you still have the medallion?"

"No. I got distracted by an intruder in the park. Next thing I knew, Snaps swam off with the coin."

"It most likely fell off that turtle's back and is lying near where you last worked," Max said, reiterating Bailey's theory.

"I looked but couldn't find it," Keri said.

Max glanced at the door. "If I can slip away from the warden, I'll break in my new toy and see if it'll turn up."

"You mean that magno thingy?" Bailey asked.

"Exactly." Max clicked a small circular light surrounding a magnifying glass and began to study the picture.

"Hmmm," he said. Then he retrieved a book buried under several others.

Keri caught a glimpse of the title, *Ancient Treasures*. "I have that edition at home," she said.

When Max found the page he was looking for, he laid the book open on the large table in the center of the room. They all reviewed a photo of an old coin.

"We're thinking the same thing," Keri said.

Max pulled another, thicker book from a stack in the corner of a large table titled *The Treasure Chest of Lost Gold*. He trailed one finger down the table of contents, found the section he wanted, and thumbed to the section he was looking for. The page displayed another picture of the same coin with a more detailed description.

Keri read the caption. "Minted in the late 1700s, this ancient gold coin is considered to be one of only several hundred ever made. Scholars believe the rendering of the woman's profile is a tribute to one of the Spanish monarchs who funded much of the exploration of the new world. These pieces of eight were last known to be aboard the *Generosidad,* the Spanish word for generosity. The ship mysteriously disappeared on her maiden voyage to the Americas in the early 1800s. Experts believe that the ship sank near what is known today as the Florida Panhandle. What caused the demise of the *Generosidad* is unknown. One theory is that the vessel capsized in an unexpected storm. Other scholars suggest *Generosidad* and her crew fell victim to Jean Lafitte's gang of pirates."

Bailey's face lit up with a quirky smile. "Is this for real?"

"Looks that way," Max answered. "Of course, you'd need the actual coin to verify it officially."

Bailey looked at her friend and smiled. "Your ship really did come in."

"Yeah, and it sank somewhere around here about two hundred years ago," Keri said.

"How many people have seen this photo?" Max asked.

"Just the three of us," Keri answered.

"And whoever printed this at your office," Bailey added.

"I doubt anyone at work noticed these," Keri said. "The techs run off so many photos, they hardly bother to look at them."

"Don't show this around town," Max said.

"Aye matey, beware of them pirates," Bailey said with a chuckle.

No one laughed at her joke.

"Oh, come on, Max, there aren't any pirates around anymore," Bailey said.

"Oh yes, there are," he replied, a dead-pan seriousness on his face. "Today's pirates just look different, that's all."

Keri imagined what could happen if word got out of a legitimate find. Professional treasure hunters were usually careful about the environment and gentle with the ecosystems while they searched. The university would also take great precautions to protect the wetlands. However, the pseudo-hunters and the wannabes who didn't know what they were doing could cause real damage to the marsh. The folks in Lost Key had already lived through the mess Thomas had made. They didn't need to contend with another one.

Keri stared again at the photo of Snaps and the coin. "I wish Tony could see this," she said softly.

"Me too," Max added. "I have an idea. Let's go find that piece of eight for Tony."

Keri liked the sound of that proposal. Her eyes glistened, and her heart warmed by the gesture. "Thank you."

"Mind if I look at the rest of the photos? It will help me know how to prepare for this search."

Keri handed Max the pack of pictures. He flipped through, nodding and grunting as if making mental notes. Then he paused. His veteran eyes lingered on the image.

"Who's this?" he asked.

"That's the trespasser I mentioned. Someone startled me. I turned to look and must have held my finger on the shutter button."

"Hmm," Max mumbled, holding the picture under the round magnifying lamp. "It's too blurry to make out much of anything, but look at this," he said.

Keri and Bailey gathered on either side and leaned in for a closer look.

"See that dark spot on the underside of her left wrist?" Max said.

"Yeah, I thought it was a smudge on the camera," Keri answered. "So, I didn't pay attention to it when we projected this slide onto the screen."

"It looks like a tattoo," the old sailor said. He pulled the photo closer, enlarging the woman's wrist, and a dark splotch transformed into a grainy skull image. "Yep, that's a tattoo. Have a look."

They leaned over the lamp again and saw the grainy image of a skull with a red bandanna. The mouth was turned upward into a sinister expression of rage. A sword curbed underneath with tiny red drops of blood dripping from the tip as if it had made a fresh wound.

"Crab balls!" Bailey exclaimed, eyes wide with surprise. "Thomas had a flag on his limo with the same image!"

"What? Are you sure?" Keri asked.

"Absolutely. I remember thinking how strange, for someone to display a gruesome symbol like that one."

"She didn't pick this out of the book," Max stated. "The design looks custom. I know most of the artists in the area. I could check around and see if the work is local."

"Thanks," Keri said. "I'd appreciate that."

"So, it can't be just a coincidence that her tattoo matches the one I saw on Thomas's limo," Bailey said.

"They probably know each other," Max concluded.

Keri shared the mystery photo with Max. "Someone intentionally left this on my windshield."

"It's obvious that she knew Tony," Bailey said. "Maybe she has information about what happened to him."

"Maybe, or maybe she was involved and is taunting you," Max stated.

"You mean like stalking me?" Keri asked.

The old sailor looked at her with a thousand-yard stare. "There are some bad elements in the world."

If Max's theory was true, things had just turned much scarier and more troubling. She needed to learn more about this stranger and why she would have left that photo of Tony. Keri thought about what Bailey said. If Thomas knows this woman, then he might also know what happened to her husband-to-be.

Keri turned to Bailey. "Feel like a trip to the psycho ward?"

CHAPTER 11

Ambiguous Loss

Appointments to see any patient at the Serenity Behavioral Rehabilitation Center where Thomas had been committed, were mandatory. So it took a couple of days before Keri could head to the SBR, as it was known. As she drove her old truck along the route, she glanced at Bailey riding quietly in the passenger seat, staring out the window.

"Hey, you okay?" Keri asked.

Bailey nodded, but she seemed anything but okay. "The last time I saw this guy, he pointed a gun at my head," she said. "I still have nightmares."

Keri's mind replayed those harrowing images of that day at the Tropical Palm when Bailey had rushed toward Thomas, aka Martin, to keep the police from gunning him down. Keri had watched helplessly, fearing that, at any moment, the madman would raise his pistol and shoot her Bailey. If not for Mark showing up when he did, she couldn't even entertain what might have happened.

"I'm surprised they didn't put Thomas in the state hospital over at Chattahoochee, or even in prison," Keri said.

"I think that's because Mark testified on behalf of his childhood friend. Sheriff Cotton backed him up."

"So, the court granted leniency," Keri said.

"Yep, the judge decided he was more broken than criminal." Bailey looked as if she'd tasted something bitter.

"At least we don't have to drive to Tallahassee, but just the other side of Pensacola."

Bailey didn't respond as they pulled into the parking lot. Recently constructed and nicely landscaped, the SBR conveyed a tranquil feel despite being a locked facility.

Keri parked her blue pickup near the door. Bailey shifted restlessly in the passenger seat. Her hands fidgeted, and her color had faded slightly.

"You sure you're alright?" Keri asked. "You don't have to go inside."

"No, I'll be alright. I'm with you."

They made their way to the entrance. After signing in at the front desk, they left any sharps and valuables with security before being allowed inside the facility. Two men dressed in white scrubs greeted them.

"Good morning, my name is Will," one said, then motioned to the other. "This is my colleague, Chuck."

After exchanging greetings, the nurses led the women to the office of Dr. Christine Kalmer, lead psychiatrist and head administrator of the SBR. Slightly under five feet tall, lean and wiry, the doctor peered up at them through black-framed glasses with thick lenses that made her eyes look bigger. The doctor's shoulder-length chestnut wig looked crooked as one of the bangs draped over one cheek more than the other. She had a disarming yet powerful presence about her.

Doctor Kalmer stood and motioned toward the couch opposite her desk. "Ladies, please have a seat. Keri, it's good to see you again. It's been a while."

Bailey and Keri sank into the couch while the doctor sat behind her desk.

"Thank you for seeing us," Keri said, deliberately not addressing the doctor's remarks.

The psychiatrist nodded. "Tell me, why do you want to see Thomas?"

Keri handed her the photograph she had taken of the stranger at the marsh. The psychiatrist studied it carefully, her face unreadable.

"Hmmm, looks more like a ghost," the doctor said. "You sure you saw somebody?"

"Yes, I definitely saw the person," Keri answered, slightly annoyed that the doctor seemed hesitant. "The image came out blurry because my camera was moving when I took the shot."

"Mmm hmm."

Keri slid the photo of Tony across the doctor's desk. "Shortly after my encounter, I found this on the windshield of my truck. Read the note on the back."

The doctor raised one eyebrow skeptically. "And you think the woman took this picture of Tony?"

"Well, that's my theory so far," Keri answered.

"So, what does this have to do with Thomas?"

"See that mark on her wrist? That's a tattoo," Keri continued.

The doctor pulled open a small desk drawer on the right side and retrieved a magnifying glass. She studied the spot in the picture. "So it is."

"The symbol is identical to the one I saw on a flag attached to Thomas's limo," Bailey added.

"That's why we think he may know her," Keri said.

"Just because her tattoo matches his flag doesn't mean there's a connection between Thomas and that woman," Doctor Kalmer said. "Maybe it's a coincidence."

"Not likely," Keri said. "Max told us that ink is custom."

"The cook at the Tropical Palm?"

"Yes, he's friends with many of the local artists."

"And if Thomas knows this woman?"

"Then he might know what happened to Tony."

The doctor nodded her head. "I know I've told you this before, but I'm so sorry about Tony."

Keri huffed. She didn't want sympathy, but answers. "Also, Bailey saw the stranger in her vision." Keri realized how crazy this must sound to a professional like the doctor.

"Did she?" the psychiatrist responded flatly.

Doctor Kalmer leaned forward, both elbows on her desk. "Losing Tony the way you did creates unimaginable suffering."

Keri suddenly felt like she had heartburn. Her jaws clamped together.

"As you and I have discussed, what makes this hellish is that you can't find closure," the doctor continued. "It's easy to get stuck in perpetual grief." She tilted her head slightly to one side as if assessing whether her message was getting through. "Part of you still expects him to walk around the corner."

Keri thought she had seen Tony several times, once at the local store, then again on a passing boat, and another time at a nearby table in a restaurant. She'd even heard his voice on several occasions before this most recent time.

"I'm not crazy," Keri protested.

"No, you're wounded. More specifically, you're suffering from—" The doctor stopped abruptly. "Well, I'll speak with you about that in private."

"It's okay, Doctor," Keri said. "You can tell Bailey anything about me."

Doctor Kalmer nodded. "You're suffering from ambiguous loss. We've talked about that before. We just didn't put a name to it."

"Ambiguous loss?" Bailey asked.

"Yes. When a loved one disappears without explanation, it can cause a kind of grief so tough that it's very difficult to find closure and any sense of peace. Your mind tells you Tony has passed, but your heart holds onto the hope that he will reappear at any moment. These two competing forces are extremely challenging to reconcile. Acceptance is always fragile."

"Exactly," Keri said. "That's why I have to talk with Thomas. I have to find out what he knows!"

"I don't think this is a good idea," Doctor Kalmer said emphatically.

"How can you say no?" Keri yelled. "This will help me get the closure I need."

The doctor grasped the photo and held it up. "This is not a clue, Keri." She took a breath. Composing herself, she continued. "This is the way you're medicating your pain. Finding clues is like margaritas for you, which I suspect you've been drinking more of lately."

Keri averted her eyes.

Bailey looked at her friend with an expression of 'How does she know all this?'

"What do people do about this ambiguous loss?" Bailey asked.

"The therapeutic goal is to help the person tolerate the ambiguity."

"How do they learn to do that?"

"Rituals help. Some people celebrate their birthdays or the anniversaries of their disappearance or do things they used to do together."

"Like setting up a memorial shrine?" Bailey asked.

The therapist nodded. "Just like that. Some find it helpful to continue a project their loved one started but didn't finish, or something they worked on together. Others even go on a quest to honor their loved ones."

Keri thought about the effort she'd put into finding whatever Tony had discovered. She hadn't just been cataloging marine life, but also exploring the nooks and crannies of the bay, looking for any link to her fiancé.

"In the more severe cases, the surviving partner can get lost in a fantasy, with unrealistic expectations," the doctor continued. "They become obsessed with searching for their personal holy grail, thinking it will finally bring them peace or maybe even find their missing loved one still alive. That course of action usually leads to worse outcomes. People can lose their jobs, even their life, by taking greater and greater risks."

Keri glanced at the wall as the doctor's sobering words chilled her down to her bones. *Am I caught in a fantasy? Have I gone down the rabbit hole?* Her body felt heavy, like she could melt into the couch.

She looked at the doctor pleadingly. "Please, I need to speak with him."

Dr. Christine Kalmer sat quietly behind her desk, her face unreadable, as if carefully evaluating the request. "The SBR is a private hospital, not a prison. However, Thomas is here under court order. So, I'll make a deal with you, Keri. We'll see him together. If he becomes upset, I'm stopping the visit. Understood?"

Both women acknowledged the conditions.

The doctor walked around her desk and gently touched Keri's shoulder. "Also, you come back into regular therapy. Agreed?"

Though Keri didn't want her head shrunk, she also knew therapy usually made her feel better. Besides, it seemed a small price to pay to get an answer from Thomas she so desperately needed.

Keri looked up at the doctor. "Agreed."

CHAPTER 12

Thomas Martin

The cinder block hallway echoed as the doctor, Keri, and Bailey walked down the gleaming, clean hallway toward the visitation room. Doctor Kalmer briefed them on the way. "Thomas is suffering from severe traumas that cause him to disassociate. So, you may hear wild stories. Sometimes he even thinks he is someone else."

"Yes, we know," Bailey responded.

Keri shot her friend a questioning glance, then asked the doctor, "You mean like multiple personalities?"

Doctor Kalmer shook her head. "Not quite that severe, but he has difficulty knowing what's real. His stories are compelling. Be careful what you believe."

"I understand," Keri said.

When they reached the visitation room, Will, the nurse, met them just outside the door. "They're ready for you," he said. "Chuck is inside with Thomas now."

Bailey turned pale.

"Don't worry," the attendant assured. "He hasn't displayed any violence."

"Except when he held a gun to my head," Bailey said in a biting tone.

"You sure you're up for this?" Keri asked.

Bailey looked as if she might pass out. She shook her head and answered, "I don't think I can go in there after all."

"No worries," Keri said. "Hang out in the hall and just listen."

Bailey sighed in relief, a pink hue returning to her cheeks.

Will pulled a nearby chair next to the doorway. "You can sit here while you wait."

"Thank you."

"I've got rounds to make," Will said. "But I'll be right down the hall if you need me." He nodded at Bailey as if making sure she was okay. Bailey returned the gesture and sat in the chair while Keri and the doctor went inside.

A couch adorned one wall. A couple of softer chairs flanked a coffee machine with a stack of paper cups and a water fountain. Thomas sat at one of the three round tables. Nurse Chuck stood watchfully a few feet behind. They had the room to themselves.

Thomas took a quick look at Keri. His brow wrinkled, and his head tilted to one side as if he was calculating who she might be and all the possible reasons for her visit.

Keri sat beside Doctor Kalmer, unable to take her eyes off the patient across the table. Thomas's black hair frizzed out in all directions. Judging from the bags under his eyes, he hadn't slept in a while. His dark pupils darted randomly, only looking at her in glances. She thought back to the day of his arrest. Nearly two dozen people had witnessed his meltdown as his bad-guy Martin façade unraveled before their eyes. The cool, seemingly unstoppable marauder was finally escorted away, crying and handcuffed. Sheriff Cotton had pledged that they would seek help for Thomas and had made good on that promise.

"Thomas, my name is Keri."

He didn't answer but kept sneaking looks in her direction.

"I'm a friend of Bailey's," Keri added.

His eyes focused on her at the mention of Bailey's name. He squinted a stare.

"You were there that day at the Tropical Palm," Thomas finally said. "I remember you."

Keri shuddered involuntarily at his observation as if she'd touched an electrical outlet. Thomas's brow wrinkled, and he continued to study his visitor. He seemed poised now.

Let's get this over with, Keri thought to herself. Her hands felt cold and shaky. She glanced at Dr. Kalmer, who nodded her approval. Keri reached into her back pocket and retrieved the photo of the stranger in the marsh.

"I'm sorry to bother you," Keri said, "but I'm hoping you can help me identify someone." She slid the picture toward him. "Do you know who this woman is?"

Thomas reached for the photo but kept his eyes locked on Keri. However, when he looked at the picture, he tilted his head to one side and scrunched his brow, then stared at nothing. Just for a few seconds, Thomas looked puzzled. Slowly he brought his focus to Keri again.

He slid the picture back across the table. "The photo's blurry. I can't even see her face. What makes you think I know her?"

Keri wasn't about to unpack her reasoning to him. Besides, his reaction suggested he might know something more.

"Are you sure you don't recognize her?" she asked. "Look again."

He seemed irritated now. "I've never seen her before in my life."

You're lying. I can see it on your face. Anger began to replace Keri's apprehension.

Thomas's countenance took on a surreal composure. "You must have been terrified that evening at the Tropical Palm," he whispered.

"What did you say?" Keri asked, her gut wrenched, and her breath grew short and rapid.

Doctor Kalmer laid her hand gently on Keri's forearm. "Take a breath," she said. Then looking concerned at her patient, "Thomas, are you feeling alright?"

Avoiding eye contact, he shuffled in his seat. Keri stared at him, her eyes fixed on every subtle moment of body language and facial expression. It took all her restraint not to leap across the table and slap that newly appeared smirk off his face.

"Thomas," the doctor said. "Look at me."

The patient complied. "Yes, Doc, I'm feeling fine. No, I don't know her."

"See the ink on her wrist?" Keri said. "She's got a tattoo that matches the symbol on your old flag."

Thomas's eyes widened. He grabbed the picture and studied it closely. His face crinkled in as if puzzled. Then with a composure that seemed forced, he flicked the photo back on the table and said, "Looks like a smudge to me."

"Thomas, if you know anything, now is the time to tell us," the doctor said.

Thomas paused, then said, "Look, the only person I know with a tattoo like that was my former boss. She died several years ago." He averted his eyes when he said the last part.

"Your boss's name?" The doctor inquired.

"Jacky Delahaye."

"Delahaye? Oh, come on! What's her real name?" Keri asked sharply.

Thomas's brow wrinkled. Instead of answering the question, he asked, "When did you take that photo?"

"Just the other night when I was working in the wetlands," Keri said impatiently. "She also left a photo of Tony I've never seen before."

Thomas squinted at the image, shaking his head. "That's not possible. That would mean that she's…" He stopped mid-sentence, his eyes bulging as he looked at something behind Keri. He gasped and said, "You!"

Keri turned, ready to lash out at whoever had interrupted this critical moment. She almost didn't recognize the woman in the doorway, standing strong, her face set toward Thomas in fierce, fearless determination. "Bailey?"

CHAPTER 13

Hurricane Bailey

"You're lying!" Bailey bellowed. "You know exactly who that woman is, don't you, Thomas!" Bailey said his name as if it were a sharp object poking him.

For a moment, the confident Thomas looked genuinely frightened by the imposing woman standing before them.

The attendant, Chuck, stepped toward Bailey. He held up one hand and said, "Ma'am, please calm down."

Bailey seemed not to hear the nurse. She stared at Thomas like laser sights locked on a target.

Doctor Kalmer stood. "Bailey, you need to wait in the hall."

Bailey ignored the doctor's order, her eyes boring into the man who had threatened her life and her town.

Thomas fidgeted. His eyes darted wildly as if looking for a safe hiding place. His breathing grew rapid. Then, suddenly, he stopped and sat perfectly still. Something about the man sitting across the table had changed. Another person with ominous confidence had replaced the tormented one. The patient slowly smiled wryly, the kind of expression that belonged to his pirate persona. He brought his focus to Bailey and said with an indifferent affect, "I should've pulled the trigger."

Bailey's face turned a darker shade of crimson. "I saved your life!" she hissed, stomping toward him, her hands curled into fists. "You sick son of a bitch!"

Chuck moved to intercept Bailey, who was now in a hurricane of rage.

Instinctively, Thomas slid his chair back as if pushed by gale-force winds. Its back leg caught Chuck's foot, causing him to stumble and Thomas to tip over backward. The pseudo-pirate landed hard on the tile floor and yelped in pain.

Keri had managed to reach Bailey and grab one of her arms. Chuck took hold of the other.

"Aaaahhhhhh!" Bailey yelled, tears spilling from her.

Chuck grabbed a phone hanging on the wall with his free hand, punched a button, and spoke into it. "Dr. Strong to visitation. Dr. Strong to visitation."

In less than a minute, Will and another attendant rushed into the room. While Chuck and Keri pulled Bailey out of the area, the other two helped Thomas off the floor and began assessing his condition.

"Wait!" Keri yelled. "Thomas, tell me, what were you going to say? That would mean she's what?"

"Get these two out of here, now!" Doctor Kalmer ordered.

The nurses escorted Bailey and Keri out of the visitation room and closed the door. After a few minutes, Will stepped into the hallway, catching his breath. "Thomas will be okay, just a nasty bump on his head. We'll get an X-ray to be sure."

Bailey rolled her eyes and pressed her lips together as if suppressing another sarcastic comment.

Will looked at Bailey. "Are you okay?"

Bailey nodded but seemed annoyed by the question. She shuffled restlessly back and forth.

"You'll both need to come with me," Will said as he motioned to the other men in white scrubs, who had just emerged from the visitation room. Each clutched one of the girls' arms and escorted them down the hallway.

"I can walk myself," Bailey protested, trying to free herself from the grip of her escort. But he held fast.

"I'm sorry," Will said. "I have to follow protocol for your safety."

Bailey scowled but didn't say anything and stopped resisting their forced exit.

Keri looked at her friend, who wouldn't make eye contact, then shook her head and clenched her teeth.

The attendants led the women to Doctor Kalmer's office, where they waited before the large mahogany desk. Within a minute, the doctor marched in and slammed the door behind her. She glared at them; her mouth pursed in a thin line.

"Sit," the doctor ordered, pacing behind her desk, trying to compose herself.

After a few back-and-forths, the psychiatrist smoothed her lab coat and sat in her chair. "Is either of you injured?" she finally asked, her voice clipped.

They both assured the physician they were fine.

"I'm sorry; I just lost my temper," Bailey said. "I don't know what came over me."

"Violence will not be tolerated in this facility," the doctor stated. She had raised her voice slightly to make her point.

Bailey hung her head. "I should've stayed in the hall."

"But you didn't," Dr. Kalmer said. "Instead, you entered the room and attacked a patient."

"It's my fault," Keri said. "I shouldn't have brought Bailey here. She was only trying to support me."

"No," the doctor said. "It's my fault for allowing this visit in the first place. You two may have undone months of progress. Thomas had begun to let go of his Martin persona." The doctor exhaled sharply. "This is a setback. I don't know how bad yet."

"I'm so sorry," Bailey said.

The doctor put her hands on her hips. "Well, at least everyone is safe. Thomas is here by court order, so I'll have to notify Sheriff Cotton of this incident, and I expect he'll want to take a look at this photo you brought. So I'm keeping it with me."

Keri felt her heart skip a beat at this news.

"You can't come back and see him anymore," Doctor Kalmer added.

"Wait," Keri blurted out. "He knows something about the woman in the photograph. You heard him."

The psychiatrist nodded. "Yeah, I heard him."

"He might know something about what happened to Tony."

The doctor stared from behind the thick lenses but said nothing.

"He's still lying," Bailey added.

"You got a feeling about that, do you?" the doctor said with a slight bite to her words.

Bailey looked away.

The doctor gently turned Keri toward her. "Look at me. I know you need closure, but your search for answers borders on obsession. It's hurting you." Then she glanced at Bailey. "And the people you love."

That last statement landed on Keri like a cup of cold water on her face. *Oh Lord, what's happening to me?* she thought. She looked over at Bailey, who seemed on the verge of tears, and felt a shard of pain in her heart.

"We'll talk more at your next session," the doctor said. Then she handed Bailey a business card. "My door is open to you too, Bailey. You're obviously struggling with some unresolved trauma. Don't try to carry this alone."

Bailey accepted the card. "Thank you, Doctor."

That ended their meeting. The nursing assistant escorted Keri and Bailey out of the facility without grasping their arms, instead just walking behind them.

Once outside, the two friends climbed into the old blue pickup.

"What the hell happened to you back there?" Keri demanded.

"I'm sorry. I'm sorry. That man drives me crazy," Bailey answered.

"Yeah, I noticed."

Bailey touched her temple. "He gives me a headache."

Keri slapped the steering wheel. "Damn it!" she yelled. "Why couldn't you have waited a few more seconds before trying to tear his head off? You interrupted him in the middle of an important sentence! Now I may never get a chance to find out what he knows."

"Sorry, my friend. I blew it."

"Yes, you did!" Keri fired back.

"Thomas is lying."

Keri saw the confidence in Bailey's demeanor. Her friend's certainty helped override the doubt she had felt since their meeting with the doctor. The thought that Thomas had deliberately withheld information meant Keri wasn't chasing rabbits. Still, frustration burned in her chest. She felt like screaming.

"I guess we'll never know," Keri said sharply, snapping the ignition key. She pulled hard on the gear shift and abruptly drove away, ignoring the ten-mile-an-hour speed limit posted in the parking lot.

CHAPTER 14

Get Out of My Car

They rode quietly for a while. Keri slumped slightly, hanging on to the steering wheel. A heavy silence filled the truck's cab like a third passenger sitting between them.

"I'm so sorry," Bailey said again.

Keri shook her head and stared at the road ahead. "A lot of good sorry does. My first chance in three years to find out what happened to Tony, and you get us kicked out."

"I feel terrible," Bailey's voice broke.

"Good, you should feel bad. The love of my life just disappeared. You know how desperately I need to find out what happened! You know how hard this time of year is on me!"

Bailey hung her head and covered her eyes with one hand.

"All you had to do was stay out in the hall. That's all you had to do!"

"I know," Bailey answered, her voice muffled.

"But no, you had come in and attack the man. What is it with you two anyway?"

Bailey didn't answer but shook her head, hand still covering her eyes. She began to cry.

"Well, it doesn't matter now. Our only lead is locked up in a mental ward and now we can't go back to see him," Keri said, frustration still smoldering. She banged the steering wheel with one hand.

Keri couldn't stand being mad at her best friend. But Bailey had messed up. *I have every right to be angry*, she told herself. Still, she hated herself for not being able to let it go. Frustration boiled inside her like a geyser ready to erupt. She felt like crying, like screaming, like driving the old pickup into the bay.

Then she glanced at Bailey for the first time since they had left the parking lot. Her anger softened as she saw her friend's head hung in shame, the watery streaks running down her cheek. Doctor Kalmer's words echoed in her mind. *You're hurting the ones you love.* Her best friend sat suffering because of this latest quest to find answers.

"Aaaahhhhh," Keri yelled and stomped on the brakes. Tires crunched against the gravel as the vehicle stopped on the shoulder of the road. She climbed out of the truck, walked to Bailey's side, and opened the door.

"Please stand out here for a second," Keri said.

"Sure. What's goin' on?" Bailey asked as she exited the truck.

Keri didn't answer her. Instead, she turned toward the truck, looked through the open passenger door, and yelled, "Get out of my car!"

Bailey's reddened eyes peeled wide at this strange behavior.

Keri stepped back as if to make room for someone to exit. Then she closed her eyes, tilted her head back, and inhaled a deep breath, letting it out slowly. Her whole body relaxed. She opened her eyes to find Bailey staring at her, a look of bewilderment etched on her face.

"You can get back in now," Keri said.

Keri walked to the driver's side and climbed behind the wheel while Bailey, still wide-eyed but not crying anymore, scooted up into the passenger seat.

Keri cranked the truck and drove off.

Bailey stared at her friend momentarily, then said, "Okay, what was that?"

"Sometimes you got to tell the devil to go away," Keri answered.

Bailey raised both eyebrows in a broader expression of surprise. "Since when do you believe in the devil?"

"I don't, at least not in the way many people seem to. Think of it more as negative energy."

"I get that," Bailey stated.

"We had some bad mojo riding in the cab with us. I needed to kick it out," Keri said.

"It's just strange to see you, the scientist, performing an exorcism on the side of the road."

Keri smiled. "I learned that trick from a Baptist minister."

Bailey snickered. "I didn't know you bought into all the religious stuff."

"You know me. I'm not a fan of conventional religion. My sanctuary will always be God's natural world. However, as a researcher, I must remain open to all the possibilities." She winked at Bailey. Then Keri made a gesture as if scooping something with one hand over her heart and tossing it into the air. "Sometimes you got to release the bad energy. Negativity sticks like barnacles on your soul."

"I'll have to try this next time I feel possessed," Bailey said, trying not to smile.

"Hey, it works, and…"

"I know. A good scientist uses what works."

"I follow your visions," Keri stated.

Bailey laughed softly. "Yes, you do."

The mood felt considerably lighter now that Keri had thrown out the unwanted hitchhiker. Bailey slumped as if she'd just let go of an enormous weight. Her shoulders relaxed, and she let her head fall against the back window.

Bailey turned her head toward Keri. "I'm so sorry, my friend. I wish I had stayed in the hallway back there."

Keri's smile faded. "I shouldn't have let you come," she replied softly.

"Like you could've stopped me."

"Yeah, I guess that's true," Keri said with a chuckle. "Still, you wouldn't have come if not for me."

"I'm a big girl. I make my own decisions," Bailey said. "I'm just kickin' myself over how I lost it back there."

"The truth is, if you hadn't gone after him, I probably would have," Keri admitted.

Bailey smiled, but a worried expression quickly replaced that. "Can you ever forgive me?"

Keri nodded and looked at her best friend. "I already have." Then she stretched her arm across the seat. Bailey raised her wrist, and they tapped friendship bracelets.

The reprieve was short-lived, as Keri felt a heaviness return.

"Am I losin' it?" Keri asked, almost afraid of the answer she might hear.

Bailey sat up and stared at her as if to put an exclamation point on her next words. "No. You're hurting, but you're not crazy."

"Maybe the doc's right. What if I'm just caught up in a painful fantasy, not wanting to face reality?"

"Not true," Bailey said without hesitation.

The conviction in Bailey's voice assured Keri that maybe she hadn't succumbed to some dark grief nightmare, at least not yet. But the intense anger she had felt toward Bailey still bothered her.

"Sometimes I feel right on the verge, you know? It would only take a nudge to push me crazy. The pain never lets up."

"As I said, you're hurting. The challenge is not to let the grief drive you insane."

"How do I do that?" Keri asked softly.

Bailey laid her hand on Keri's arm. "We'll figure it out, my friend."

Keri only nodded as tears pooled behind her eyes. Her heart swelled with gratitude for her friend. *What would I do without you?* she thought to herself. They rode in silence again for several miles.

"Do you have a destination in mind?" Bailey asked. "Or are we just gonna drive around all day?"

Keri started to answer when her stomach rumbled so loudly they could hear it over the hum of the tires. With surprise registering on her face, she laughed.

Bailey laughed too. "Sounds good to me."

Absent of other clues to follow, and in response to Keri's grumbling stomach, they drove to the one place where their world always made sense, the Tropical Palm.

CHAPTER 15

Sea Sparkles

The next evening, Bailey and Keri sat on her house-boat deck, nursing a pair of salt-rimmed margaritas, while the music of Jimmy Buffet serenaded them on the radio.

The song faded, and the DJ's voice said, "You're listening to WJLQ, your number one station for cool beach tunes. Batten down the hatches. It looks like we got another storm brewing in the Gulf. Get them shutters up and your raincoats ready. Stay tuned for all the latest updates. Now, here's a little more of that Gulf Coast vibe." An island-sounding song with steel drums began to play.

"Where's the storm headed?" Bailey asked.

"They say it has a good chance of hitting right here," Keri said.

"Well, I hope it's nothing like Hurricane Andrew. That one was brutal."

"Yeah, a nasty one. The forecast says this isn't likely to reach hurricane strength, but still, there'll be a lot of wind and rain."

As the evening air cooled, Bailey donned her favorite faded gray sweatshirt. Keri pulled on one of the strings dangling from the old pullover. "You may wanna change shirts before the storm hits." She laughed.

"Cut that out. This thing's got some life to it yet," Bailey said. Then she gestured to the old radio. "Look who's talkin'. They make newer models, you know."

"No way, never gettin' rid of that thing," Keri said, licking the salt off her lips. "Dad gave me that."

"I know, I'm just sayin'. It looks like it's on its last song."

"We'll see. It's been playing continuously for three years straight now."

Bailey choked as she sipped her drink. "What! You're kidding."

"Used to run on batteries. When I moved in here, I got Clem to hardwire it to the power. I leave it on 24/7. It helps me feel closer to Papa. It's never stopped playing."

"What about when the power goes out?" Bailey asked.

"Last time that happened, it stayed on until they restored it. I guess those batteries still had some juice."

"That's so cool."

They listened to the tunes as if paying reverence to the memory the music box represented. Keri downed her drink and poured a second one. She caught her friend's concerned stare.

"It's just temporary," Keri said, sounding defensive.

Bailey gave her a skeptical look, then said, "I'm worried about you."

Keri started to dismiss the comment, then paused. A feeling of gratitude replaced her defensiveness. "I'll be okay."

Bailey nodded slightly but didn't look convinced.

"You know that picture the stranger left on my truck?"

Bailey nodded. "Yeah, what about it?"

Keri glanced at her friend. "Tony looks so happy," she said tentatively.

"Don't go there, girlfriend," Bailey said.

"You have to admit; it's a possibility. Why leave me this pic? Maybe Max is right. What if she's taunting me."

Bailey turned to face her friend. "Tony did not run off with another woman. No way. You were the love of his life."

Keri's eyes glistened as she leaned on the assurance of her closest friend. "Thank you. It's just that a few weeks before he disappeared, he came home one night all excited about an investor who'd offered to fund his exploration to find lost Spanish treasure."

"Did you ever meet this person?"

"No. Tony said she insisted on remaining a silent partner."

"She?"

Keri nodded. "His enthusiasm didn't last long. He became increasingly moody and withdrawn, even secretive. He finally said the deal wasn't going to work out."

"Hmmm, that's not like Tony."

"Something was eating at him."

"Well, one thing I know for sure, is how Tony felt about you. He would never cheat on you." Bailey pulled Dr. Kalmer's business card from her pocket. "If you believe he would, then you need to call the doc right now and get your head straight." Bailey glanced at the card, then did a double-take. "Did you see this?" she asked.

"What?"

She handed the calling card to Keri. "Dr. Kalmer's slogan is the same as what you heard from the voice the other night."

Keri grabbed the card and read it aloud. "Going Blue? Call me."

"Going Blue is yours and Tony's special phrase."

"Yeah. What are the odds?"

"Well, I'm sure when Tony said it, he didn't mean go to therapy."

"No, Tony was referring to the bluish bioluminescent algae. He believed it could lead to lost treasure."

"You'd think he was a treasure hunter rather than an underwater archaeologist," Bailey quipped.

Keri smiled. "He would say, 'I'm going blue tonight. Come on and join me.' Funny, but my dad used to say the same thing. When I was growing up, he always promised to show me what 'going blue' truly meant, but he died before he got around to that. They were both big fans of the sea sparkles."

"Sea sparkles?"

"That's my nickname for this wonder of nature. Scientifically speaking, it's simply a chemical reaction from some species of algae that occurs mostly on summer nights. They emit a glow. A lot of times it gets churned up in the wake of a boat, or by the waves along the shoreline."

"Cool."

"Some folks, like Tony, take a more mythical view. They believe that bioluminescence can lead you to hidden fortunes. Certain cultures even believe that the glowing algae are loved ones returned from the beyond for a visit."

"And, as Max told us, for one Navy Pilot, that bioluminescence guided him home. Maybe it's God's flashlight."

"Amazing story," Keri agreed.

"So, what do you think?" Bailey asked.

"It's a natural phenomenon," Keri answered. "However, when I followed Buddy the other night, the water glowed blue just up the channel toward the bay."

"Whoa! You saw it?"

"Yeah, and not just then. Buddy left a shimmering trail in his wake. But the B&B wasn't churning up any glowing algae. It's like I was being led, and I don't mean by just a dolphin. As fantastic as that is, it felt like another ethereal force was guiding me. Like… Tony was calling me."

"You weren't hoping to find a shipwreck or lost gold either."

Keri shook, and her eyes glistened. "No," she said softly. "I saw it one more time as I was getting ready to head home. A bluish-green glow caught my eye. When I turned to look, I swear, for a second, I saw Tony."

"That's why you ended up in the water. You were distracted."

"The odd thing is that the glow just appeared. Nothing stirred it up. Sounds crazy, huh?"

Bailey laid her hand on Keri's knee. "Sounds like you miss him fiercely."

Keri let out a long sigh. "I have no words."

"I don't want to see you go down a dark path again where I can't reach you for days. I also can't sit back and watch you drown your sorrows in bottles of tequila and empty quests."

Keri considered her friend's words. What if all this meant that she needed to go back into therapy? That seemed more realistic than chasing ghosts, and much safer. Counseling had helped her before when Tony had gone missing, but ultimately, it had only dulled the pain for a while.

"Maybe the doc was right," Keri said. "I need to talk with her. Maybe that's what going blue means for me—going into therapy."

"Well, as much as I'm concerned for you, I've also got a feeling I can't shake," Bailey said, now clutching the cross at the end of her necklace. "I just know that the next step will present itself."

"Going barefoot is your strength, not mine."

Bailey smiled and then turned serious. "The coin, the voice, and the doc's card, these aren't just coincidences."

"I know. Those things are connected somehow. I get it," Keri said. "Part of me is screaming to keep searching until I find answers. But you heard the doc. Maybe I'm becoming obsessed. So far, these quests have only led me to more pain and frustration. I don't know that I can take another disappointment."

Bailey held up the doctor's calling card. "This is a sign if I ever saw one."

Keri let out a gasp and grabbed it from Bailey's hand. She blinked as if to make sure she hadn't seen a mirage. The back of the card depicted a photo of a beach near sunset. The dunes and sea grass looked familiar, but what stood out were tiny lights in the water.

"Bioluminescence!" Keri said, showing Bailey the image.

"What!" Bailey stared at the back. "Looks like a photo! Is this for real?"

"This is Johnson's beach. I'd recognize that place anywhere!" Keri said. She remembered Tony's playful excitement whenever he talked about the sea sparkles and felt guilty that she had never quite believed him. *You were right, my love.*

"Crab balls! This is unbelievable." Bailey's eyes gleamed with excitement.

Keri's mind raced, her senses on full alert. She saw a big bright moon suspended in a clear night sky. She sat up and turned toward Bailey. "Maybe we are being guided. We need to find these lights."

"Right now?"

"Come on," Keri bellowed over her shoulder as she grabbed a life jacket and jumped on board her watercraft.

"Wait a minute!" Bailey yelled, scrambling to follow. "What makes you think we'll find the glowing water?"

"It's as good a time as any. Hurry up."

Scooping up a second preserver, Bailey hopped on the back just as Keri cranked the engine. The watercraft lurched forward as the throttle stuck open again. If Bailey hadn't grabbed the handle on the back of the seat with one hand and Keri's life vest with the other, the sudden surge would have thrown her into the channel.

"Is this what going barefoot feels like?" Keri shouted over one shoulder.

Bailey chuckled. "No! We haven't even kicked off our shoes yet."

CHAPTER 16

Keri's Lighthouse

Keri's heart pounded with anticipation. Hope burned within her that somehow Tony had reached her from wherever he was, in this world or the next. Yet doubt rode alongside as a constant critic. She had followed this kind of impulse before, only to be crushed. This time, however, felt different. She wasn't alone; her best friend sat right behind her. Seeing the bioluminescence on the back of the doctor's card had tipped the scales to the I'm-not-crazy side. The craft glided out of her cove and into Perdido Bay. She started to turn toward Johnson's beach when a light flashed in the distance to her right.

"You've got to be kidding me!" Keri said, easing off the throttle. She stood and pointed. "Do you see that?"

Just as Bailey turned to look, the light flashed again. The white beam moved in a circle, came around, and blinked again. "Yeah, I see it," Bailey said. "Is that coming from your…"

"My little lighthouse!" Keri exclaimed.

"I thought you said the lamp didn't work."

"It doesn't."

The beacon in her tower hadn't functioned in several years, but tonight it whirled all over the bay. *No way*, Keri thought. *Even if someone found the hidden entrance to the lamp room, you have to know how to open it. No one could randomly wander up there and fix the thing. Besides, who would bother anyway?* She could think of only one person with the know-how and the desire—*Tony. Of course! His perfect way to send me a message.* She tried to dismiss this idea, to save herself the torture of another grief-induced fantasy. *There's gotta be another logical explanation,* she thought. But her heart wanted to believe. She turned the watercraft toward the pulsing beacon and pulled back on the accelerator.

"We gotta follow that light," Keri spoke over her shoulder.

"I'm with ya, girlfriend. Let's go."

They rounded the corner that opened into the larger bay and turned northeast. Keri's old house sat on a point surrounded by water on three sides—a black fuzzy silhouette that grew more distinctive as they got closer. Soon, Keri could see the outlines of the deck and the angles on the roof and outer walls. The tower at the corner, where the beam would have come from, now seemed like it hadn't been operating in years, with no glow or circling beacon. Suddenly, she felt apprehensive and uncertain, as if her reality scales were tipping back in favor of the I'm-losin'-it side. "We saw it working, right?" she asked.

"Yeah, we did," Bailey answered.

As Keri leered at the dark windows, the present receded into the past to a time when light and love had filled her home. She remembered the day Tony had first shown her the place.

"Are we there yet?" Keri had asked, eager to take off the blindfold.

"Almost," Tony had replied. "No peeking."

Keri bounced in random directions, forward, then sideways, in the passenger seat of Tony's truck. The sound and feel of the ride changed as they veered off the road, her body jerking forward when they stopped.

"Keep your eyes shut," Tony reminded her as he exited. He walked around to her side, opened the door, took her hand, and helped her out. Long grass tickled her ankles as they walked. They stopped, and Tony stood behind Keri. Grabbing her shoulders, he adjusted her position. Then he gently grasped the blindfold on both sides and lifted it away.

"Voilà!" he said proudly.

Keri faced an old, dilapidated house with several broken windows and wood rotted in some spots, missing in others. Much of it needed more than repainting. She couldn't tell if the original color had been gray or if it had turned that way from age and weather. By some designer's logic, which she couldn't decipher, one end of the house had been constructed at a curved angle that rose to a point. The only question that came to her mind was 'why?'.

"This is gonna be our home," Tony whispered.

Keri's heart sank. *Oh, please, no.* Water surrounded the property on three sides—the only redeeming quality about this run-down pile of trash her fiancé had just called home.

Tony stood beside her, one arm around her shoulder.

"I know it needs a little TLC," he said, waving his free arm in a sweeping motion as he talked.

A little? Might as well level it and start over, Keri thought.

"Can you see it? We can fix the windows. Imagine a full wrap-around porch leading to a dock big enough for all our water stuff."

Despite her best efforts, Keri couldn't envision the picture her fiancé was painting, but she loved hearing his dreams about what this abandoned shell could be.

"See how the house goes up to a curved point on one side?"

"Yeah. What is that supposed to be?" Keri asked.

"I don't know what they had in mind, but you know what that could be?"

Keri shook her head.

Tony turned to face her. "A lighthouse," he said.

As if Tony had just pulled off the cover, hiding his actual rendering, Keri could suddenly see the home he had in mind. Rotted wood restored itself green and young; windows shimmered with new glass. The pointed end of the house transformed into a rounded shape with a bay window topped off with a small lighthouse tower. She saw every detail of Tony's vision, right down to the soft green grass in the yard.

Keri looked at him, her heart bursting with adoration for this sweet man. "I love it," she said with a wide smile.

That seemed like another life. A bounce on a wave jolted Keri from her warm memory, and the dark, barren, abandoned structure loomed once again. A chill swept through her, and she felt sadness returning. They hit a swell, and water splashed.

"Hey! Watch it!" Bailey yelled.

"Sorry," Keri shouted, but held the throttle at full.

No, he has to be there, Keri told herself, squelching the sorrow that threatened to spill over again. *No one else could have turned on the light.*

"Don't leave," Keri said. "I'm on the way."

"What?" Bailey asked. "I couldn't hear you."

"Hang on. We're almost there," Keri yelled over her shoulder.

It was odd to see her dream home so lifeless and foreboding. Keri stared at the window to the kitchen, and in her mind, another scene replayed from better days. She remembered Tony cooking while she sat nestled up to the counter. He had just finished preparing dinner, and as he turned his handsome face toward her, Keri tingled all over and thought, surely, she must be glowing. At that moment, she fell even deeper in love with him. She'd follow this man anywhere and love him with all her soul till the end of time. *Isn't it strange how the simplest gestures can have the most impact on one's life?* she thought at the time. Even now, his kind act of cooking for her remained one of Keri's most treasured moments.

Tony had smiled as he gently laid the plate in front of her—a fresh crab cake blended with herbs, coated with just a touch of breading, sautéed to perfection, then drizzled with a homemade brown pecan sauce. Each savory bite had been intoxicating.

The memory faded, leaving only dark windows and the last of a dusky day.

Why doesn't he turn the light on?

Keri had felt safe then. She could hardly wait to return to their home each day. Her heart raced, and her shoulders tensed as the once peaceful sanctuary evoked a brackish pool of conflicting emotions. When they got close enough, she cut the power and drifted the last few yards to the bank.

"Careful, we don't know if someone might be in there," Bailey said, leaning forward.

Keri looked over her shoulder at Bailey. "Seriously? You're telling me to be careful. You're one to talk."

Still, Bailey had a point. An intruder made the most logical sense. Regardless, Keri felt something else, the excitement of possibility, even though that feeling didn't match the cold reality of her dark, empty house.

Am I getting so desperate that I'll believe anything?

"Maybe we can peek…" Bailey began, her sentence interrupted when Keri jumped off the B&B and splashed toward the house.

"Tony!" Keri yelled.

Bailey shouted after her, but Keri kept running. She leaped the stairs to the deck in a single stride, bent down to retrieve a hidden key, then hurriedly unlocked the door and disappeared inside.

CHAPTER 17

The Lamp Room

Keri stood between the living room and kitchen, strangely disoriented. Although she recognized the furniture, she wondered if she hadn't entered someone else's home by mistake. A corked, half-full bottle of wine and a red-stained empty glass sat on the island countertop.

It must have been sitting there for two or three years, Keri thought.

She could almost smell the rich bouquet as the cabernet had splashed into the goblet that night. She'd just taken a sip when Sheriff Cotton knocked on her door.

"Sorry to disturb you, but we're looking for Tony. Is he here?" the sheriff had asked in his natural commanding voice. He took his hat off when she answered the door, otherwise he would have had to duck under the top of the frame.

Keri felt as if a giant hand had gripped her chest. "No, he's still working. Is something wrong?"

"We're not sure. A patrolman found his truck out by the marsh. The door was open, and keys were still in the ignition, but no sign of Tony."

The hand tightened, and Keri struggled to breathe. The rest of the officer's words faded into a muffled background. Keri awoke a few minutes later to find herself lying on the couch.

"Keri, you alright?" she heard the sheriff ask.

She wasn't, and would soon discover that she'd never be the same again.

"Hey, what's happening girl?" Bailey gasped as she reached the doorway.

Bailey's voice brought Keri back from that dreadful night several years ago to the emptiness of now. Tears leaked uncontrollably, and pain overwhelmed Keri like a strong riptide threatening to drown her. She had no answer to give Bailey. After a glance at her friend, Keri sprinted through the dining area, took the steps to the second floor three at a time, and stopped in the middle of the main bedroom. Bailey clambered after her, pausing at the top of the stairs.

Keri stared blankly at the giant bay window and the bed nestled in the center. Usually, she would have been captivated by the view of the bay, but tonight she only saw the memories of her and Tony's cozy moments. Keri could see him in her mind, sleeping in bed, then laughing with her. She closed her eyes and grabbed both arms across her body, feeling as if Tony's ghost had walked up behind her and wrapped her in a loving embrace. Another wave of grief cascaded over her before she felt the gentle comfort of Bailey's hand on her back. She looked at her friend with a nod of appreciation and took several slow breaths.

Keri needed a few moments to collect herself. Finally, she was able to look around. She half-smiled as she walked over to the bookcase on the left wall. An old ship's wheel hung next to the shelves. It had faded from exposure to weather, and a couple of spokes had been replaced by clear plastic tubing.

Keri glanced at Bailey as she grabbed the wheel and turned it one click to the right. They heard the clang of a latch releasing, and one side of the bookcase moved a few inches from the wall. Keri pulled it open, revealing a narrow spiral staircase.

Bailey raised one eyebrow. "A secret passage. So that's how you get to the top of the lighthouse."

"Yep," Keri answered, winking one of her red puffy eyes. She stared at Bailey and said, "Tony and I were the only two people who knew about this hidden doorway."

Bailey's eyes widened. "There's no other way to get up there?"

Keri shook her head. "No."

"Either the beacon came on by itself, or someone turned it on," Bailey said.

"Or… maybe *he* did." Keri's voice betrayed an uncanny certainty.

Bailey's expression suggested that she understood and was open to the possibility that Tony could have turned on the light. "Unless he told someone about it," she added.

Keri furrowed her brow. "I suppose so."

"That someone might still be up there," Bailey said, glancing at the open passageway.

"There's one way to find out."

They hurriedly ascended the narrow swirling steps, Keri leading the way. When she reached the top, she shoved the wooden hatch open, which landed a loud crack. The friends quickly scurried up into the octagonal room of the lighthouse, unsure of who or what they'd find. But nothing awaited them.

"Wow," Bailey whispered as she surveyed the breathtaking 360-degree view. They could even see the Gulf.

But Keri only saw a vacuous room and the panoramic vista of a world without Tony. Her shoulders slumped, and she suddenly felt heavy, tired. Sighing, she leaned back against the railing.

"Yup. I'm losin' it," Keri said.

"No, you're grieving," Bailey answered. Then she came over to Keri and put one hand on her shoulder. She pointed toward the big lamp in the middle of the room and said, "That light was on."

Keri walked over to the switch on the near wall and flicked it up and down several times. Nothing happened. Again, she let out a heavy sigh.

"Maybe we saw another light?" Keri said. Frustration gripped her, and she found it difficult to breathe. *No, not again.* Another clue, another dead end, and she'd brought her best friend into her delusion this time.

Bailey shook her head. "Where? No, it had to be coming from here."

Keri touched the glass covering. "It's still warm!"

Bailey placed her hand on the big lamp and gasped.

Keri shivered as a chill ran down her spine. "You feel it too!"

Bailey nodded her head but didn't answer. She looked both excited and spooked at the same time.

"Okay, so I'm not going crazy. What does this mean?" Keri asked.

Bailey shrugged.

Looking at one another, they simultaneously said, "It's another sign!"

"It has to be," Keri said. "You gettin' any visions?"

"No," Bailey said, shaking her head and looking around to make sure they were alone.

"What if…" Keri started, but then swallowed the rest of her words.

"What if what?" Bailey asked.

"What if it is a message from Tony."

The question hung in the air between the friends. While they'd considered the possibility that Tony might have been trying to contact Keri, the ability of a ghost to turn on a broken light fell in a whole other league beyond whispers and brief glimpses.

"Let's assume he's trying to contact you," Bailey said with a moderate tone. "Why not just visit you? Why turn on a broken beacon?"

Keri shrugged.

Suddenly, they heard the whir of rotors and gears moving. Bright white light beamed from the device, and it began turning.

"Aahhhhhh!" Keri screamed, along with Bailey. As if the circling light had a force pushing them, they both backpedaled till they hit with a thud against a window.

"The switch is still off!" Keri yelled.

"Whrrump, whrrump," the light sounded as it turned rhythmically.

"Let's get out of here!" Bailey shouted.

"Good idea," Keri agreed.

The whrrump sound stopped with a loud clang, the light now fixed and shining into the bay. Then the whirring died down, and the light faded, leaving them in the silent darkness again. Keri peered through the window in the direction the beam had been and saw a faint glow in the water.

"Wait!" Keri said, grabbing her friend's arm.

"What?"

"Look. See that?" Keri asked, pointing to the window where the beam had stopped.

Bailey squinted her eyes, scanning the bay. "No, I don't see anything."

"It was right there," Keri said, poking the glass. "It was a sparkly blue/greenish glow in the water."

"Sea sparkles?"

"Could be. You sure you didn't see it?"

"Sorry, I didn't see anything." She blinked, trying to clear the aftereffects of the giant light shining in her eyes.

Keri stared out the window and caressed the ring Antonio had given her, which hung on her necklace. "Come on. We gotta go," she said, rushing down the stairs.

"Where are you going?" Bailey called after her, trying to keep up.

"The glowing light was close to Snake Island."

"Okay. So what?"

Keri stopped and grabbed her friend. Excitement twinkled in her eyes. "It means this *is* real! Tony brought us up here to show us this!" She pulled Bailey toward the hatch and said, "Come on. We're kickin' off our shoes."

CHAPTER 18

Snake Island

The moon hung bright and low in the Gulf Coast sky, casting a long, shimmering line on the bay water. When they arrived where Keri thought she saw the luminescence, she cut power to the engine and drifted silently, looking for the mysterious glow.

"See anything?" she asked.

"Not a thing," Bailey answered while scanning the water.

"We must be close," Keri said. "I just know it." She glanced at Bailey. "You sure you didn't see it?"

"No, I didn't, but I believe you."

Keri sighed heavily, then felt Bailey's hand on her shoulder.

"Breathe," Bailey said.

Keri let out a low groan and patted Bailey's hand, grateful for a friend who truly had her back.

"You sure the light came from glowing algae?" Bailey asked.

Keri replayed the memory in her mind. "Hmmm, maybe not," she conceded. "I saw the light reflecting on the water, more green than blue. Then it abruptly went dark. The naturally occurring phenomenon usually fades. It doesn't just turn off like someone flipped a switch."

"Could it be artificial? Another boat?"

"Maybe," Keri said as she considered several possibilities. Bailey's suggestion made sense. The reflection could have come from another boat. Still, why would someone turn off their running lights unless they didn't want to be seen?

"Whoever it was couldn't have gone far," Keri said over her shoulder.

The scientist cranked the watercraft and began to methodically circle the small, nearby island. With very few palm trees and almost no beach, the place didn't fit the image one usually held of a tropical island. Instead, short pines and scrub brush comprised most of the thick foliage, as if a piece of lower Alabama had broken off and floated into the bay. In recent years, Snake Island had become a favorite haunt for teenagers. However, their partying stopped when a couple of kids almost died from snake bites. The Florida Fish and Wildlife commission discovered that the place had become home to three of Florida's most venomous snakes. The reptiles didn't like visitors, and the local government agreed. Since the near-fatal incidents, the authorities had declared the island off-limits to humans. It now belonged to the serpents.

Keri circled the forbidden patch of land, looking for any sign of a beached boat, while Bailey kept her eyes on the more expansive bay. Neither saw any other craft nor any glows in the water.

How could a boat disappear? Keri felt a strange sense of déjà vu, like when she had seen the stranger in the marsh.

They idled, facing one of several signs posted around the island warning visitors to stay away.

Bailey leaned forward and asked, "You're not thinking what I think you're thinking, are you?"

"There's a passageway just to the right of that sign," Keri said.

"You mean that sign that says *Keep out? Extremely dangerous wildlife?*"

"That's the one," Keri answered as she clicked off the running lights and eased the throttle back.

"It's called Snake Island for a reason," Bailey stated.

"Nah, that's the wildlife commission scaring away the unwanted teenagers. The real Snake Island is in Brazil. You don't want to set foot on that one. Still, keep your eyes peeled."

Keri steered through a break in the virtually impenetrable thicket, unless you were traveling at idle speed or happened to be a marine biologist like Keri, who had studied the area. The entrance opened only wide enough for her small craft. Branches scraped against their arms and back, causing them to jump now and again. Their heightened imagination turned the tentacles of the brush into slithery reptiles, ready to strike. The dense growth soon opened into a more expansive cove.

"Wow! A hidden hideaway, how cool," Bailey said. "I can see why the kids hung out here."

"Tony and I snuck away to this spot, too, on occasion," Keri said, as the memories swirled in her mind.

She shut off the engine, and they drifted to the shoreline. Keri pulled a flashlight from a central storage compartment and fanned the beam in the surrounding water and nearby beach. All clear. She splashed into ankle-deep shallows and dragged the B&B onto the bank.

"We camped here overnight a couple of times," Keri said.

"Cozy," Bailey said, smiling.

An old fire pit nested before them, with the lagoon just beyond. No one had burned a fire here in some time.

Suddenly, they heard a strange squeaky cry—the kind of sound that made you wonder if you'd heard it or not. They looked at each other in surprise.

"There it is again!" Keri exclaimed.

"Is that a bird?" Bailey asked, turning to her friend for an explanation.

"Sounds like a tree frog crying," Keri said.

"That's so sad. Why is it crying?"

"Probably being eaten by a snake."

"That's not funny."

"I'm not joking."

Bailey looked up and around. "There are snakes in the trees?"

"Yeah, and sometimes they can fall on your head."

While Bailey turned, Keri reached out and poked her shoulder.

"AHHHHH!" Bailey screamed and jumped. "Hey! Not cool!"

"Sorry," Keri said, suppressing a laugh.

Bailey glared, then looked away, trying to hide a grin. She let out a chuckle.

Suddenly, they heard a rustle behind Keri.

Bailey gasped and froze. "Something's there!" she said, pointing behind Keri.

Keri turned, clicked on the small flashlight again, and shined it in the direction Bailey was pointing. "That's a turtle," Keri said, surprised. The marine biologist stepped toward the creature, keeping it in the spotlight, and saw a heart-shaped discoloration atop his shell. "It's Snaps!"

Startled, the turtle froze, then scurried into the water.

"Seems a long way from the cove he normally hangs around," Bailey said.

"I've never seen him here, though this island is not out of his range of migration."

"What's the digging for?"

"Well, turtles dig holes for several reasons," Keri began. "To lay eggs, but since he's a male, he's not doing that. Or to look for food, or to hide for protection."

"We're talking about Snaps, so maybe he was digging for treasure," Bailey said with a quiet laugh.

Keri chuckled. "Yeah, right." She focused the beam on the spot where Snaps had been digging, finding nothing but a shallow hole. She felt nostalgic.

"What?" Bailey asked.

She glanced at Bailey. "You don't suppose…"

Bailey shrugged. "As I said, we are talking about Snaps."

They both knelt closer to the hole their turtle friend had just made. Keri began to dig with her hands while Bailey shined the light on her progress. After a few minutes, Keri's hand struck a hard object.

"There's something here!" Keri said, digging more fervently.

"What is it?"

"Not sure yet." She excitedly cleared more sand away, exposing a small wooden box. She carefully retrieved it and brushed it clean. She noticed an etching on the lid. Keri took one corner of her shirt and wiped it across the top. Two sapphire-colored words glittered in the beam of the flashlight. *Go Blue.*

CHAPTER 19

Keepsakes

Keri's mouth fell open as she stared at the box. "We always said we'd bury a memory box here, but we never got around to it."

"Well, Tony clearly made time," Bailey said. "Open it."

Keri held her breath and slowly pried up the lid. She retrieved a folded piece of paper from inside with a shaky hand and quickly unfurled it. The parchment had been torn as if ripped from a book, creating a jagged edge. A handwritten note sprawled across the top. She clasped a hand over her mouth as tears filled her eyes.

"It's from Tony!" Keri said, barely able to speak.

She read the note silently, her lips mouthing the words under the dim glow of her small flashlight. Then she hung her head and sobbed.

Bailey hugged her friend for several minutes.

Finally, more composed, Keri handed her the paper and the light.

Bailey read it aloud.

My dearest,

Our ship has come in! Go blue with me, and I'll show it to you!

Yours Always, Antonio.

Bailey put her hand over her mouth and looked compassionately at her friend. "It's a drawing of you and a pretty good one. You look pretty content in that sketch."

Wow, he must have taken his time with this, Keri thought. Tony had paid loving attention to detail, capturing the wisps in her hair as if the wind were gently blowing. Her beloved had even drawn her wearing the engagement ring on her left hand. Keri smiled and touched the real one, hanging around her neck as usual. The note and the drawing threw fresh kindling on a smoldering fire of grief for Keri. She mourned the exploits they would never have. She would have loved sharing his great discovery, not for any gold, but just for the adventure with him.

Keri noticed an arrow extended from the engagement band to the right edge of the page. Flipping it over, she discovered several more hand-drawn sketches and written descriptions, not of her but of ancient Spanish medallions.

Bailey reached into the wooden container again and brought out an old gold coin. "This looks similar to the one in your photo!"

Eyes wide, Keri grabbed it from Bailey. The artifact seemed to match the piece of eight Snaps had brought her the other night. Someone had cleaned this one, so the gold shined. She looked at Bailey and said, "You're right! It's the same. It has to be."

"Crab balls!" Bailey exclaimed. "Tony actually found treasure. Incredible!"

"It would seem so."

"Look! There's something else in here," Bailey said, reaching inside the box. She retrieved a weathered piece of wood, jagged edges on both ends, with the letters DEL M carved on one side. Someone or something had broken the plank, cutting off the rest of the word and perhaps more.

"What do you make of this?" Bailey asked.

Keri shook her head as she ran her fingers across the engraving. "I don't know. It looks like a piece of wood I've got back home."

"You think it goes with this one?"

"Not sure, but we definitely should compare the two."

A sudden crack and snap made them jump.

Bailey quickly switched off the flashlight. "Did you hear that?"

Keri sat rigidly, facing the general direction of the noise. "Yeah," she whispered. "It came from somewhere in the brush."

"That ain't no snake," Bailey said. "Maybe it's just a wild animal."

A faint rustling sound came from the brush, closer this time. Bailey clicked on the flashlight and shined it in the direction of the noise. Someone or something ducked behind the foliage.

"Or maybe not," Keri said. "Let's get out of here."

They both sprang to their feet and ran, Keri cradling the memento box under one arm. The rustling noise grew louder. Keri looked back to see who or what followed them and tripped on an old log near the fire pit. She landed with a thud, fumbling the box, its contents spilling onto the sand. Bailey helped her friend up and then quickly scooped the loose items and some sand back into the wooden case. She tucked it under one arm, and they raced toward the B&B.

A shadowy shape emerged from the brush and chased after them.

"Someone's coming!" Keri yelled. "We gotta go now!"

Quickly Keri pushed the jet craft into the water and hopped on board.

Bailey jumped on the back, clutching the small treasure box in one hand and holding on tight with the other.

"Hang on!" Keri yelled. She made sure Bailey had a firm grip before cranking the engine. Now was not the time for her friend to be thrown off the back, as had happened a few months before when they were getting away from a menacing gunman. As the craft lurched forward, Keri glanced over her shoulder. She spotted their pursuer moving gracefully and swiftly toward them. She couldn't make out any facial features, but judging by the curved, shapely legs cutting a path in the sand and the long hair bobbing back and forth, Keri figured their pursuer to be a woman.

Branches scratched as the watercraft entered the narrow passage, pulling Keri's attention forward.

"Ooowww!" Bailey yelped. "Wait! Stop!"

Keri cut the engine and turned to check on her friend. Bailey held her right hand over her left forearm. Tiny droplets of blood trickled from underneath her fingers. "You okay?"

"Yeah," Bailey answered. "But I dropped the box."

Keri spotted the keepsake floating right side up, about halfway between them and the beach. The mysterious person stood at the water's edge.

"Who is that?" Bailey asked.

"I don't know."

The stranger sprinted into the lagoon, dove into the murky pool, and swam toward them.

"She's after Tony's mementos!" Keri said. She couldn't turn their craft around, and the passage was too narrow to paddle back in time. She began to take off her shoes, but Bailey stood.

"I got this," Bailey said.

"Wait," Keri protested.

"Be ready to get us out of here!"

Before Keri could respond, Bailey dove off the back and swam toward the precious cargo. Keri's heart raced as she watched her friend put herself in harm's way. While Bailey would reach the box first, could she make it back to the B&B before the mystery woman caught her? The stranger seemed like a stronger swimmer.

As expected, Bailey did get to the prize first. Grabbing it under one arm, she paddled with the other, kicking and pulling frantically toward the watercraft. Given her compromised state, the stranger quickly gained on her, leaving no doubt that she would overtake Bailey before she returned safely aboard. Keri opened the seat compartment, pulled out a nylon rope, and fastened one end to the handle on the back of the seat.

"Hey! Grab this and hold on tight!" Keri said, swinging the coiled rope in large circles. *I'm only gonna get one shot at this.*

One final swing, and she let loose, praying that the lifeline's path was true. The rope slapped the water right next to Bailey, who grabbed it with her free hand and wrapped it around her wrist. Squeezing the box, she held the rope tight and yelled, "Got—" Her sentence was cut off as the attacker caught up with Bailey and pushed her under.

"Hang on!" Keri yelled as she cranked the engine and pulled back on the throttle. The craft strained forward, which meant Bailey still had a hold of the rope. Keri glanced back to see her friend surface, rope entwined around one wrist, Tony's treasure under her other arm.

As the stranger treaded water and watched, the craft pushed through the small passage and darted into the bay, pulling Bailey and the box behind them.

CHAPTER 20

After Bailey climbed back aboard, their water-craft glided effortlessly through the glassy, still water. Keri glanced behind her for the fifth time since their harrowing escape. No one pursued them. She let out a long breath.

"All clear; I just checked," Bailey said.

"I can't lose you," Keri said. "I just can't lose another person I love."

"You're not gonna lose me," Bailey assured, displaying her friendship bracelet like a superhero.

Keri sighed. The wristband seemed like childish protection against the nefarious forces weighing upon her. "Are you alright?"

"My shoulder hurts, but I'll be fine."

"So, that was a woman who attacked you?" Keri asked.

"Not just any woman. It's *her*."

"The one who left the picture after spying on me in the marsh?"

"Yes."

"Did you get a good look at her face?"

"Only a glimpse, but she is definitely the same person I saw in my vision. I know it." Bailey rested her head on Keri's back.

"Hang on," Keri said. "We're almost there."

Keri felt an unsettledness down to her core. She wondered how long the mystery woman had been watching her. How did she know Tony? Even more unnerving, this stranger had become aggressive while charging after them and even tried to drown Bailey. The attacker also seemed fearless, diving into a snake-infested lagoon. Her movements had been powerful as she pursued them. But why would she be interested in the keepsake box?

As they approached the houseboat, Keri spotted someone on the deck. She banged her hand against the throttle several times until it released, and the craft slowed.

"Who's that?" Bailey asked, pointing.

Keri squinted, fearing the worst, then smiled. "Oh, it's Clem." She sighed, realizing she had been holding her breath.

"Ahh, I didn't recognize him. It looks like he's rearranging your furniture or something."

She nudged the throttle, resuming her course toward her houseboat. Once docked, they bounded up the stairs. A tall, broad-shouldered, muscular man greeted them with a big bear hug. He wore an American flag bandanna over his head and a neatly trimmed, blond/grayish beard.

"How's it going, Clem?" Bailey asked.

"Well, I ain't buying any green bananas, but other than that, doin' better than I deserve.

"What's happened here?" Keri asked.

"I heard a loud noise that seemed to originate from your deck. I thought I saw someone over here and came to check it out."

Keri looked around. Everything seemed in order, except one end of the small desk sat away from the wall.

"My desk looks like it's been moved."

"Yeah," Clem said. "And your shrine was on the floor; some of the contents spilled. I picked it up and put it back."

"You found the skull!" Keri said, and hugged the old SEAL. "Thank you."

"You bet, kid," Clem said.

"You think your speedboat boyfriend came roaring through?" Bailey asked.

"He's not my boyfriend," Keri said.

"I know, but he's still got a thing for you."

"Forget it. He's just not…"

"Tony," Bailey said.

"That's right," Keri said, with a look that warned both her friends not to challenge her on this.

"I would've noticed his big orange boat," Clem said. "Knocking over that desk would take a pretty good-size wake."

Keri examined the desk. One corner had a chip off where it had hit the deck. Someone could have gone through the drawers, or maybe the jumbled contents resulted from the desk falling over. Otherwise, the antique looked intact.

She scanned the rest of the living space. Hard to tell if things had been disturbed. Keri wasn't the neatest housekeeper.

"Maybe some kids out looking for a quick buck," Keri said.

"Hmmm," Clem grunted, looking even more concerned. "You gals been in a fight?"

Keri noticed several scratches on her forearms from the thicket. She brushed her hand through her hair, pulling out a variety of splinters and spurs. Bailey looked no better, holding her left shoulder. The rope had burned a red circle around Bailey's wrist.

"We went a few rounds with nature," Keri answered.

Clem squinted as though he knew there was more to the story. He trained his eyes on the box tucked under Bailey's arm. "Find some treasure?"

"Oh, um, yes. We found some of Tony's mementos," Keri said, gesturing to the box Bailey cradled under one arm.

Clem raised one eyebrow, then nodded. "Well, that is special. I'll leave y'all to your business."

"You think it's safe for me to stay here tonight?" Keri asked.

"Well, you're not staying by yourself, girlfriend," Bailey said. "I'm camping out with you."

They both looked at Clem as if asking permission.

"Yeah, I suppose y'all will be safe here," Clem said cautiously. "I doubt they'll come back. Hoodlums prefer staying in the shadows. I'll sleep with one eye open." He winked. "One more thing, Tony's mom came by today. She asked me to give this to you." He handed Keri a card.

Emotions swelled as Keri read the note. Gathering her composure, she said, "It's an invitation to their Day of the Dead celebrations."

"You've got a family that cares about you, Keri," Clem said.

"I appreciate this," Keri said as she laid the card aside.

The old vet hugged them both and left.

"Hey!" Keri called to him. When he stopped and turned, she said, "Thank you for taking care of my house."

He nodded and ambled home.

Once Clem reached his house, Keri quickly grabbed the box and poured the contents onto the table. Sand and debris spilled, along with a medallion and a piece of paper. Ignoring the coin, Keri picked up the parchment, eager to read Tony's handwriting in a better light.

Her expression quickly soured. "This isn't the note! It's just an old piece of trash." Tossing the paper aside, she rifled her hands through the remaining sand, finally turning the empty box upside down. Then she checked for any secret hideaway places inside but found none. "Where's Tony's message?" she asked. "And his drawing of me?"

"I don't know," Bailey answered. "It was dark. I panicked. I scooped up everything I could."

"I have to go back," Keri protested. "I have to find it."

"You're not serious," Bailey said.

"Damn right, I'm serious," Keri said, moving toward the dock.

Bailey grabbed her arm. "You're not going back out there. Not tonight."

"Yes, I am," Keri said, freeing her arm. "I'm not leaving him out there!"

Bailey stepped in front of her, blocking the way to the dock. "Him? Listen to yourself."

"Get out of my way, Bailey!"

"Someone is on that island, and they just tried to drown me! It's too dangerous. There's also a bunch of snakes, in case you forgot."

"I can handle myself." Keri stared at her friend. "Don't make me take you down."

Bailey met Keri's glower with equal fierceness. "You take one more step, and I'll tell Clem everything. We'll tie you to the deck, call the doc, and have you committed. You're talking crazy."

Anger boiled inside Keri. Every muscle tightened, ready for a fight. But she wasn't about to launch an assault on her friend. Never.

"Just wait till morning," Bailey said more softly. "Please. You're gonna find the note. I know it."

"Serious, serious?" Keri asked.

"Serious, serious," Bailey answered.

"You can't be kidding around with a serious, serious. You know that," Keri said.

"I know the rule, girlfriend."

"Alright, I'll wait till morning," Keri said.

"Thank you."

A feeling of remorse suddenly ached in Keri's chest. She'd almost physically fought with her best friend.

"I'm sorry," Keri said.

"It's okay."

The two friends hugged. Bailey winced and rubbed her sore shoulder.

"You sure you're not injured?" Keri asked.

"Felt like my arm was being torn off my body back there. But, better than the alternative."

"Definitely."

Bailey looked scared. "The lady was strong. If you hadn't thrown me the rope…"

"But I did throw you that rope, and you held on."

Bailey moved her wounded joint in a circular motion, grimacing with each rotation. "I'm never riding on the back of your stupid B&B again. Every time I do, somehow, I end up in the water."

Keri shrugged. "Let's take a look at our treasures," she said. "Bring the box inside. I have something else I want to show you."

Bailey placed the wooden box on the antique writing table.

"You know my grandmother, Bertha Mae, gave me this desk," Keri said.

"Yeah, it belonged to Captain Davenport. You told me. Was he a pirate?"

"No, but he was a captain, a British merchant. A furniture company made this for him, and it became a popular style."

"I can see why," Bailey said. "It's compact with lots of neat drawers on the side, and the top lifts up for storage underneath."

Keri smiled. "That's correct, and there's more." She reached around the back and pressed a small wooden button, then gently pulled the entire desktop forward.

"Cool! A secret compartment."

Keri stuck her hand into one of the small hideaways and handed Bailey the photo of Snaps with the coin on his back. They compared it to the medallion Tony had left in the box.

"They look the same!" Bailey exclaimed.

Next, Keri retrieved a piece of old wood from the same hidden niche. It looked almost identical in shape and color to the one from the keepsake box, except for the letters **GEN** carved across it.

"Tony found this before he disappeared," Keri said. "He believed it was from a previously unidentified shipwreck. Not knowing the full name, it became next to impossible to track it down in the records."

Keri laid the two fragments on the desk. They looked like matching pieces of a puzzle, only with a section missing in between. GEN had been engraved in the same font and size as the one with DEL M. Keri slid the two scraps closer.

"Hmm," Keri said. "Looks like Tony didn't just find treasure. I think he found a shipwreck."

CHAPTER 21

Self Defense

The following morning, Keri cooked breakfast while Bailey stirred awake on the couch.

"What time is it?" Bailey asked, her voice muffled under the blanket.

"It's 9:30, sleepyhead. Time to get up."

Bailey groaned and slowly sat upright on the couch.

"Fresh coffee waiting for ya," Keri said, tilting her head toward the pot on the counter. She divided the scrambled eggs onto two plates, then added toast and crispy bacon.

"Sorry I slept so late," Bailey said, pouring herself a cup of steamy java. "I know you want to get back to Snake Island as soon as possible."

Keri shrugged, sighed heavily, and chewed on a bit of bacon. She avoided looking at her friend.

"Your eyes are puffy. Have you been crying?" Bailey asked.

"Just a tough morning. I don't want to talk about it." Keri pushed the opposite chair back from the table with one foot. "Sit down and eat."

Bailey's expression changed from concern to surprise. "Is that sand on your ankle?" Bailey looked out the front door. "Why are there wet footprints on the deck?"

"I had to run an errand for work," Keri replied, biting down on a piece of toast.

Bailey set her cup on the counter. "You didn't."

Keri took another bite of breakfast.

"Keri, tell me you didn't," Bailey commanded.

Keri leveled her eyes on Bailey. "I did."

Bailey's face turned crimson. "I can't believe you!" she yelled, pushing the chair back under the table. "You said you'd wait!"

"I did wait. You were asleep."

Bailey shoved the table, spilling Keri's coffee. "Don't give me that. You know what I'm talking about!"

Keri stood abruptly, her chair slamming into the bookcase behind her. "You said the note would be there! It wasn't!"

Bailey's aspect softened. "You didn't find the note?"

"No! You said I would. You said, 'Serious, serious.' "

"I know what I said!" Bailey spat back.

"Well, you were wrong!" Keri threw her napkin on top of her food.

Bailey paused before answering. "No, I'm not wrong. You will find that note. But obviously not on Snake Island."

Her friend's certainty surprised Keri, but Bailey's intuition was rarely wrong. Part of her hoped again, but she squelched that as quickly as it had emerged. *No,* she thought, trying to control the grief. *No more. Time to accept things. What am I upset at Bailey for?*

"It doesn't matter," Keri said. "To hell with it."

"I can't believe you went out there alone!"

"Well, I did. Deal with it."

Bailey looked ready to leap over the table and come after her. Keri hadn't seen her this mad since Thomas had gotten under her skin.

"Good morning," a husky voice said.

The greeting interrupted the anger that seemed to have reached a boiling point within Bailey.

"Good morning, Clem," Keri said.

Bailey mumbled a welcome and moved toward the couch.

Clem handed Keri a brown paper sack. "I bought y'all some of your favorite treats."

Keri opened the bag and sniffed the sweet aroma of warm bread coated with cinnamon and sugar, cooked apples baked inside. "You're the best, Clem," she said.

Clem nodded and glanced at the two. "Y'all okay?" he asked.

Keri looked at Bailey and answered, "Yeah, we're okay. We're just sorting out a disagreement."

Clem looked at Bailey, who nodded.

"Yeah, we're good, Clem," Bailey said with a sigh and what seemed like a forced smile.

"Alright then, holler if y'all need anything."

As he stepped onto the deck, the Navy vet pointed toward the latch and said, "You keep locking that door, you hear?"

"Will do," Keri promised.

"Oh, and stay away from Snake Island. That's a dangerous place."

"What?" Keri tried to feign innocence, but the shock clearly gave her away.

"Where else would Tony hide a gift for you except in y'all's special place." He winked and left.

"No wonder he'd had such a successful career as a Navy SEAL. That guy knows his stuff," Keri said. She smiled as she watched him hobble home. "He's never really told me how he injured his leg. He's spun some stories about tripping at home or falling off a ladder. I think it's an old war injury."

"Even with a hitch in his get-along, he looks pretty tough," Bailey added.

"A what?"

"You know, a limp."

Keri smiled and shook her head. "Clem's a former Navy SEAL, tough as they come. If I were a burglar, I wouldn't dare take him on. He could kick ten men's butts with a hitch in his… how does that go?"

"His get-along. Just call it a limp." Bailey rolled her eyes and sipped her coffee.

Keri looked at her friend and said, "He taught me a self-defense move. Wanna see it?"

Bailey shook her head. "You don't wanna mess with me. I ain't even had coffee yet, and I'm not very happy with you right now."

"Come on," Keri said as she stepped outside. She grabbed a cushion off one of the lounge chairs and threw it on the deck. "That's so you won't get hurt when I drop you."

Bailey raised one eyebrow and looked annoyed.

"Get behind me and pull one of my arms behind my back," Keri instructed.

Bailey seemed eager to do as she asked.

Keri continued, "Now press me against the wall so I can't move."

Bailey stared at her.

"Don't worry, you're not gonna hurt me," Keri reassured. "Pretend you're a pirate."

Bailey pinned her against one wall of the houseboat, then smugly said, "Now give me the gold."

Keri twisted and stepped back between Bailey's legs, forcing her friend's weight to shift more to one side. As she turned, she grabbed Bailey's other leg and yanked hard, using her body weight to knock Bailey off balance. The move sent them both tumbling onto the cushion with a loud squish. Keri landed on top and rolled, her elbow poised to strike.

Bailey's eyes opened wide. "Wow!" she said. "That was awesome."

Keri smiled smugly as her aggressive expression faded. "Yeah, it's a pretty cool move. I'm supposed to finish you off with an elbow to the nose."

"Thanks for holding back. You should have seen the look in your eyes. You were fierce, girlfriend."

"You good?" Keri asked, offering a helping hand.

Bailey took her hand. "Yep, fine," she said, but her tone had an empty quality.

Keri's eyes glistened. "I'm sorry. I'm sorry I went out there without you."

Bailey's lip quivered as she fought back her own tears. "I forgive you."

The two friends hugged each other.

"I hate being mad at you," Bailey said.

"I don't ever want to fight with you."

"Well, remind me never to pin you against the wall."

Keri spread her mouth in a satisfied grin. "I told you I can take care of myself." As much as she welcomed the lighthearted moment, it quickly evaporated like the rising sun burning the morning mist. She opened the memory box Tony had left for her on Snake Island and retrieved the coin. She compared it to the one in the photo on Snaps's back.

"They do look identical," Keri commented.

"That's a real Spanish medallion."

"Maybe," Keri said flatly.

"I don't get it. How come you're not more excited about this?"

"I'd rather have his note." A familiar ache burned in Keri's chest, and once again a longing for her lost love overtook her. Keri stared blankly as she caressed the engagement ring hanging around her neck.

"Talk to me," Bailey said.

Keri took a breath and motioned for Bailey to sit in one of the empty lounges. Keri sat opposite. "One night, Tony wanted me to meet him. 'Come see the lights,' he said. 'Come and go blue with me.' But I just wasn't up for it. I'd had a long day at work. All I wanted to do was shower and go to bed. So, I told him I'd take a rain check."

Bailey shrugged her shoulders. "Nothing wrong with taking care of yourself."

"That was the night he disappeared."

Bailey covered her mouth with one hand. "Oh, my God," came her muffled reply.

"If I'd gone… If I had just been with him."

"No, no," Bailey said, laying her hand on Keri's arm. "It's not your fault."

Keri seemed lost in a memory. Bailey gently shook her attention back to their conversation. "It's not your fault. You hear me?"

Keri nodded. "I know, but I can't help but wonder."

"Listen to me," Bailey said. "It's… not… your… fault."

Keri took a minute as if trying to absorb the comforting words that Bailey had given her.

"I took you to Snake Island," Keri said. "I put you in danger. I had to go back and look at Tony's message. But I just couldn't let you come with me."

"I can understand that, but I'm still mad at you."

Eager to avoid repeated confrontation, Keri squeezed Bailey's arm and looked at the books scattered about the deck and living room. "I haven't stayed up half the night doing research since college when I was cramming for a test."

"And we are still no closer to locating Tony's mystery shipwreck. Let's show Max what we found. Maybe he can tell us more." Bailey proposed.

"Okay, but no one else needs to know right now."

"Agreed."

Keri put the scrap wood marked with DEL M back into the keepsake box, then handed it to Bailey. "Would you keep the memento box for a while?" Keri asked. "It doesn't feel safe here."

"Of course. I'll take good care of it."

"Thanks. I'll hold onto this." Keri pocketed the coin Tony had left for her. She recognized that focused, determined look in Bailey's eyes. "Don't dive into the danger like you did on Snake Island ever again."

"Really? After what you just pulled?" Bailey said, putting her hand on her hip.

Keri pursed her lips and stared at her friend. "I mean it. Don't go barefoot on this one. Promise me."

"On one condition," Bailey answered. "You don't go chasing clues by yourself either."

"Deal," Keri said. "I'll meet you at the Tropical Palm."

"Sounds good. I just need to go by the office for a bit first. I'm already late."

"I'll meet you there early afternoon, say 1:30?"

"Alright, but lunch is on you this time," Bailey muttered as she walked toward her Jeep. "Your ship finally comes in, and Snaps is the only one who knows where it is."

CHAPTER 22

Bounty of the Sea

Keri's stomach growled as she pulled into the parking lot of the Tropical Palm. Though she had cooked breakfast, she hadn't eaten much of it. Keri scanned the other cars—no sign of Bailey's Jeep. A refreshing blast of cool air greeted her as she walked through the front door. The diner buzzed with the low hum of several table conversations and clinking utensils. Keri settled into one of the stools at the counter. Her mouth watered from the aroma of freshly cooked delights. A loud male voice echoed from the kitchen, seemingly bragging about his culinary abilities.

"Y'all got a new cook?" Keri asked.

Mary smiled as she poured Keri a cup of coffee. "Yep. Max is training him."

They heard another boisterous exchange from the kitchen.

"Kind of loud, ain't he?" Keri asked.

Mary leaned down and lowered her voice. "He's kind of smitten with Katie. So, he's struttin' his peacock feathers."

Katie walked by, carrying a tray of dirty dishes. She glanced toward the serving window and rolled her eyes.

"All men are jerks," Katie whispered.

"Not all men, dear," Mary stated, smiling. "Young and in love."

Max appeared from the back, wiping his hands. "Well, there's a ray of sunshine," he said, looking at Keri with a bright, welcoming smile. He walked over and gave her a grandfatherly hug. He glanced around the diner. "Where's our newest convert to treasure hunting?" he said, lowering his voice.

"Sales call, of course, and we're not hunting for gold." Max winked.

"We've found something. Bailey is bringing part of it with her," Keri said.

She took out her cell phone, dialed Bailey's number, and got her voice message again. *Surely, she's not still mad at me.* "Hey, it's me. Where are you? I'm at the Tropical Palm. Hurry up and bring the box."

Keri looked at Max and said, "I guess she got caught up at work. Anyway, I wondered what you thought of this?" She slid a scrap of wood, with the letters GEN carved into it, toward the old cook.

Max studied the driftwood. "Where did you get this?"

"Tony found it a few months before he disappeared. He was convinced it was part of an old shipwreck."

Max raised both eyebrows in surprise. "Come on around back. Let's see if we can find out what ship this came from."

Mary stood a few feet away, hands on her hips. "Go on. I'll keep the coffee warm."

A plate with hot food appeared in the serving window. When Katie reached for it, the young male voice said, "Now there's a work of art."

Katie picked up the dish and tilted her head as if annoyed. "It's just an omelet," she said, walking away.

"I wasn't talking about breakfast," the voice yelled after her.

Katie shook her head. "Oh, please." Her cheeks turned slightly pink, and she pressed her lips together as if hiding a smile.

"I think she likes him," Keri said.

Mary chuckled. "I think you're right."

Keri followed Max around the back of the restaurant to the rustic wooden shack now serving as Max's map room and man cave. She checked her phone to ensure she hadn't missed a call from Bailey. Nope, no messages.

Max stepped through the entrance of his hideout, waving her inside. Several renderings of Lost Key covered the top of the large wooden table in the center of the room.

"Here's a reprint of the map hanging in my diner," he said, pointing to one on the table. Then he reached for the one next to it. When he held it up, the dim light shined through it. The paper was thin, almost transparent. Max laid this one atop the other. "And this is a modern-day, more precise map of the bay."

"Wow, the old one is surprisingly accurate," Keri said.

"Yeah," Max agreed. "And without the help of the modern technology we have today in the '90s."

He reached for another large drawing and stacked it with the others. This one displayed several curvy lines drawn from the Gulf and winding into the bay.

"Here are the routes of the known shipwrecks in the area," Max said. Each line had a name beside it, marking the ship believed to have taken that particular path.

"Interesting," Keri said, scanning the cartography.

Max pulled another piece of paper stashed in the pages of a thick book. He unfolded the paper and laid it flat, revealing a drawing of the bay in more detail, with several arrow-like paths sketched across it in various directions, along with several rows of numbers.

"I showed this to Tony right before he disappeared," Max said. "He took detailed notes in a journal he was carrying."

Emotions swirled within Keri. After months of searching, she felt like she'd just found a tiny piece of a giant puzzle. "That means he wrote the note after meeting you," she said, almost whispering to herself.

"What note?" Max asked.

"Tony wrote me a message saying our ship had come in. It seemed like someone had ripped a page right out of a notebook. Bailey and I found it in a keepsake box he left."

"Let's take a look. Do you have the note with you?" Max asked.

"No, we lost it when we were leaving Snake Island."

Max shot her a disapproving look, but Keri held up her hand before he could protest.

"I know. We shouldn't have gone there," Keri said. "Tony and I used to go there as our secret getaway before they quarantine the place. This time we found a memento box Tony had left for me. The note was inside."

Max looked concerned and waited for more explanation.

"Bailey and I saw someone out there that night. We got spooked and ran. I tripped and spilled the contents onto the beach. We scooped up the items as fast as we could before racing off, and later learned we had left the note. I went back the next morning but found nothing."

"So, someone else knows about your discovery."

"Yes," Keri said.

"What else did y'all find besides the note?"

Keri's eyes darted around the room before addressing his question. She reached into her pocket, retrieved the gold coin she'd been carrying, and handed it to Max.

"We found another piece of eight."

Max's mouth opened slightly, eyes fixed on the medallion as he slowly rotated it. "This is nearly identical to the one in the photo you showed me. They're clearly from the same mint," he said.

Max looked at Keri with an icy, hair-raising expression, walked over, and closed the door to the shack.

"Finding one authentic Spanish medallion is rare, but two is remarkable," Max said with excitement and apprehension.

Keri saw Tony's face in her mind, giddy and excited like a little boy at play.

"Tony also found another old scrap of wood with the letters DEL M carved into the broken pieces," she said. "He speculated the first word stood for Genesis, but now I wonder…"

Max reached for a small pile of loose papers and leafed through the stack. "I did some more research on the lost ship, *Generosidad*," he said. "Remember, scholars believe these coins to have been on board that ship when it disappeared."

Keri nodded, remembering the old treasure hunter's explanation from before.

Max grabbed another book titled *Ships of the New World* and opened it to a page he had previously bookmarked. He held the image of an ancient sailing vessel under the magnifying light. "Here's a drawing of the *Generosidad*."

Keri joined Max, peering through the glass. They could see the ship's name carved out of wood and mounted on the side.

Keri read the name aloud. "*Generosidad Del Mar.* It means the bounty of the sea."

"Look at the style of the script," Max held up the scrap of wood next to the magnified name.

"They're a match!" Keri said.

"This piece of wood is from that ship." Max's eyes gleamed as he spoke.

"Tony found the *Generosidad*!" Keri exclaimed.

"It looks that way."

They returned to the big table with the maps and overlays.

"Here," Max said, tracing his finger along one of the lines. "This is believed to be the path of the *Generosidad*."

Keri wished that her best friend was here to share this news.

Max continued, "This coin is from one of the most valuable troves on record. Finding the rest would be worth millions, more than what they uncovered in Sebastian."

"Wow!" Keri exclaimed, making a mental note to research the treasure discovered off Florida's Gold Coast.

"Listen to me carefully. Tell the sheriff immediately, but don't show anyone else what you have discovered. I'd also advise you to stop hunting for it too. There are likely some very dangerous characters looking for this."

Despite the warning, Keri felt the urge to pick up the search again. This second coin confirmed she hadn't been crazy chasing after clues of Tony's disappearance. Still, the cryptic tone in Max's voice gave her pause.

"Don't worry, I'm done with all that," Keri said. "I mean, I wouldn't say no to millions of dollars, but I was chasing a memory more than a sunken ship of gold."

"Please let Sheriff Cotton know what you found," he said.

"Okay," Keri said. "Will do."

"I have to admit, this is exciting," the old cook said, eyes gleaming.

Keri noticed that she felt more worried than thrilled. "I don't know, lost treasures, old pirate tales, and mysterious assailants. I hope we don't end up walking some plank."

CHAPTER 23

The New Lost Key

A large turtle-shaped swimming pool occupied most of the old parking lot at Lost Key Realty. Boardwalk trails led off in several directions from the pool and the office. Although not yet complete, these plank paths would eventually lead to the new cottages and scenic walks through the nature preserve.

"Bailey went to show a lot to some prospective buyers. Then she'd planned to meet you for lunch." MJ frowned with a look of concern.

"She never made the lunch," Keri replied.

MJ looked at her watch. "She left about three hours ago. She should have been done by now."

Keri had learned long ago that time is measured differently in real estate. Fifteen minutes might mean two hours, and client meetings always took longer than expected. Still, she felt uneasy.

"Let me grab my cell phone and see if Bailey's checked in," MJ said. "Mark is over there in the tiki bar if you want to say hello."

"Thanks. I'll head over there."

Keri walked toward the back. The rear wall of the original office had been replaced by a cute, tropical tiki bar, complete with a grass roof and hanging lights. *Whew, this place reeks of alcohol,* Keri thought. The odor was even more pungent than it had been in Bailey's new office. It smelled like someone had spilled a bottle of booze mixed with rotting fruit.

The makeover of Lost Key Realty included several wildlife carvings in the concrete walkways surrounding a large community swimming pool. A figure of a sea turtle with a heart shape on its back stood out among the others. *Snaps! You're famous now, just like an actor with a star in Hollywood.*

She found Mark standing next to the pool just beyond the bar. Sketchpad in hand, he was talking intently to a couple of other men in construction garb. They nodded as if he had just given orders and left.

"Hey, handsome," Keri said playfully. They both knew she wasn't flirting. She would never interfere with her best friend's boyfriend.

"Well, hey yourself," Mark replied, high-fiving her.

Keri liked Mark, not in a romantic way, but because he treated her friend well and made her smile. He and Bailey had been dating now for several months, the longest relationship Bailey had had since her former husband ran off with another woman, taking the two kids Bailey had helped raise with him. So, yes, Keri liked Mark. Any man who looked after Bailey automatically made 'the friends list' in Keri's book.

"Your vision is coming to life," she said.

Marked nodded with a look of extreme satisfaction. "It's like a dream."

Mark's creative designs, which evoked a storybook feel, had become the new plans for Lost Key. While beautiful and fun on paper, they had proven even more so in real life. Keri imagined how it must feel to see his sketches take shape before his eyes.

"It may seem like a dream, but it certainly smells real," Keri teased.

Mark rolled his eyes and shook his head. "No one can figure out where that dang odor is coming from. But at least you expect a tiki bar to smell like a… tiki bar."

"A couple of shots, and folks won't care."

Mark chuckled. "Yeah, I suppose that's true. Where's Bailey?"

"Still at a showing, apparently."

Mark looked at his watch and scrunched his brow. "She left a few hours ago."

"Well, real estate has its own time," Keri said, the anxious feeling in her gut growing.

"Yeah, I'm learning," Mark replied. "And evidently, its own dress code too. I couldn't believe she wore that old sweatshirt to meet a new client."

"The one unraveling?"

"The very same."

"That's our Bailey. Free spirit." Keri placed her hands on her hips and let out a huff. Her eyes landed on an alligator statue about five feet away. She took a few steps closer. "Wow! That's a very lifelike sculpture. Where'd you find that?"

"What sculpture?"

The statue moved as he turned to see what Keri was referring to. The lumpy green head opened its jaws and hissed as its bulbous eyes locked in their direction.

"Ahhhh!" Keri screamed.

She and Mark backed up till they slammed into the tiki bar, knocking a stool over. The crash of the bar seat only further agitated the gator. It stood on all four legs, ready to charge.

MJ burst around the corner. "What's happening?" Then she saw the reptile. "Oh my! Hang on! I'll get Eddie." MJ disappeared, yelling for her employee.

In less than thirty seconds, Eddie came running from the inside, wearing his customary cargo shorts and a loud floral shirt. MJ trailed behind. Eddie didn't usually move that fast nor get very excited about anything. He had a reputation for falling asleep on the job. Real estate wasn't his passion, but alligators brought out the wonder in him. Eddie stopped a few feet from the reptile, his eyes alert, and a smile spread from ear to ear.

"Well, look at that!" he said excitedly. "Must be a four-footer at least."

"I didn't bring you out here to admire it," MJ said. "Do your gator thing and get rid of it."

"I gotta to call my brother," Eddie said, "He'd love this."

The reptile took steps toward Keri and Mark. They screamed.

"Call your brother later!" Keri yelled.

"Get that thing outta here, and I'll draw you a picture so you can show your brother what it looked like," Mark added pleadingly.

"Oh, all right," Eddie mumbled. He took several confident strides up to the menacing gator and casually slapped its snout with one hand. The reptile hissed but also seemed disoriented. Eddie maneuvered behind its head, grabbed its tail and neck simultaneously, and picked it up. The creature struggled but quickly yielded to Eddie's relentless grip.

"Wow!" Keri exclaimed. "That's unbelievable."

"Ahh, not really," Eddie replied. My brother and I handle gators this size all the time. I'll just put him in the back of my truck and release him into the swamp."

"Thanks, Eddie," MJ said.

"Good thing Bailey wasn't here to see that," Mark said. "It would have freaked her out for sure. Especially after that big one chased us in the water back off Dauphin Island."

MJ dialed her cell. As it rang, she said, "Speaking of Bailey, has anyone heard from her?"

"I left her a message a while ago," Keri said.

Mark shook his head.

MJ hung up. "Got her voice mail again." Then she shouted over to the office assistant. "Eddie, would you bring me my pager, please? It's on my desk."

"Sure thing," he answered as he slammed the tailgate shut on his truck.

A loud clang echoed from the bed of his pickup as the gator's tail swatted the side.

"Can it climb outta there?" Keri asked.

"Na, I don't think so," Mark replied. But his eyes remained fixed on Eddie's truck as if he didn't trust his answer.

Keri noticed the concerned look on MJ's face had intensified. The uneasy feeling turned into a knot in her stomach. "What is it?" Keri asked.

"We have new safety protocols in place now," MJ said. "Agents are to check in regularly and always let the office know where they are. In case of emergency, they send out a 911 page."

"Then we should have heard from Bailey by now," Mark looked as worried as MJ.

Eddie returned with the pager. "Here you go."

MJ pressed the button to retrieve any pages. "Bailey sent me a message about two hours ago," she said, and her face looked even more distressed. "How did I not see this?" The broker showed them the device.

Mark read the numbers on the small display screen. "Ninety-one. What does that mean?"

"You don't think that's…" Keri began, but couldn't bring herself to articulate the thought.

"Bailey could have gotten cut off as she was trying to send the emergency code," MJ said.

The knot cinched down further, and Keri began to feel queasy. "No, please, no."

Mark's face turned pale.

MJ's cell chimed. She answered. "Hello?" Her eyes bulged and her mouth dropped open. She looked aghast. "Oh Lord, please, no. Thank you, Sheriff."

"What is it?" Keri asked, all her senses attuned.

MJ glanced back and forth between Mark and Keri. "Bailey's missing."

CHAPTER 24

Bailey's Missing

"What do you mean Bailey's missing?" Mark said, his face contorted in a look of sheer terror.

"An officer on his routine patrol came across Bailey's Jeep, the door open and engine turned off. They said it seemed like she had parked hurriedly."

"Where was her last appointment?" Keri asked, head forward, intensely listening.

"Out at the far end of this development," MJ said. "There's some vacant land that juts next to the bay—pretty remote."

Keri bolted toward her old pickup, panic surging through every nerve. "No, no, no. You have to be alright. You have to be alright!" she kept saying.

"I'm going with you," Mark yelled, chasing after her.

Keri jumped into the truck and cranked the engine. "Where exactly is the property she was showing?"

"Way out, off Boggy Bayou Road," Mark answered, hopping into the passenger seat. "It's a dirt road and marsh, but you can get there in your truck." He leaned forward as he spoke, as if to nudge the truck forward, then stared out the window anxiously.

Keri's stomach hurt now. A feeling of dread now filled her. She knew the place Mark was describing, knew it all too well. "Why would you build anything out there?"

Keri didn't wait for an answer. She shoved the gear-shift into drive and sped off, ignoring stop signs and speed limits as she rushed to the scene.

The truck skidded to a stop upon reaching the dirt road to the bayou. A deputy's car blocked the path, lights flashing, and a patrolman stood next to the vehicle. His hand fell to his gun as they approached. He relaxed when he recognized Keri and walked toward their truck. She rolled down the window, intently focused on what he might say next.

"The officer bent down. "Sorry, but I can't let any-one through here. We've got a possible crime scene, and they need…"

His words were lost as she jammed the gas pedal to the floor. Waiting was not an option. She knew precisely where the scene would be, the same place her fiancé had disappeared. Keri felt a horrible déjà vu. The last time she had ridden down a similar road was with the sheriff, the night Tony went missing, never to return—the night that had changed her life forever. More flashing red and blue lights greeted them as they neared the location. She slammed the brake, shoved the gearshift into park, and bolted out the door, running toward the scene. She could no longer hold back the tears. Terror overwhelmed her.

"Bailey!" she screamed.

Mark's voice echoed just behind her. "Bailey!"

Sheriff Cotton quickly intercepted them, grabbing Keri in a big bear hug. He held up his arm, signaling Mark to stop too. Another officer at the scene stepped between Mark and Bailey's yellow Jeep.

"Where is she?" Mark yelled.

"Hey, listen to me," the sheriff said, still trying to restrain Keri.

She struggled, not heeding the officer's words. "Bailey!" she yelled again.

"She's not here!" the sheriff shouted.

Keri's mind swirled as images of Tony's truck flashed over Bailey's Jeep, but the sternness in Sheriff Cotton's voice commanded her attention.

"She's not here," he said more softly. "All we've found is her abandoned vehicle."

"She would never leave her Jeep," she said with a ragged breath.

The sheriff nodded and released Keri from his protective hug. "I know."

Keri looked at her friend's beloved sheet metal companion. The front tires were half-submerged in the marshy water as if she had driven too far out. Or had she been forced off the road? The scene gave her the same terrifying feeling as when they had found Tony's truck that fateful night. She glanced at the sheriff, who nodded his approval. "Come on. You can take a closer look. But don't touch anything. We're still processing the scene."

When Keri agreed, the sheriff looked to Mark, who nodded.

The sheriff nodded, then escorted them toward the scene. Keri's eyes remained fixed in disbelief. Except for the vehicle being parked too far out in the water, nothing seemed out of place—no other signs of a wreck, no new dings as far as she could tell. The lights were off, and the door had been left ajar. She placed her hand on the hood; the engine was cold.

"Don't touch the vehicle," the sheriff said, pulling her back.

She nodded and peeked inside. She found no keys in the ignition.

"Notice anything unusual?" the sheriff asked.

Keri shook her head. "No."

She started to climb into the driver's seat, and the sheriff blocked her with one arm. "Keri, I can't let you do that."

"Alright, alright. I'm just gonna stand here for a bit if that's okay."

"Fine, take a few minutes," the sheriff answered.

She wanted to stay near the Jeep and as close to Bailey as she could. *Oh, my Bailey. Please be okay, please.* It took every ounce of resistance not to hug the steering wheel.

"Maybe she went for a walk," Keri said, her voice crackly with desperation.

The sheriff raised an eyebrow and tilted his head as if to say anything was possible, but he clearly didn't believe that Bailey had just wandered off.

"What are you doing to find her?" Mark asked sharply.

The sheriff took note of his tone but seemed to temper his own response. "Everything we can."

One deputy handed the sheriff a small, square electronic device. "We found this in a grassy marsh just over there," the officer said, pointing about ten feet away.

The sheriff showed the gadget to Keri.

"That's her pager," she said.

"Would she go for a walk without her pager?"

Keri shook her head. "That means something bad happened to her, doesn't it?"

"Let's not jump to any conclusions. Right now, we're still assessing the situation."

"What else could it mean?" Mark asked, his face red with an angry glow.

Again, the sheriff remained composed. "We're gonna do everything we can to find her and bring her home safe."

Mark huffed, pacing restlessly back and forth.

The world around Keri grew fuzzy, the noises silenced, and her emotions numbed. She'd heard that promise before. *I can't believe this is happening again.* In her mind, she stood on a beach, a giant wave approaching. There was no time to run, nowhere to escape. She wouldn't survive this one. Keri felt a hand on her shoulder—it was Sheriff Cotton. When she looked at him, his voice became clear.

"You okay, Keri?" he asked, apparently not for the first time.

Keri stared blankly, then managed to shrug her shoulders, unable to answer or even assess her well-being.

The sheriff looked at Mark and said, "Make sure she gets home safely."

"I will," Mark said, nodding his head.

In his deep, reassuring voice, the sheriff said to both, "We'll find her."

His words landed flat with Keri. She appreciated the pledge but had little confidence he could deliver. She trusted the sheriff; he'd proven a very caring and capable officer. Yet, she couldn't get past the fact that he had said the same thing when Tony vanished. Since then, she'd learned that missing persons often remain missing, even with our brightest and best on the case.

Time seemed to stop as Keri stared at the sunshine-colored vehicle that Bailey loved so much.

If you could only talk, you could tell me what happened to my Bailey.

A strange numbness enveloped her like an invisible protective shield. Keri didn't know how she felt now or if she felt anything. She blinked, unable to accept what her eyes perceived—an abandoned Jeep, a discarded pager, and no sign of Bailey.

CHAPTER 25

A Message

Keri didn't remember dropping Mark at the office or making any of the several turns required to return to her houseboat. Yet somehow, she had arrived at the picket fence gate of her home, truck idling.

How long have I been sitting here?

Robotically, she turned off the engine and walked inside.

Go to bed, a voice in her mind whispered.

She didn't know how she'd manage sleep until she heard her best friend was home safe. She tried to comfort herself with the thought that maybe Bailey needed some alone time.

Yeah, sure, that's why she tossed her pager in the marsh, to make sure no one would interrupt her.

Keri's mind flashed to the Jeep parked slightly too far in the water, engine cold, and the door left open.

Maybe Snaps got into trouble, and Bailey had to scramble to save him. Yeah, and an alligator dragged her off.

No scenario could explain away the dreadful feeling that something terrible had happened. She dialed Bailey's cell number for the tenth time. No answer.

Come on, Bailey. Please give me some sign you're okay.

She spotted a small wooden box on the table as she stepped onto the deck. It looked similar to the one she and Bailey had found on Snake Island. As she drew closer, she stopped and gasped. The words 'Go Blue' glittered in the evening light.

"Bailey!" she yelled, looking around and peeking inside the living room. "Bailey, are you here?"

No one answered other than the usual cadence of the night creatures. *She must have left it here as a message for me,* Keri thought.

She rushed to the box and opened it. Her heart leaped with hope when she saw a note inside. Keri unfolded the paper, hoping that it was from Bailey. It wasn't. The card revealed an hourglass symbol half full of sand that seemed draining. Fear jumped to her throat as she read the message, *TIME'S UP!* spelled in cut-out hand-pasted letters. Thomas (aka Martin) had left Bailey that exact message before her troubles with the sinister privateer had started.

Sticker letters spelled a second message on the other side: *TONY'S JOURNAL FOR HER LIFE. TELL NO ONE OR SHE DIES.*

Keri read the note several times, blinking in disbelief. "Tony's journal?"

Conflicting emotions collided within her. On the one hand, she knew her best friend was still alive, at least for now. On the other, she now had confirmation of her worst fear. Bailey hadn't taken a walk or a time-out from the world. She'd been abducted. More disturbing, her disappearance seemed connected to Tony. These kidnappers, whoever they were, thought Keri had what they wanted. If Bailey's disappearance were even indirectly her fault, Keri would never forgive herself.

Her mind flashed to the stranger who had attacked them on Snake Island. *Did she write this?* Keri wondered. The type of note was Thomas's MO, but he was currently locked up in a mental ward. He couldn't have written it. *Could he?*

"What did ya find?" a curt voice asked, startling Keri.

She turned and saw Clem standing at her fence. Putting one hand over her heart, she said, "Oh, thank goodness it's you. You know, you really need to stop sneaking up on people."

"Sorry, old habits. I saw you pull up and thought I'd come to check on ya." He glanced down at the note she was holding. "I heard about Bailey. The sheriff called me and wanted me to watch for you coming home."

"Did he have any new information?"

Clem shook his head. "No, they're still processing the scene."

Keri realized she was clutching the mysterious message close to her chest as if caught reading someone else's mail.

"Find something?" the imposing ex-SEAL asked.

Keri glanced at the note. The words *tell no one, or else she dies* blared. Looking at Clem, she said, "Bailey and I found a letter from Tony. It brought up some old memories."

"Hmmm. Tough stuff. I don't know any loss harder to get past than your loved one disappearing. You're always looking for 'em."

A lake of grief and fear brimmed behind her eyes. "It's brutal."

"I heard you calling for Bailey as I walked up." Clem's statement sounded more like a question.

"Yeah. I thought she might be here 'cause I gave her this box to hold until we were sure my place was safe. You didn't see anyone around earlier, did you?"

"No, the only fresh tire tracks belong to your truck," he said, pointing behind him.

"Maybe Bailey dropped this off earlier," Keri said, her voice filled with doubt.

"As I said, those aren't Jeep tracks, and I don't see any footprints either," Clem replied. "Whoever left that must have come by boat."

"Who could that be?" Keri said, but the feeling in her gut told her it had to be the mysterious stranger.

"The abductors left that as proof they have Bailey," Clem answered. "That box is evidence. The sheriff needs to see this."

"I'll make sure he knows," Keri offered.

"I don't like anyone coming around unannounced. Even the delivery people respect that about me. I vary my times going out, so people can't predict when I'm gone." The vet wrinkled his brow. "To get past me, they either have training in stealth techniques, or they're watching this place. This strangeness keeps up, and I'm not gonna go anywhere. I'll start growing my own food."

Clem always thought strategically about everything, even grocery shopping. You can take the man out of the Navy, but you can't take the SEAL-training out of the man. He sometimes seemed paranoid, yet Keri felt comforted by his caution, especially tonight.

"I'm glad you're here, my friend."

"Keri, is there something else?" Clem asked, his blue eyes fixed on her.

Yes, there is, but I can't tell. Please understand. "No," Keri answered, feeling a stab of guilt for the concealment.

Clem squinted ever so slightly, then slowly nodded his head. She hoped that meant he understood her dilemma.

"Be careful," Clem said sternly. "I got an uneasy feelin' I can't shake."

"I will. Thanks, Clem."

As he walked away, she wanted to run and tell him everything, but she couldn't. She needed to learn more and play it safe for Bailey's sake. She didn't know for sure who had sent the cryptic note. She didn't even know her fiancé had information of such importance someone would resort to kidnapping to get their hands on it. Even if she did find the journal, where was she supposed to take it?

Why Bailey? Why not just abduct me?

The answers she sought wouldn't come from a book this time. She'd go crazy waiting for Bailey's kidnappers to contact her again or hoping the sheriff would solve this.

She saw Clem step through the door of his house. She took a step after him and stopped.

No, I can't involve him yet.

She reread the card—*Time's up.* Suddenly, it occurred to her that one person might have some answers. Thomas. He knew more than he let on. *Hell, he might be behind this one too.* The more she thought about this possibility, the more her blood began to boil. *I don't know if—or how—you did this, Thomas. But I'm gonna find out!*

CHAPTER 26

She's Alive

Rain plinked against the tin roof. Keri stared out her bedroom window. Through the water-streaked haze, she saw a figure moving toward her. The blurry edges took shape and color as the grayish mass drew near. A woman emerged, with long red hair and sharp but delicate features. Her ocean-blue eyes peered at Keri from the other side of the glass. Strange, but her hair wasn't wet from the downpour. Her lips spread in a spectral grin. Tap, tap, tap, the stranger rapped on the pane. The noise sounded deafening. The mysterious woman struck the glass again, harder, and repeatedly, until it shattered. Keri's eyes snapped open to discover she wasn't on her houseboat but sitting in her truck. Tap, tap, tap came the sound again. Large brown eyes behind thick glasses stared at her from the other side of the driver's window. The lady's brown wig, soaked by the rain, dripped onto her jacket. Keri breathed a sigh of relief at the sight of Doctor Kalmer. *I'm really here. I thought I dreamt about it.*

Pulling the door open, the psychiatrist asked, "Keri, are you okay? What are you doing here?"

Keri grabbed the doctor's coat. "Something's happened to Bailey!"

"Oh Lord, please, no," the doctor replied as she put her arm around Keri. "Come on inside."

An attendant greeted them at the reception desk. Keri removed all sharp objects and signed in. The familiar face of Will, a charge nurse, came around the corner.

"Good morning, Doctor," he said. "Hello again, Keri."

"Hey, Will," Keri managed to say.

"Will, cancel my morning group meeting," the psychiatrist ordered. "I've got an emergency to attend to."

"Yes, ma'am." Will glanced at the reception staff, who nodded that Keri was cleared to go.

The doctor took Keri's hand and led her down the hallway. "I'm so sorry, my dear." She squeezed Keri's hands.

Emotion choked off any words for Keri. "I'm not sure where to turn."

"You did the right thing coming to see me. Don't carry this alone."

Once inside the office, Keri sat on the couch, and the doctor took one of the chairs across from her.

"Did you spend the whole night in the parking lot?"

"I'm not sure. Half the night, maybe. I can't rest until I find Bailey," Keri said, noticing how much energy it took for her to respond. "What day is it?"

"It's Monday, my dear. Do the authorities know anything yet?" the doctor asked.

Keri shook her head, feeling desperate and afraid.

"The sheriff and his deputies won't stop until they find Bailey," Doctor Kalmer assured.

"There is one new development," Keri said. "Our conversation is confidential, right?"

The psychiatrist furrowed her brow in a serious look. "Of course," she answered.

Keri handed her the note left for her back on the houseboat.

The doctor's eyes opened wide, and her posture straightened as she read.

"You got this from the kidnappers?"

"Yeah, they placed a message along with the memento box we'd found. Clem says they left it as proof they have Bailey."

"I have to report this to the sheriff," Doctor Kalmer stated.

"You said this was confidential."

"I'm a mandatory reporter. You've presented new evidence in a current missing person case and a life-threatening situation."

"You read the note; I'm taking a risk just telling you."

Doctor Kalmer squinted her eyes and said, "You didn't come here to see me. You want to see Thomas."

"Yes, partly," Keri answered defiantly.

The professional took a deep breath.

"Look, this is the same tactic Thomas used before with Bailey," Keri said. "He either sent this himself or can tell us who did. Please, I have to talk with him!"

The doctor stared at Keri excruciatingly long, then said, "I'll allow you a short visit."

"You will?" Keri replied, caught off guard by the doctor's answer.

"Yes, but I'll be in the room with you."

"Sounds fair."

Doctor Kalmer sat up straight again. "After our visit, I will report this to the authorities."

"You can't tell anyone! Bailey's life depends on it."

The psychiatrist leaned forward. "That's precisely why I must say something."

Keri recognized that particular look in the doctor's eyes—discussion over. Though she'd gotten her meeting with Thomas, whoever had written the message would likely learn that she'd violated their demand to tell no one. *I had no choice,* she told herself. *Still, this meeting had better pay off with enough information to save my friend. And fast!*

The psychiatrist picked up her phone and called her attendant. "Will, bring Thomas to the visitation room. Thank you."

The doctor looked at Keri. "Thomas has been doing well, making progress. Let's keep the discussion civil. We'll present him the note and ask for his help."

"Ask for help? That approach didn't do any good last time," Keri said as if she'd just eaten sour candy.

"Don't provoke him. Stress might trigger Thomas to disassociate and regress to his alter ego."

Keri felt no concern for Thomas's well-being. She didn't give a damn about whether he felt comfortable or not. She just wanted any information he had on Bailey's disappearance. On the other hand, she knew his Martin persona would be of no help whatsoever.

"Okay," she said flatly.

"Let's go then."

They met the patient in the same visitation area as before. Once again, he sat at a round table. Will, the attendant, waited outside the door. The doctor and Keri took seats opposite the patient. Thomas looked more rested than the last time Keri had seen him—his eyes less puffy and hair combed—and he seemed more composed.

Keri found herself glaring at him, contempt rising. She glanced at the doctor, then back to Thomas, and said, "I need your help."

Thomas raised an eyebrow. He looked at the doctor, who nodded.

"What can I do for you?" he asked, his mouth curving as if holding back a smirk.

"My friend Bailey is missing."

"How unfortunate," he answered with a tone of indifference.

"Yes, that is unfortunate," Keri said sharply. She felt Doctor Kalmer's hand on her forearm.

"What's this got to do with me?" Thomas asked.

Keri flung the note with pasted letters across the table. It skidded to a stop in front of him. "You don't recognize your handiwork?" she asked sarcastically.

"Keri," the doctor said sternly.

Thomas's forehead wrinkled in concentration as he slowly picked up the note, studying it carefully. He looked away as if trying to remember something he'd forgotten. Then he brought his focus back to Keri. "I didn't send this." He spoke evenly, but as if he were forcing himself to stay steady and focused.

"Don't lie to me," Keri said, her anger rising. "This is exactly the kind of note you sent to Bailey when trying to scare her away so you could run your crazy scheme to cheat my friends and ruin my marsh."

He sat back, more puzzled than provoked by her accusation. His reaction only angered Keri more.

"Where is she?" Keri demanded.

He shook his head and said, "I don't know what you're—"

"Cut the crap! What have you done with Bailey?"

"Keri!" the doctor said. "Get a hold of yourself, right now."

"I've been here," Thomas said. "This note didn't come from me."

"Bullshit!" Keri yelled. "That's what you said last time when you tried to kill Bailey and Mark."

"No! I didn't do that! Like I told the police, I never ordered my men to shoot at them."

Thomas's denial only enraged Keri further. She imagined what it would feel like to put her hands around his neck and shake the truth out of him. So what if he was a crazy pirate?

"Y'all need to calm down," the doctor said. "Or I'm ending this meeting."

Thomas's puzzled expression deepened. He shifted restlessly in his seat. He looked confused, almost frightened. Then he gasped, eyes wide. "She *is* alive!" he exclaimed.

"Who's alive?" Keri asked, her jaw clenched, and face flushed.

Thomas shook his head. "No, that's not possible."

"What!" Keri exclaimed. "What's not possible?"

Thomas focused again on Keri, but now he looked distressed. His hands began to shake.

Keri slammed her fist on the table. "Answer me!"

"Keri!" Doctor Kalmer yelled. "One more outburst, and this meeting is over."

"I didn't hurt your friends." Thomas almost spat the words, his eyes boring into Keri. He glanced at the doctor and took a breath. "I didn't hurt Tony either."

"What did you say?" Keri asked. She blinked several times and shook her head. "You know what happened to Tony?"

"Not exactly," he managed to say.

Hot volcanic anger bubbled in the pit of Keri's stomach. "What the hell does that mean?"

"He should've never gotten involved with her." Thomas's breaths grew rapid and short.

Keri's face turned pale and she felt all semblance of control slipping away. "Involved? With who?" she yelled. "Tell me! What happened to Tony?"

"I think he's having an episode. We need to stop." Doctor Kalmer touched Keri's shoulder as she spoke. Keri recoiled at the doctor's caring gesture, then batted away her arm. Eyes ablaze, she sprang from her seat so fast that the chair flew behind her. Rage replaced all reason, and one thought dominated—to throttle him and force a confession. It took every ounce of restraint to keep from flying across the table at the pseudo pirate.

The attendant immediately moved to Keri's side and placed a firm hand on her shoulder. Doctor Kalmer rushed to Thomas who seemed on the verge of a full mental meltdown.

Keri couldn't think. Her body felt like a twisted knot of raw emotion, a tsunami of grief threatening to spill over the dam of her eyelids. The nurse gently pulled her toward the door. She held Thomas in a watery, defeated gaze. It was hard to be sure in her hysterical state, but Thomas's face had softened into a look resembling compassion.

"I didn't hurt your boyfriend," he repeated, his voice quivering. "Maybe she did." His tone sounded almost remorseful.

"He was the love of my life!" Keri yelled, grabbing the door frame, tears spilling freely.

Then, unexpectedly, Thomas's wrinkled brow smoothed. His body stopped shaking and he sat back as if defeated. He shook his head slowly as the nurse escorted Keri from the room. She just caught the words he spat out in a barely audible voice. "She used me."

CHAPTER 27

The Hunt of Lost Key

Keri drove aimlessly, kicking herself for losing her temper with Thomas. *That guy's a psycho anyway,* she thought, trying to console herself. The incident still rattled in her mind, and her embarrassment filled the truck's cabin. Strangely, the doctor seemed encouraged by their meeting with Thomas.

"You may have cracked open that protective wall he's built around his psyche," Doctor Kalmer had said. "You were right, Keri. He knows more than he's been telling."

Keri struggled to focus on the psychiatrist's words, but unwelcome thoughts pulled her like a riptide. She didn't see progress—just another dead end and a blown opportunity to find out what happened to Tony.

"The sheriff and I will follow up with Thomas. I promise," Doctor Kalmer said. "Sharing his feelings and telling the truth will be an important step in his recovery."

Keri's attention returned to the dull hum of the tires gripping the road. She grabbed her cell phone from the passenger seat and dialed Bailey. She wanted to hear the comforting voice of her friend, even if that meant a pre-recorded voicemail. There was no answer. She dialed Bailey's work.

"Lost Key Realty, this is Eddie."

"Hey Eddie, it's Keri. Anyone heard from Bailey?"

"No, I'm afraid not," Eddie answered. "They found her pager near the Jeep."

"Yeah, I know. What about Bailey's cell phone?"

"It hasn't turned up yet, but they think somebody may have tossed it into the marsh."

This news landed like a rock on a fragile emotional bubble. Any hope of contacting Bailey evaporated. Keri felt entirely at the mercy of the abductors.

"Call me the second you hear anything."

"Will do. You okay?"

"No, I'm not," Keri said and hung up.

The world blurred except for the narrow vision of the road ahead. The lovely crystal beaches, the lush tropical foliage, and even her romantic island escape now felt strange, as if her home had betrayed her by hiding kidnappers. A familiar structure, the Red Barn, drew her vision off to the right.

Bailey's Aunt Lee and Uncle Jed owned and operated this local Gulf Beach Road fixture and lived right next to it, making it easy to run. The Red Barn had started as Uncle Jed's home garage for fixing and building race cars. After that, it became a game room for teens. Graffiti from Bailey's childhood still adorned the walls. At present, it served as a flea market. Usually, all three garage doors would be open, antiques and knickknacks spilling out, and lots of people browsing for a gem. Instead, the barn/flea market was closed. Keri turned into the gravel parking lot to see Aunt Lee talking intently with a shorter woman wearing a stiff nest of black hair atop her head.

In her usual sweatsuit pants and top, Bailey's aunt stood a good three inches taller than the visitor.

"Look, we are closed until further notice," Aunt Lee said, her face flushed. "In case you've been living under a rock, my niece Bailey is missing!"

"Oh yes, I did hear about that," the lady said, her puffed-up hair unmoving in the wind and her long ankle-length dress not quite Sunday attire but too formal for shopping at the Red Barn. She put one hand over her heart while the other cradled her purse at the elbow. "I'm just so sorry about that; it's truly awful." The woman's overly sweet tone seemed like jelly on week-old pastry. "I do hope they find that poor girl."

"Me too," Lee answered.

"If I could just come in for five minutes," the lady persisted. "I know exactly what I'm looking for; it's that piece—"

"Oh, hell's bells! You got wax in your ears? Did you not hear what I just said?" Aunt Lee fired back.

"Well, I never…" the lady began.

"Never what? Put someone else's needs before your own?"

The woman scoffed and marched back to her car. "See if I ever come here again!"

"You promise?" Aunt Lee yelled. "You wanna find something priceless, then go search for my Bailey!"

Lee spotted Keri and seemed to forget about the woman she'd just been yelling at. Bailey's aunt hurried over and wrapped her arms around Keri. "I've gotcha, hon. I gotcha."

Keri let her head fall on Lee's shoulders and melted into her embrace.

"I just can't believe it," Keri managed to say once she stopped crying.

"Come on into the barn, hon," Lee said, cradling Keri with one arm like a protective mother hen, just as she'd done with so many other young folks. At some time or another, most of the kids in Lost Key found their way to the Red Barn. Lee and Jed were not just Bailey's kin. They'd become an adopted aunt and uncle and sometimes surrogate parents to most of the youth in the area. Their house was a safe place to play and a trusted haven if you found yourself in trouble.

Aunt Lee opened the door. Just as Keri stepped inside, the woman yelled from her car.

"Oh, I see. You're not really closed. Only special people can shop today."

Lee's face turned crimson. Her eyes ablaze, she snatched a broom leaning against the wall and marched toward the lady's car.

"Get the hell out of here!" Aunt Lee yelled, brandishing the cleaning tool like a sword.

Lee's charge clearly surprised the woman, who sat frozen behind the wheel. Aunt Lee swung her wooden straw sword and slammed it into the side of the driver's door.

"I said, get the hell out of here!"

The lady screamed, hurriedly cranked her car, and sped off, nearly hitting an oncoming truck on Gulf Beach Highway.

Keri watched the drama unfold between Warrior Lee and the stranger.

"Sorry you had to see that, dear," Aunt Lee said as she closed the door to the Red Barn and put her broom/sword away.

"I'm glad you're on my side," Keri said with a half-smile. She felt grateful to have such strong guardians and wondered who would be more formidable, Clem or Aunt Lee.

"I'm always on your team," Lee replied.

"Well, I guess you lost a customer."

"Nah. She'll be back—been coming here for years. She's too cheap to stay away."

They sat in two folding chairs around a black card table beside the wall.

"You look like hell. When's the last time you slept?"

Keri bristled at Lee's comment but appreciated the honesty, even if she didn't want to hear it. She shrugged her shoulders in answer to the question. Then her heart skipped as she spotted Bailey's artwork on the wall—a hand-painted set of pool balls corralled in their triangle rack.

"You'd think Bailey would have painted a mini soccer table as much as she likes that game," Keri remarked.

"Yeah, especially since she's so damn good at it, too."

Keri smiled. "She's not half bad at pool, either. I always loved when she'd take on those cocky local boys and wipe the table with them."

"Sheriff called earlier, looking for you," Lee said.

Keri concluded that the doctor had made good on her pledge to contact the authorities.

"I need to tell you something, but you have to keep it secret," Keri said.

"It won't leave this barn, hon."

Keri considered how much she should reveal. She trusted Bailey's aunt but felt too many people already knew about the note. More would surely follow. Lost Key was a small town, so at the end of the day, most everyone knew your business. Even so, Keri recounted the recent events to Lee. She told her about the lighthouse, finding the note on Snake Island, the mysterious reappearance of the memento box with the cryptic message inside, and her disastrous meeting with Thomas.

"You're lucky they didn't admit you to the center," Lee said.

"Oh, Doctor Kalmer wanted to. That's what finally calmed me down. It took some acting to convince her to let me go home."

"Christine knew you'd come here," Lee said and winked. "She called me right after you left."

The comment surprised Keri both because Lee had referred to the doctor by her first name, and that Christine would call the aunt of the Lost Key.

"You know Doctor Kalmer?"

"For years. I knew Christine before she became a head shrinker and way before she wore wigs. She stressed herself out getting that degree. If you ask me, that's why her hair fell out."

Keri scrunched her forehead. "Anyway, somehow I ended up here. I don't even remember the drive."

"That's because you were supposed to come here today," Aunt Lee stated, as if it were the most obvious fact in the world.

"Really?" Keri asked.

The aunt of Lost Key nodded. Then her countenance changed as if she'd suddenly remembered something vital. Lee walked over to a section of old books and rifled through them till she landed on one. She pulled it from the others and walked back to the table.

"I'm not supposed to give this to you," Lee said, holding up the book. "But now, I feel I must."

Lee sat it in front of Keri. The worn leather cover suggested lots of use and exposure to weather. Keri opened the book to a random page. Her puffy eyes sprung open as she leaned down for a closer look. She blinked in disbelief, quickly turning to another page, then several more.

Keri gasped and said, "This is Tony's handwriting!" She looked up at Bailey's aunt for an explanation.

Lee said, "That's his journal."

CHAPTER 28

The Journal

Keri read the pages of Tony's journal slowly, savoring every word. She could hear his voice as if he were speaking directly to her with each sentence. She longed for her beloved and the heartache poured over her reddened eyelids.

Lee slid her chair to the other side of the table and wrapped one arm around Keri's shoulder.

Keri closed her eyes, held the journal close to her heart, and gently kissed it.

"It's like I can feel him," she whispered. "You don't know how much this means to me."

"I've got a pretty good idea," Aunt Lee answered.

"Thank you."

Lee hugged her tightly. "You're welcome, my dear," she said apprehensively.

Keri read another line and vividly imagined Tony's voice narrating to her. She couldn't believe the comfort she felt, as well as an intense ache for his embrace. *Oh God, I miss you.* She'd have read it daily if she'd had this when he disappeared. Her life might not have been so chaotic these last few years.

Keri spun her chair around to face her surrogate aunt.

"Why did you wait till now to give me this? It's been three years since Tony vanished."

Lee raised her eyebrows, clearly surprised by this sudden change. "Because Tony told me not to," she answered.

Keri's face turned a shade pinker. "What are you talking about?" she said sharply.

"He made me promise to never give this to anyone, and especially not to you."

The words stung. "Why the hell not?" Keri shouted.

"Let me finish explaining!" Lee fired back, then composed herself again. "Tony came by the Red Barn a few days before he disappeared, very upset, and he wouldn't tell me what it was about. He just made me swear to never show this to anyone."

"You could have at least told the sheriff. There could be information in here that might explain what happened to him. Or what he had found. Damn it! I've been searching for answers for years, and you've been holding onto the most clues of anyone."

"Believe me, going to the sheriff was the first thing I considered," Lee continued. "I wanted to tell you many times, to share this burden with somebody. I came close to burning it more than once, but something in my intuition told me to honor my promise. So I hid it—tucked it away in plain sight."

Conflicting emotions collided within Keri as she tried to take in this news.

Lee laid her hand gently on Keri's arm, then coolly said, "Hon, I sure didn't want to cause you any more suffering, but if you could have seen the look in his eyes.

Tony was terrified. He believed that the information in there would put you in danger."

Keri grimaced, still bewildered that Aunt Lee had kept this secret.

"Tony also made me promise not to even read it."

"You haven't looked at this?"

"Never."

Keri clutched the journal tighter. It now felt more like a love letter for her eyes only. Though Keri had no words to express her profound gratitude for having these last writings from her fiancé, she couldn't get over feeling angry at Aunt Lee, and now Tony, for their overprotection.

"I still wish you'd shared this with me earlier," Keri said. "Why now?"

"Well, things always happen for more reasons than we know. One thing that is now clear, you're gonna need Tony's diary to save Bailey, and yourself."

Keri felt a hot burning of anger again. "If I'd had this all along, Bailey might not be missing now. Did you ever consider that?"

"Or you might not be here either," Lee said sharply, her lips pursed in a tight line of defiance.

Keri didn't want to be mad at Aunt Lee, but she couldn't help it. She also felt furious at Tony for leaving her, and both scared and ticked at Bailey for disappearing, even though neither had been at fault. They were victims. She knew that. But you feel what you feel. When it came to the journal, Keri understood that Tony and Lee had thought they were protecting her. Bailey's disappearance confirmed Tony's concern; these notes contained dangerous information that had led to the kidnapping.

Keri closed her eyes and held up her hand apologetically.

Lee quickly grasped Keri's hand in hers. "It's okay, hon," she said. "I'd be madder than hell if I were in your seat."

Keri nodded her appreciation.

"Have you heard from Bailey's abductors?" Lee asked.

"Not yet."

"Our Bailey's in trouble, and you're going to be the one to save her," Lee said cryptically. She looked at the wall as if watching a private movie.

"What are you talking about? I can't even help myself. How am I supposed to rescue Bailey?"

Lee gazed at Keri, yet her eyes seemed unfocused.

"I see a struggle between you and another woman," Lee said. "You both fall off a platform into the ocean… blue lights… I see Bailey… frightened." She looked up. "Sorry, but that's all I've got."

Keri sat up straighter, her attention rapt on Lee's words. Bailey had seen some of the same images. "Does Bailey come through this?"

Aunt Lee shook her head. "I honestly don't know."

"Oh, come on. There has to be more. When does this happen? Where?" Keri asked.

Lee looked away, then back. "I'm not sure where, but… it's during a storm."

"What does the woman look like?"

"She's fit and strong, long crimson red hair. Her face is painted like a skeleton."

Bailey had also seen a red-headed lady in her vision, though not that last part—a skeleton face.

"Keri, be careful," Lee said. "This woman is extremely dangerous. There's a lot of dark energy surrounding her."

Bailey had spoken of Aunt Lee's visions, but Keri had never experienced them until now. Keri felt a chill and folded her arms together. "Okay. I'll take extra care."

Convinced even more that these images were not just flights of imagination, Keri's mind began considering connections and clues. The next step had to be somewhere in Tony's journal. She turned through the pages again. This time she noticed lots of handwritten notes, strings of numbers written alongside rough sketches of ships and landmarks. Dr. Kalmer's voice echoed again in her mind. *There will always be another clue.*

"No, this is different," Keri said.

"What's different?" Lee asked.

Keri realized she'd spoken her thoughts. "Oh, I'm just thinking out loud."

She searched his notes, wondering what the kidnappers could want from them. A particular notation? Buried treasure? Then she abruptly stopped scanning.

"Aunt Lee, look at this," Keri said. "There's a page missing!"

"Looks like someone ripped it out," Lee replied.

"That must be the page Tony wrote his note on!" Keri exclaimed.

"Oh Lordy, hon. There's something on that page he wanted you to know."

"It was a drawing of me and detailed information about gold medallions on the other side. We found it in the keepsake box Tony left for me." Keri fondled her necklace as a distant memory replayed in her mind.

Lee listened attentively.

"Wait a minute," Keri said. "In that sketch, Tony depicted me wearing my engagement ring, and he drew an arrow from my ring to the side of the page."

"Hmm. Maybe Tony was leading you to those coins by marking this spot in the notebook," Lee concluded.

Keri focused again on the journal. The page before the missing one contained several details about a ship named *Generosidad*. Six numbers, 303478, ran vertically, close to the spine, with an arrow alongside pointing to the top of the page.

"What is it, hon?"

Do I tell her about the coins? Keri wondered. *No, too many people know already.* But she needed to confide at least part of the truth.

"Tony may have discovered sunken treasure," Keri answered.

Lee didn't say anything at first. She looked at Keri with an ominous stare. "So, pirates have returned to Lost Key."

CHAPTER 29

Partners

Later that evening, Keri delved into the notebook Tony had written till the words and numbers jumbled together. Exhaustion overwhelmed her. When she couldn't muster any more brain power to sort through these recent events or investigate the diary looking for hidden clues, Keri lay down on the couch. *Just a quick nap,* she thought. Cradling the journal like a beloved stuffed animal, she fell asleep. However, frightening dreams invaded her slumber. Thomas transformed into a hideous monster. Pirates stormed her boathouse. She saw Bailey's arm outstretched, desperately reaching for her. She heard her friend scream. Only it wasn't Bailey's voice but that of a man.

Abruptly, she awoke, catching her breath, fully dressed in the clothes she had worn the day before. All the lights in the houseboat were still on. The clock read 10 a.m. Muffled voices outside drew her attention.

She tucked the journal under a cushion and opened the door to see Clem scowling at Mark, who looked terrified, his back pressed against his car. She realized the scream must have come from Mark.

"Hey, guys, what's up?"

"Do you know this man?" Clem asked.

"Yeah. Mark's my friend and Bailey's boyfriend," Keri said, walking to the gate.

"Well, pardon me then. I've heard good things about you," Clem said, his expression softening. "Nice to finally meet ya." He slapped Mark's shoulder, who jumped at his touch.

"Yeah, nice to meet you too," Mark said shakily.

Keri thought Mark might pass out right there beside his car. She opened the gate. "Come on in."

Clem nodded somberly at Keri. Before returning to his house, he said, "Sheriff Cotton called looking for you. They want to send some officers here to monitor your phone in case the kidnappers call."

"Oh, okay. Thanks," Keri said to the old sailor.

"Sorry to drop by like this, but I didn't know who else to talk to," Mark said, breathing a bit easier now.

"No problem. Come by anytime."

Mark shook his head as he glanced toward Clem's house. "No, that's… too dangerous. Next time I'll call first."

Keri saw Clem sitting on his porch, rocking, and watching.

She managed a half-smile. "Some people have a Doberman pinscher protecting them," she said. "I have an ex-Navy SEAL. Good thing you're not a burglar."

"He came out of nowhere when I drove up. For a moment, I thought he might actually take me out."

Keri raised an eyebrow and motioned for Mark to sit as she took the second chair. "How are you holding up?"

The dark circles under his eyes suggested Mark hadn't slept much either. "I just can't believe…" he began, but choked with emotion.

"Me too. Any news?"

He shook his head. "I just… I wish I could do something besides wait."

"I feel ya," Keri said.

Mark shifted in his seat and made intermittent eye contact.

"What is it, Mark?" Keri asked.

He looked at her and said, "I went to see Thomas."

Keri adjusted her position, ruffled by the revelation.

"I've been visiting about once a week since he was admitted to the center," he continued.

"Yeah?"

"Doc wouldn't let me see him yesterday. She said he had an episode after a bad visit from somebody."

"Oh?" Keri said, shuffling again. Oddly, she felt pleased that Thomas had been bothered by her.

"Doctor Kalmer finally let me see him this morning," he continued. "She thinks my visits help him let go of his Martin persona. The hospital wouldn't say who had come by, but Thomas told me it was a local woman accusing him of kidnapping Bailey."

"That would be me," Keri admitted.

"I figured," Mark replied.

Keri sighed. If it hadn't been Mark asking, she might have told him to jump in the channel. "That didn't go well," she said. "After I got that note, I became convinced Thomas was behind all this mess." She closed her eyes regretfully. *Damn! I shouldn't have told him about the message.*

"I saw the note," Mark said.

"You did?"

"Dr. Kalmer kept a copy and showed it to me. She and the sheriff thought that if Thomas did know anything more, he might talk to me."

Keri looked at Mark, pleading, "Please don't tell anyone. You read the warning."

He touched her arm reassuringly. "Don't worry, the sheriff briefed me. I won't say a word."

"You can understand why I went to talk with him, can't you?" Keri said. "He's using the same intimidation technique he did with Bailey before her trouble began."

Mark nodded his understanding.

Keri continued, "When I saw Thomas, he acted like he didn't have a clue about what happened to Bailey. Then he let on that he knew about Tony's disappearance. I got so mad I wanted to take his head off."

"Thomas told me about that," Mark said. "The thing is, I believe him."

Keri felt a cold chill run down her spine. "What?"

"I think he's telling the truth," Mark said in a whispery voice leaning closer.

"Oh, come on. How can you?"

"Something has shifted. He's Thomas again. He doesn't speak to me as that phony alter ego character he created, but as my friend, the one I grew up with in Lost Key. We even reminisced about old times."

Keri felt an acid burning in her chest again. "Has the whole world gone freakin' nuts?" she yelled.

While Keri appreciated Mark's loyalty to his childhood friend, she didn't trust anything from that lunatic at SBR. Yet, if Mark's perceptions were accurate, she might have blown any chance of getting help from

Thomas. *Help from Thomas.* She scoffed at the thought. *He's probably just trying to cover his butt.* Still, Mark's friend knew more than he had told anyone and, most importantly, he obviously knew something about what had happened to Bailey. If Mark was the one to get that information from him, then so be it. Keri was going to follow every lead.

"Well, if Thomas didn't send the demand, then who did?" Keri asked.

Mark turned to face Keri, leaning his elbows on both knees. "Someone who calls herself Jaquolette sent that message and kidnapped Bailey."

Keri scrunched her brow. "As in Jaquolette Delahaye?"

"Yeah, exactly. Delahaye, that's what he said."

"Oh, for crying out loud, Mark! That's the name of a notorious female pirate who died three hundred years ago. You're caught up in his fantasy world."

"Listen to me. I know Thomas. My friend is back."

"Yeah, except when he's pretending to be Martin Delahaye, a marauder wannabe." Keri's voice had a cutting tone, not so much aimed at Mark but stemming from her enormous frustration and anxiety over this ordeal.

"Hey, look. I know Thomas is messed up right now, and he has caused a lot of angst for folks," Mark continued. "I also know he's hurting. I'm telling you, he truly believes what he is saying."

"That doesn't make it real."

"Well, we know Bailey's missing and that someone has her. Is that real enough for you?" Mark said sharply, then held up his hands in an apologetic gesture. "Let's just get to the truth."

On that point, Keri agreed. She needed answers. More importantly, she had to find her beloved Bailey. The thought of her friend being held captive hurt so much she thought she might explode any minute. Yet, by luck or fate, Keri had a partner now. She hoped whoever had sent that note didn't know the word had spread.

"Just in case a terrifying lady pirate *is* lurking, let's keep this our secret. Agreed?"

"Yeah," Mark said. "But we can't sit back and wait. We have to find Bailey."

"I agree with that. But how?"

The melody of a wind chime filled the silence.

Just as Keri considered whether to share Tony's journal, a voice said, "You're gonna need a boat."

Both turned abruptly to see a man, decked out in a fishing vest and an old camo-colored ball cap, standing atop the stairs that led to the lower dock. The words on the cap read 'I'd Rather Be Fishin'.'

Mark's eyes opened wide with surprise at first, then slowly, his mouth curved into a smile. "Cricket!"

CHAPTER 30

Friends

"Cricket! What are you doing here?" Keri gave him a giant hug, grateful for another friendly face.

"I heard Bailey's missing. Y'all know darn well she ain't lost. Whoever's snatched her, they're not gonna git away with this."

Keri and Mark looked at each other. The good thing about small towns is that everyone knows everything that's happening, even before it makes the news, and everyone knows everything about your business. Sometimes the bad thing about small towns is the same.

"How did you get past the special forces?" Mark asked, tipping his head toward the veteran's house.

"I didn't," Cricket answered. "Clem saw me comin' 'fore I even got close. Gave me a wave and a salute. Me and him go way back. Good neighbor you got there, Keri."

"Don't I know it," Keri said, then she hugged him again. "Good to see you."

Mark rested his hand on Cricket's shoulder. "This man saved Bailey and me back on Dauphin Island. Those hooligans would have shot us for sure."

"I think the gator would've eaten ya first," Cricket said in a deadpan manner.

Keri remembered how Bailey and Mark had fallen into the water and come face-to-face with a ten-foot alligator. Cricket's sudden appearance frightened the creature away.

"Cricket also spotted those goons dumping fake oil into the marsh," Keri said. "He thwarted their plans to drive real estate prices down so Martin could take over Lost Key."

"This man knows these waters better than anybody," Mark said, gently patting the fisherman's shoulder. "If it hadn't been for that secret passage through the brush, I don't know if we'd even be here now."

Mark seemed to have found a new confidence. He stretched his arm between them, hand open. "Let's find Bailey."

Cricket put his hand on top of Mark's. "I'm in!"

They both looked at Keri. Now three knew about the message from the kidnappers, six if you counted the doctor, the sheriff, and Thomas. Way too many, according to the cryptic instructions. Still, Keri decided to embrace this turn of good fate. Despite the warning, she felt hopeful.

Of course, we could all be deluding ourselves, but at least I'm not alone.

Keri stacked her hand atop theirs. "All right, let's go!"

They raised their bond in unison, held it high for a few seconds, then pushed down and let go with a cheer. Three lives had come together with one united purpose—to save their friend. Then, the would-be rescuers stood, looking at one another.

"Where we goin'?" Cricket asked.

"I don't know," Mark said.

They turned to Keri. Her blank expression said she had no clue what to do next.

"We need a plan," she said, trying to assume a reassuring leadership role.

Keri's new partners mumbled their agreement.

Although touched by their gallant enthusiasm, a growing uneasiness churned in her stomach. She felt like an implacable storm surge was pushing them into actions they were not qualified for, nor ready to take. They seemed to her three bumbling stooges on their way to meeting a gang of seasoned swashbucklers.

We don't stand a chance, she thought.

Having no clue what to do next, she said, "The note says they're willing to trade Bailey's life for Tony's journal."

"Do you know where his journal is?" Mark asked.

Keri found herself reluctant to answer the question. She needed more time to study it, savor every word of her fiancé's notes, and hear Tony's voice as she read it as if they were sharing a last leisurely visit. However, as painful as it would be to let it go, she'd trade the diary for Bailey's life any day. The greater risk seemed to be not sharing it.

"Yes, I have his journal inside," Keri answered.

Mark breathed a sigh of relief. "Thank goodness. At least we have something the pirates want in exchange for Bailey."

"Pirates?" Cricket asked.

"Well, that's one theory. We think whoever took Bailey might believe they are some sort of buccaneer," Mark answered.

"Them sea rats will only want one thang, gold," Cricket said. "Yer better off finding what those notes lead to. Then ya got somethin' to bargain with."

Neither man knew of the gold coin Snaps had brought her that had been swallowed by the bay. Nor did they know of the second medallion she carried in her pocket. The one Tony had left for her in their memento box.

It might be better if they didn't know about either, at least for now, Keri reasoned.

"Finding lost treasure could take a lifetime," Keri said. "I'm not a professional like that Mel Fisher guy."

Both men acted as if they understood, but their puzzled looks revealed they had never heard of the famous treasure hunter.

Keri retrieved the notebook from underneath the couch cushion. She let Mark leaf through it while Cricket looked on.

"So, these abductors want the journal to know where to look?" Mark asked.

"Exactly," Keri said.

"I'm tellin' ya, we need to look in there and ferret out any clues Tony left behind," Cricket said.

"Look, we're gonna give these kidnappers exactly what they want," Mark shouted. "We're not gonna risk Bailey's life on some treasure hunt."

"That's not what I'm sayin'," Cricket replied, his voice a little louder.

"Hey, both of y'all, just hold up a minute," Keri said. "Of course, we'll exchange this journal for Bailey. But we have until they contact me again to learn anything we can from Tony's diary."

"There's a lot of stuff here," Mark said, scanning the pages. "Tony took meticulous notes."

"Yes, and we don't have much time to decipher any clues he might have left behind," Keri said. "And I should make a copy of this."

"Let's at least search a little before you have to give that up," Cricket stated.

"Even if we picked up Tony's treasure trail, Tropical Storm Karl is gonna make it difficult to look for anything," Mark added.

"Actually, the storm might make it easier to find something," Keri exclaimed.

"What do ya mean?" Cricket asked.

"Big storms stir up a lot of sand and move things around. They've been known to wash ancient artifacts inland or even uncover lost ships. Tony used to tell me there was no better time for treasure hunting than right after a hurricane. Anyway, it doesn't matter. I searched for months after Tony disappeared and found nothing."

"But now you got a first-rate guidebook," Cricket said.

"Look, let's get something straight. I only care about finding Bailey; this book might hold clues as to where they are holding her," Keri said adamantly.

Cricket held up his hands in a gesture of surrender. "Just tryin' to help."

"We need someone to interpret these notes quickly," Keri continued. "The kidnappers could call at any time."

"Okay," Mark said. "So, who do you have in mind?"

Keri paused thoughtfully, then said, "Max. He can help us and will keep this on the down-low."

"You mean the cook at the Tropical Palm?" Mark asked.

"The same," Keri answered. "He's also a treasure hunter." Raising the journal, she continued, "He can probably understand this quicker than anyone."

Keri grabbed her keys and hurried for the truck. Mark followed her.

Cricket bounded down the steps and hopped into his boat. "I'll meet y'all there," he yelled.

Keri clutched Tony's journal close, aching to read it. *I want to hear every word, my dear. But first, I need you to save my Bailey.*

CHAPTER 31

Latitude & Longitude

ailey's friends convened in Max's man cave around the back of the Tropical Palm. Cricket and Mark gawked at the maps and various artifacts adorning the wall. They looked awestruck, like little boys who'd just found a secret clubhouse. Both seemed especially enchanted by the autographed picture of the astronaut. Meanwhile, Max fixated on Tony's notebook like it was the greatest novel he'd ever put his hands on, one of those books you just can't put down. Each page evoked some response from him.

"This is incredible," Max whispered. "I've never seen such detailed, current research of explorations in this area."

"I knew you could make sense of Tony's work," Keri said, glancing at her new partners.

"It's exquisite," Max said. Then he scrunched his brow in puzzlement. "There's a page missing."

"Yeah," Keri replied. "Apparently, Tony tore it out to send me that message I mentioned."

"Is that the same note you left on Snake Island?"

"Yes."

"You went to Snake Island?" Mark asked.

"What in the world ya go there for?" Cricket chimed in. "Don't you know how dangerous that is?"

"Long story for another time. Focus, guys," Keri ordered.

"Keri, have you heard anything from the abductors?" Max asked.

She shook her head. "Not since that cryptic demand for Tony's journal. This is the fifth day now. I'm about to lose my freakin' mind!"

"Hey, listen to me. They took Bailey for a reason," Max said with certainty.

"I hope she's okay."

Max laid the diary open on the table. "Why would Tony choose this specific page to send you a message?" Max asked.

Keri shrugged. "I figured he just tore one at random."

"Maybe," Max said. "Or it could be a clue."

They all scrunched closer as Max continued his observations.

"See, the page before has some numbers along the edge with an arrow pointing up." Max traced the figures with one finger as he spoke.

"Yeah, I noticed that earlier. What does that mean?" Keri asked.

"Could the numbers be for a combination lock?" Mark asked.

"Hmmm. What if you add a period after 30? The numbers will read 30.3478. Then let's assume the arrow pointing up means north. I think this is a latitude," Max stated.

"Wow," Cricket whispered.

Max flipped the next page back and forth. "There's no corresponding longitude. After the torn page is a drawing of an old Spanish medallion. Hmmm, looks familiar."

"Wait a minute," Mark said. "Are you suggesting that Tony found some gold?"

Max glanced at Keri, who nodded her approval, then said, "Yeah, I believe he did." He tilted his head toward Keri. "Her medallion proves it."

Mark and Cricket looked at her quizzically.

Reluctantly, Keri reached into her pocket, withdrew the ancient coin, and set it on the table.

"Tony left this for me along with the note," she said.

Mark gaped, then picked up the piece, turning it over in his hand. Cricket leaned in to get a closer look.

"Is this for real?" Mark asked.

"You better believe it," Max answered. "It could be from the *Generosidad*, the most valuable treasure ever lost."

"That's what I'm talkin' 'bout," Cricket exclaimed. "We find that, and we got somethin' to trade."

"What part of NO don't you understand?" Keri shouted. "We've been over this! We don't have time to find lost treasure."

"She's right," Max said. "We don't even know where to look." He waved the diary. "There's no 'X marks the spot' in here. It will take quite a bit of research to decipher Tony's notes and pick up his trail."

"At least we got some idea where to start," Cricket said.

Max looked slightly annoyed. He pulled a map of Perdido Key from a stack of papers and opened it on the table. Pointing to one of the thin horizontal black lines, Max began slowly tracing it with one finger. "Here's the latitude 30.35. Whatever Tony found might lie right near this line, but without the other coordinate, we have no idea where to look."

"Keri, did you see any numbers on the page Tony left for you?"

"No," she answered. "Tony drew a sketch of me." Her voice choked with grief. After composing herself, she continued. "A message to me announced that our ship had come in. Go Blue with me, and I'll show it to you."

Mark and Cricket looked to Keri for further explanation.

"Going Blue was Tony's nickname for searching for the bioluminescence," Keri answered.

"You mean that glowing water?" Cricket asked.

"Yeah, you seen it?" Keri asked.

"Sure, but not lately."

"Tony believed it held mystical powers," Keri said. "Sometimes, he would joke that the luminescence could guide one to lost fortunes."

"Sounds like something your dad used to say, Keri," Max stated.

"My dad told you that?"

Max nodded. "Yeah, he used to go on about it. The thing is, he was right. The bioluminescence occurs here in Perdido Bay. I've seen it too. However, its appearances are rare and random. I don't see how Tony could use it as a marker to find anything."

Keri could hear her dad's voice and see his playful smile as he talked about going blue. She always thought Tony and her dad had conspired to tease her with stories of the glowing water. Keri would always roll her eyes at the notion. Now, she wanted more than anything to believe they were right.

"I saw it, too," Keri said. "At least, I think I did. The other night around Snake Island. By the time I got there, it had disappeared."

"Y'all aren't suggestin' we go 'round looking for glowing the dark algae, are ya?" Cricket asked.

"No, of course not," Keri answered. Yet if she had not followed the glow that night, she wouldn't have gone to Snake Island nor found the keepsake box. *Did the glowing algae lead me there?* she wondered.

The conversation between the men had descended toward a full-blown argument. They began talking over one another, getting louder to make their points.

"Quiet!" Keri yelled, her face flushed with frustration. "Just let me think."

The guys hushed.

Max stared at her, his jaw clenched. He handed her the note and the journal. "You need to get this to the sheriff right now."

Her eyes met his with a desperate look. "Max, we can't go to the authorities. Bailey's life depends on it."

The old sailor seemed as immovable as a ship's anchor.

"Please," she added more softly.

Keri realized how scared she sounded. She could only hope he'd keep this secret long enough for her to rescue Bailey.

"Will you help us?" Keri asked.

Max held her in his gaze. She couldn't tell if he was profoundly concerned or about to explode in anger. The look on his face said he didn't like where this was leading.

Then he gently squeezed her arm with one of his calloused hands. "Alright, but on one condition," he said. "Whatever you do, I'm going with you." His eyes looked focused and determined. He nodded reassuringly to the others.

"We all are," Mark said.

"We're with ya," Cricket echoed.

She exhaled in relief, just realizing she'd been holding her breath. "Thank you," she whispered.

"Just promise that from now on, you won't keep any more secrets from us anymore," Mark said. "We're a team, right?"

"No more secrets," Keri promised.

Keri felt a mixture of apprehension and relief. She nearly cried. Here stood the rescue team. She looked at each one, the local fisherman, Bailey's artist boyfriend, and the Navy vet-turned-cook. Four friends who loved Bailey so much they were willing to sail head-on into the face of certain danger. Her heart swelled with gratitude.

Keri's mind drifted to the missing page and the lovely rendering her fiancé had created. She remembered the arrow extending from her engagement ring to the other side of the paper, connecting it to the coins. She gasped and clutched the ring she wore around her neck. Raising it to eye level, she looked at the engraving on the inside. A string of six numbers, *a longitude!* "Hey guys, you're not gonna believe this."

"Brrrinnnng," Keri's cell phone chimed.

She looked at the number calling. "Oh, my God!" She punched the button and answered. "Bailey?"

"Guess again."

CHAPTER 32

Contact

A blood-curdling chill radiated through Keri's body. Her hand trembled as she held the phone to her ear. "Who is this?" she managed to ask.

A woman's voice, smooth and confident, said, "Lose your friends and call me back. You have five minutes."

"Wait!" Keri said, but heard only silence. The caller hung up.

Oh my God, she's watching me! Keri thought. *How long has she been spying on me?*

As her eyes darted around the room, she noticed the growing concern on the faces of her new partners. Forcing herself to remain composed, Keri pretended to continue the call.

"Oh, Sheriff Cotton, I didn't recognize you…" Her voice had become raspy now. "What?… Oh, that's just awful… okay, yes. I'll be right there. Thank you."

Her three friends awaited an explanation.

"That was Sheriff Cotton," Keri said.

"Yeah, we heard that much," Max stated.

"Did he have news about Bailey?" Mark asked.

"No, um, well, um, he, he uh." Keri tried to form a sentence, but the words eluded her.

"What is it?" Mark asked. He pulled back his shoulders as if bracing for the worst.

"Oh, nothing new about Bailey," Keri said. "Except they found her cell phone, obviously. Since he just called me on it."

"What did he say that was awful?" Cricket asked.

"Oh, it's MJ. The sheriff said she got sick and ended up in the hospital."

"Sounds bad," Max said.

"That's unexpected," Mark added. "She's been doing great lately."

"I'm not sure what's going on," Keri said.

"Hmm, I wonder why the sheriff didn't call me? I'm working with her these days," Mark said. "I didn't realize you and MJ were that close."

"Umm… I gotta go," Keri said, starting for the door.

Mark followed after her. "Come on. I'll ride with ya."

Keri stopped him abruptly. "No! I mean, thanks, but no. I wanna go see her before visiting hours are over."

Mark glanced at his watch. "It's only 7:30. You've got another hour."

"No!" Keri shouted. Panic gathered in her throat as she struggled to come up with a plausible story. The scientist in her had never been good at lying.

"I want to go alone… and I gotta run an errand downtown," Keri said.

"You don't wanna go downtown tonight," Cricket said. "With all the new Halloween festivities, traffic will be a nightmare."

"Halloween isn't until Saturday. It's only Thursday," Mark noted.

"Don't ask me," the fisherman said. "I don't plan those thangs."

"Whatever," Keri said. "Y'all stay here and come up with a plan or… something." Then she scooped up the journal in one hand and bolted out the door.

"Hey, wait!" Max called after her. "I need that notebook if I'm gonna help y'all."

"I'll make a copy and get it back to you," Keri shouted over her shoulder, kicking herself for not having already done so.

She sprinted toward her truck, heart pounding. Keri felt on the verge of hysteria. Her hands shook more now, causing her to drop the keys on the floorboard. Retrieving them, Keri sat up startled by Mark now standing next to the driver's window.

"What's going on, Keri?" Mark said, leaning closer. "What are you not telling us?"

Keri fumbled with the keys, finally jabbing them into the ignition and starting the vehicle.

"I'm sorry, I'll explain everything later. I gotta go."

Max and Cricket stood outside the shack, watching with bewildered faces.

A sharp pang of guilt stabbed her as she realized she'd just kept something from the team again after just promising never to do that. It didn't comfort her that she had no choice.

"Sorry guys," Keri whispered, then sped off.

She dialed her phone, calling Bailey's number. "Hello, it's me. I'm alone."

"Go to the Plaza de Ferdinand," the cold voice said. "Take the haunted walking tour."

"How will I find you?"

"You won't. I'll find you."

"Let me speak with Bailey," Keri stated.

"Don't test me," the voice answered, clearly annoyed.

"Let me talk to Bailey, or I'll stop this truck right now." Keri had mustered all the courage she could, yet her tone sounded timid, and her ultimatum seemed weak. However, she wasn't about to give away Tony's journal without proof that Bailey was alive.

"Keri?" The response was timid and soft, but she'd recognize that voice anywhere.

"Bailey!" Keri's eyes pooled with water, and tears spilled down her cheeks. "Are you okay?"

"No," Bailey said, crying. "Please help me."

"Hang in there, Bailey! I'm on my way! ...Bailey?"

"Bring me the journal if you want to see your friend alive again," the abductor said.

"If you harm one hair on her head, I'll swear... I'll hunt you down."

"That's cute," the woman sneered.

Fear gave way to molten hot anger. "If you don't let Bailey go, I promise I'll get you!" Keri yelled.

"Tour starts at eight. Better hurry," the voice said placidly.

"Eight o'clock! That's not enough time."

"Come alone. You know what happens if you don't."

Keri heard a heavy click, then nothing. "Aaaaahh-hhh!" she screamed and shoved the accelerator to the floor.

The truck swerved on the dirt roads like a scared wildcat. Keri drove right past the stop sign at Sorrento Road, tires screeching as she made the left turn toward downtown. An oncoming car honked in protest and quickly veered off, narrowly avoiding a collision that could have ended the trip right there.

Keri took a deliberate, slow breath. *Easy now. You gotta get there in one piece if you're gonna help Bailey.*

Downtown was a straight shot east from Perdido Key. Her truck raced along State Highway 292, aka Sorrento/Barrancas Road, over the Bayou Chico Bridge, then bounced over the railroad tracks and veered right onto Main Street. She figured it would be the least crowded. Her plan almost worked till a line of traffic at least five blocks long brought her to a dead stop.

No, no, no. I'm not gonna make it in time.

She redialed Bailey's number. She just needed about five more minutes, a reasonable request.

"Pick up! Pick up!" No answer. "Oh, come on!" she screamed.

Officials had opened the vacant, littered field to the right for overflow parking. Keri found the nearest spot. She shoved the gear shift into park, grabbed the journal, and ran down the street, terrified she wouldn't make it in time.

I don't believe this is happening!

CHAPTER 33

Ghosts and Pirates

The festivities attracted a large crowd, so most down-town streets were closed to traffic, just as Cricket had predicted. Several horse-drawn carriages offered nostalgic rides through historic Pensacola, a tribute to simpler days.

Despite the multitude of people and the jubilant atmosphere, Keri felt startled each time she bumped into someone. Any one of these bizarre characters could be a henchman or, worse, the kidnapper herself.

Still, she snaked through the thick gathering of zombies, vampires, pirates, and more. Most of the Halloween outfits seemed homemade, as if thrown together from bits and pieces of mismatched clothes lying in the back of somebody's closet. Others were much more professional looking. Keri peered at each one, trying to see beneath the costumes and masks for any sign of the woman who held Bailey's life in her hands. None felt like the sinister marauder.

Daylight lingered from the setting sun as the shadows grew longer and the alleyways darker. Finally, she reached the Plaza de Ferdinand. The park occupied a city block of downtown and, being only a short walk to Seville Quarter and the Historic District, provided the ideal starting place for the haunted tour.

A group had already gathered around a lady dressed in a faded cream-colored Victorian outfit that looked aged and authentic, her face painted a pale white. Their guide for this haunted excursion would be a ghost from that time.

The lady waited with an almost unnatural stillness for the group to gather and grow quiet.

"Welcome, mortals," she began, her greeting accented with a ghostly smile. "We are so pleased you wish to spend some of your precious moments with the undead tonight. The warmth of your life force is so…" She tilted her head back, breathed deeply, and exhaled slowly. "Intoxicating to us."

A light chuckle escaped the group.

"I've been appointed to be your guide this evening. Be assured, you will see dead people—faces in the window of souls long gone. Restless spirits haunt these streets and old houses. Some seek solace, others justice for wrongs committed against them. And I must warn you, some of you may not return tonight."

Several in the crowd ooohed, playing along with the entertainment. One young woman turned and scurried away, apparently too spooked for this adventure. The crowd cackled.

"Hmm, we lost one already," the elegant ghostly guide said.

The crowd seemed even more eager to be scared.

"Welcome, I might add, to America's first city. Many do not know that Pensacola was founded in 1559 by the Spanish explorer Don Tristán de Luna, before Saint Augustine and almost fifty years before Jamestown. The settlement initially didn't last long and tends to get overlooked, but we know. Come with me if you dare. Let's see who's out and about tonight."

Although most certainly a fascinating history, Keri didn't hear a word. She couldn't stop thinking about the upcoming meeting with Jaquolette, the most frightening encounter that would happen tonight. *I have to know my Bailey is alright.*

The group began to walk a block toward the east to what is known as Seville Square. Alert for signs of the dreaded invaders, Keri kept her eyes peeled for any movement out of the ordinary, an impossible task. She missed her new partners but had no choice but to brave this adventure alone. This whole night wasn't typical.

"Look! In the window!" someone shouted, pointing to a second-story window in one of the old buildings on Government Street.

Others began to point and murmur. A faint light glowed from an upstairs window in an otherwise dark building. The light grew brighter and seemed to be moving toward the old casement. Then, the face of a man appeared. Dressed in a drab top hat, tattered coat, and shirt, he carried an oil lantern. The shadows concealed the lower half of his body as if he were only a floating torso. Many gasped. Then the image suddenly disappeared, as if someone had extinguished the lamp.

"Come, we mustn't linger," the guide instructed.

The group continued along Government Street for a couple of blocks till they reached another park, Seville Square. They gathered near one of the oaks, whose thick branch curved close to the ground before stretching out in various directions.

The guide pointed to one of the houses across the street.

"Legend has it that used to be the home of a maritime captain. He would lock his wife in that house while he was away at sea for months at a time. She finally broke free of his prison. When the nefarious captain learned of her disobedience, he killed her. Now, you can often hear her mourning songs if you stand here after dark."

Everyone grew quiet, listening. A melodic voice began to sing, swirling around the group. Keri figured there must be hidden speakers in the park echoing the ethereal song. Murmurs spread throughout the party, and some couples grabbed on to one another. Then came a sound most unexpected.

"Keri," a voice whispered.

Instinctively she turned, but she couldn't tell who might have spoken her name. The spectators all seemed caught up in the ghost story. She spotted a figure walking away. She was about to dismiss this as her overactive imagination, but when the person reached the corner, he turned and looked directly at her. The brim of his top hat shadowed his eyes, but she could tell he was a man by his jawline and physique. Everyone else was facing the other way, focused on the haunted house and ghostly song. This stranger had to be the one who had whispered her name. He gestured toward an empty carriage hitched to a single horse, an invitation. As if a hand had gently nudged her, something compelled her forward. She left the group and walked toward the stranger.

Her heart pounded. *It's starting.* Keri cautiously approached him. Dressed in a black tuxedo, white gloves, and a tall top hat, he stood statue-like, staring at her. His face had been painted white, with dark circles around the eyes and teeth outlined in black around his lips. He looked like a walking skeleton. Though she'd never seen this man, she knew the one thing that mattered. *You're with her.*

"Where's Bailey?" Keri asked. She felt weak and shaky.

The tuxedo ghoul didn't speak. He glanced at her notebook, then fixated back on her. Silently, he motioned again for her to climb into the carriage.

Emotion and energy surged through every fiber of her being right down to her fingertips. A million thoughts swirled in her mind. While it went against every bit of common sense to ride off into the night with a frightening skeleton man, her desire to save her friend outweighed the fear thundering through her body.

She climbed into the open-air carriage, comforting herself with the thought that she could bail at any time if things got too dicey.

Silently, the ghoulish guide climbed up front, grabbed the reins in both hands, and whipped them with a flick of his arms. The carriage jerked forward and then moved at a slow, steady pace. The clopping sound of the hooves echoed as they headed north, away from the festivities. When they reached the Saint Michael's Cemetery, the man pulled on the reins, stopping the ride in front of the entrance.

He turned over his shoulder and spoke in a raspy voice, "She's waiting for you."

CHAPTER 34

Back from the Dead

Every nerve in Keri's body tingled, causing her fingers to twitch slightly. She climbed down from the carriage and stood facing the entrance to the graveyard, home to thirty-two hundred headstones. Saint Michael's Cemetery is the resting place of captains and victims, the privileged and the poor. *Is this where I meet my end?* Keri wondered.

She peered into the darkness, trying to find whomever was waiting for her. The distant streetlamps, however, didn't provide enough light for her to make out much of anything in the forbidding graveyard.

Suddenly, her skeleton guide grabbed her by one arm and began pulling her into the burial grounds.

"Aaahhh," Keri screamed. "You're hurting me. Let me go!"

The mysterious escort ignored her demand, eyes fixed ahead and his grasp firm. As they walked briskly into the burial grounds, Keri's gate became sluggish and weak. The next few minutes could determine Bailey's fate and possibly her own. Suddenly, she could no longer keep pace with the henchman. His grip, a vice, now dragged her along.

The overdressed minion guided her toward a dark, quiet corner on the northeast side. She could hear the faint sounds of happy people having fun downtown, but that might as well have been miles away. Her mind flashed on Mark, Max, and Cricket staring at her as she had hurriedly driven away. *I wish y'all were here.*

Just up ahead, a shadowy silhouette waited. A feeling of dread overwhelmed Keri. The man held fast to her arm even once they finally stood before the sinister lady. She wasn't dressed like a pirate but more like an exotic ghost. Her face, too, had been painted white; dark circles encompassed her eyes, skeleton teeth outlined her lips, and a spiderweb design crept across her forehead. Thick hair cascaded down her shoulders and glinted red in the faint glow of streetlights. A form-fitting, dark leather mid-length coat wrapped her voluptuous body. The shirt and tight pants seemed especially fashioned for her. Black, shin-high boots completed her outfit. She stepped toward Keri, each stride confident and assured. Her movements and her red hair reminded Keri of the woman who chased them on Snake Island. Her features could easily match the profile of the blurry picture Keri took that night in the marsh. Could this also be Thomas's old boss?

So, you're Jaquolette, Keri thought. "Back From the Dead Red," she blurted, just above a whisper.

The stranger paused, her skeleton face tilting slightly. She studied Keri for a moment before taking another step toward her.

"Where's my journal?" she demanded.

"Where's Bailey?" Keri's retort didn't have any force of conviction behind it. Trying to stop her shaking knees seemed to take all her energy.

The lady gave Keri a dismissive stare and remained silent.

Fear leaped to Keri's throat. She swallowed it back down. *Don't give up the notebook until you see Bailey.*

"My friend first," Keri somehow managed to say, holding Tony's diary behind her back.

The skeleton lady gave an almost imperceptible nod to her follower, who grasped Keri's other shoulder with his free hand and shoved her hard, knocking her to the ground. She fell with a thud next to an old grave, the tombstone blank of any identifiers. Her right shoulder painfully absorbed most of the fall and the notebook jarred loose, landing a few feet away.

Jaquolette squatted in front of Keri like a tiger over her prey. "Don't mess with me, little girl, or I'll carve your name on that headstone."

Any resolve drained from Keri's body. Even lying down, her legs shook. A tightness gripped her like someone had pulled a belt around her chest. Her breathing became rapid and shallow, and she felt lightheaded. The skeleton lips curved into a spectral smirk.

Suddenly, a cold chill enveloped Keri as if the temperature had just dropped ten degrees.

"Keri," a voice said softly. It sounded similar to the whisper she had heard on her houseboat.

Then Keri saw him. "Tony?"

He stood about ten feet behind Jaquolette, who abruptly rose, gasping, "You! But you're…"

"Back from the dead?" the man mocked.

A green aura surrounded Tony. Keri didn't know if the glow was supernatural or if dim lights combined with the tears in her eyes were playing a trick on her mind. She scrambled to her feet, ignoring the pain in her shoulder and the fear in her gut. As soon as she stood, the man vanished.

"No!" she shouted, reaching toward the now empty space.

Jaquolette turned toward her, the smug smile gone, a look of bewilderment evident through the makeup. She suddenly didn't seem so menacing. Even her henchman was backing away, seemingly in fear.

"You saw him too, didn't you?" Keri said.

The lady ignored the question, her eyes searching the graveyard.

Standing taller, her legs firm beneath her, Keri grabbed the notebook and slung it as far as she could behind her and out of the pirate's reach. It was a bold move and a considerable risk, she knew. Yet, the vision of her beloved infused Keri with a new resolve.

"Bring me Bailey. Then I'll give you the journal."

The skeleton's eyes blazed as she reached for a knife sheathed on her belt and took a step toward Keri.

Oh shit! Keri thought as the blade glinted. She had figured she didn't stand a chance anyway, but now she was in a knife fight with no knife of her own. Even so, inexplicable courage quickly replaced the fear in her gut. She raised her arms in a defensive gesture and crouched slightly, every muscle tightened, poised for combat.

"Hey! You there!" a voice shouted. "Stay away from my friend!"

I know that voice. Keri turned to see Cricket running toward them, followed by Mark and Max. Hope saturated her whole being. For the first time, she had the upper hand. Further behind the three friends, the tour group appeared, apparently making their way to the cemetery.

Jaquolette stood for a moment, then sprinted toward the journal. As if charged with new energy, Keri ran to intercept. They reached the notebook at the same time, simultaneously grabbing it by opposite covers. The skeleton lady turned her body into Keri, sending her flying backward. Keri landed hard, her shoulder catching the edge of a tombstone.

"Aaaahhhh!" she screamed as the impact sent a searing pain down her right side and knocked the wind from her.

By then, Keri's friends had almost reached them. Jaquolette had started to run away but stopped when she noticed that Keri had somehow managed to hang on to half of the journal, effectively ripping the book in two. The skeleton face stared at Keri as if attempting to bore a hole right through her. "Say goodbye to your friend!" she exclaimed, her voice filled with rage. Then she ran out the back gate.

Whatever courage Keri had felt now vanished as horror overwhelmed her. She tried to move, but the pain radiating from her shoulder proved too much. She managed to lift her head.

"No! Wait!" Keri yelled. "I'll give you what you want!" Then she fell back on the ground.

CHAPTER 35

It's Not Over

The skeleton marauder disappeared into the lamp-lit, misty night. Keri sobbed. *What have I done?* She lay back in pain from her shoulder and the knowledge that her best friend in the world would soon die. It was her fault, all her fault.

"Keri, you okay?" Cricket asked, bending over her and trying to catch his breath.

"I killed her, Cricket! Bailey's dead because of me!"

She felt a firm hand on her wounded shoulder. Max had knelt on the other side of her.

"Your shoulder's dislocated," he said. His voice sounded like he was in a tunnel.

Keri felt cold and heavy as if she might sink into a grave and disappear among the dead. Right now, that sounded appealing.

"We gotta get you to a doctor," Max said, his voice receding farther away. "But first, I'm gonna pop your shoulder back into place so we can move you."

Keri didn't nod that she either understood or agreed with what Max had said. She just cried. He might as well have been talking to someone else. Keri felt a pair of hands underneath her upper back on either side, lifting her to a sitting position. Then Max pulled her right arm up and gave it a slight twist while his other hand pressed the dislocated shoulder ball back into its socket. She heard a pop.

"AAAAAAHHHH!" Keri screamed. Unimaginable pain enveloped her body, followed by blackness and, finally, the relief of nothingness.

Keri opened her eyes minutes later to find Cricket and Max staring down at her.

"How you feelin'?" Cricket asked.

Keri didn't know how to answer that. She stared blankly.

"Come on, let's sit her up," Max said.

Gently, they helped her to a sitting position and held supportive hands on her back. The pain was still there, but it had lessened substantially.

Keri looked around the graveyard, dropped her head, and wept. Sobbing so hard her shoulders shook, she covered her face with her hands. "I killed her. It's my fault," she repeated in a muffled voice.

"We don't know that yet," Cricket said, trying to console her.

Max laid his hand on her shoulder gently. "Keri, look at me."

She brought her focus to the old sailor. "I failed Bailey."

Max held up the half of the diary that Keri had ripped free from Jaquolette.

"No, you didn't," he replied.

His confidence disoriented her. Keri scrunched her forehead and stared at the veteran.

"I don't know how you managed this," Max continued, "but you held onto half the notebook. I might agree with you if that criminal had gotten her hands on all of it. But you still have something she wants."

Keri focused on Max through a watery haze of tears. "Really?" she asked softly.

"I know it," Max replied firmly.

"I hope you're right," Keri said.

Max leaned toward her. "I am."

Keri scanned every nuance of his facial expression and tone of voice, searching for any sign that he might just be placating her. Instead, his manner conveyed a granite conviction and certainty. She borrowed his assurance because she had none left. After this encounter with Jaquolette, she feared there wouldn't be a shred of mercy left in that twisted lady's heart.

"Hey, did y'all see Tony?" Keri asked.

Cricket straightened and looked around nervously. "Naw, can't say that I did."

"He was standing right over there." Keri tried to lift her right arm but it was still too sore.

Max and Cricket glanced at each other. Then Max said, "We didn't see him."

Keri felt the ache for her fiancé afresh. She wondered if she had imagined him. *No. He was real. I know it.* "That lady saw him too," Keri said. "And so did her scary stooge. Tony scared him off."

"So that's who we saw riding away in the old carriage," Cricket said.

"That confirms there's more than one kidnapper. She has an accomplice," Max added. "Maybe several."

"I can't believe y'all didn't see Tony. He was right there," Keri said again, pointing with her good arm this time. "I promise."

"We believe you," Max said.

She wasn't convinced they did, but she couldn't deny her experience. Keri looked longingly at where she'd seen the apparition. "It was the clearest vision I've ever had of him. He called my name." She touched the engagement ring she wore around her neck as she spoke.

A man ran toward them from the back gate where Jaquolette had fled. For a moment, Keri would have sworn it was her beloved coming to visit again. But as he drew closer, she recognized Mark.

He fell to his knees, panting. "I couldn't find her."

Keri realized that Mark had chased after the elusive skeleton lady. *You really do love Bailey.*

Finding his breath, Mark continued. "She ran through that neighborhood. I lost her in the midst of the trick-or-treaters."

Keri looked at the streets that flowed with families joining the festivities. The entire scene felt like a haunted house to her.

"If y'all hadn't come along…" Keri began, but couldn't finish the sentence.

"We got ya," Max said.

Gathering her composure, she asked, "Speaking of that, how did y'all find me?"

"It was obvious you were hiding something when you took off. So, I called MJ," Mark said. "That's when we knew it wasn't the sheriff who had contacted you."

"Max gits most of the credit," Cricket said. "His military mind figured the kidnappers would use the festival as cover to make the exchange, or worse."

Keri nodded to the veteran.

"We would have been here sooner if we hadn't had to park so damn far away," Max added.

Keri let her eyes linger upon her friends. A feeling of gratitude began to assuage her grief, and her mouth curved in a slight smile. The three of them had taken such a risk for her and Bailey. It was rare to find friends like these.

"Thank y'all," she said.

"I told you, we're with ya," Cricket assured.

"I'm glad you're safe," Mark said on the verge of tears. "But we didn't do Bailey much good." His voice broke, and his jaw clenched. "I had that crook in my sights." He pounded the ground. "How could she just disappear like that?"

"Just like the real Jaquolette," Keri answered.

Mark plopped down, exhausted as if crushed by a heavy weight. Choked with emotion, he said, "I've lost my Bailey." Tears streamed down his cheeks.

"Mark," Max said, laying a hand on the young man's shoulder.

Bailey's boyfriend continued to cry.

"Mark, look at me," Max said, shaking him gently.

Mark gazed at the old sailor like a wounded soldier on the battlefield. Keeping one hand on Mark's shoulder, Max held the remaining half of Tony's notebook in the other. He lifted it in front of Mark and said, "It's not over."

Max turned toward Keri and Cricket. "Y'all hear me?" he said. "It's not over."

CHAPTER 36

Dreams

After several hours at the emergency room, doctors confirmed that Keri had dislocated her shoulder. They prescribed pain meds and sent her home with a prescription for rest. She welcomed that advice, though she'd never relax until Bailey returned safely.

Recent events felt surreal, like they had happened to someone else. The sighting of Keri's beloved had left her breathless and stunned, the whole experience draining her to exhaustion. Safely back on her houseboat, she fell into a restless sleep. She dreamed of the encounter at Saint Michael's. Images flashed of the lady's painted face and her fierce, deathly expression. Keri's sleeping body jerked and turned as she relived Jaquolette knocking her to the ground with a forceful body blow. Still asleep, Keri grasped her shoulder in pain, as if she'd just injured it again. This time, however, a new detail stood out—a small tattoo inside her attacker's wrist, a sword with a drop of blood dripping from the tip.

The nightmare ended as it had in real life. The marauder fled through the gate, then dissolved into the night as if she were part of the misty rain. Just before she awoke, Keri saw a vivid image of her beloved, heard him say "back from the dead," and felt the power of his presence.

"Tony!" she yelled. Startled from sleep, she sat up with a gasp, one arm reaching for her fiancé. She looked around at the familiar items in her bedroom. Suddenly, she heard the deck chair creak. She looked up to see Clem leaning forward and peering inside the houseboat.

"I'm alright," she said.

Clem had insisted on keeping watch to protect Keri from any more trouble. Knowing he sat just outside had helped her finally fall asleep. She started to roll over when she suddenly recalled the last vision in her dream.

The tattoo! Keri spotted the memorabilia box across the room. Throwing off the covers, she sprang from the bed. She grabbed the container, flung open the lid, and began rummaging through the pictures.

"Come on, where are you?" she muttered, then closed the box and shoved it back on the shelf. She hurried to the living room area and began rifling through several drawers, yanking them open, then slamming them shut.

Clem poked his head inside the door. "What's up?"

"I know who attacked me," Keri stated. "It's the same lady who stalked me in the park. I've got a picture of her." Her eyes searched the room. *Oh, where the hell did I put that?* She turned over magazines on the end table. A couple slid off the edge and onto the floor.

"How do you know it's the same person?"

"She has the same tattoo on her left wrist," Keri answered.

"You saw this last night on her arm?"

"Well, yeah, although I wasn't aware I saw it. I just woke from a vivid nightmare about all that. When the lady reached out to grab me, I saw the tattoo on the underside of her wrist."

"You noticed this detail while you were sleeping?" Clem asked, with a hint of a skeptical tone.

"Well, yes, I dreamt it, but that mark is real. I know it." Keri realized how defensive she sounded. Her story had a desperate quality, but she couldn't shake the feeling of its authenticity. "Look, I'm not making this up.

"You haven't slept in several days now," Clem said.

Though Keri felt more tired than ever, she knew this new detail wasn't a product of her fatigue.

"That photo will confirm my dream. That lady's got the same ink on her wrist. I'd bet money on it. We're one step closer to discovering who she is and where they may have taken Bailey." Keri bent down, looking under the couch cushions and side table. "Oh, come on!" she yelled.

"Keri," Clem interrupted. "Get some rest. You're no good to anyone if you're exhausted."

"I'll rest when we have Bailey back. Right now, it's time to gather the team."

Clem gently grabbed her arm. "Time to tell the sheriff what you've discovered."

"What's he gonna do? Too many people are involved already. Besides, all that will take way longer. We can handle this."

"Like y'all handled her last night?" Clem's tone conveyed a stern warning. "Next time, you might not be so lucky."

Keri bit back the words she wanted to say. She felt angry, but Clem was right. Skill hadn't saved her in the graveyard. However, she hadn't felt lucky either. Instead, it seemed like angels had been watching out for her—as if Tony had protected her.

"Clem, I saw him. I saw Tony."

The veteran's stern stare revealed nothing. She'd seen that look on his face before when he first found her floating in a skiff near where Tony had disappeared.

"The pirate lady, she saw him too," Keri continued. "It rattled her."

Though Keri couldn't read his expression, he seemed to take her at her word.

"Good thing Cricket showed up when he did," Clem said. "Damn brave of him, too."

"I know how this sounds. But I'm telling you, Tony was there."

Clem squinted as if considering the possibilities. "Understood," he responded gently. "But you can't count on a ghost in a knife fight."

And I can't discount what I saw, Keri thought. She didn't challenge her friend. Clem always kept it honest and gave real-world advice. Yet Keri couldn't deny that her loved one had appeared at the right moment. Tony had saved her. She hugged Clem, grateful for his protective care. Then she sat on the couch while he stood in the doorway.

"Times like these, I wish I had Bailey's intuition," Keri said. "Then I could see the next steps to take."

"You may not be psychic, but you're a scientist," Clem encouraged. "Trust your skills. You're trained to make observations and connections."

His praise landed like a balm on Keri's anxious heart. "Thank you."

Clem shook his head. "I'm not trying to make you feel better. I'm very concerned. We don't know this enemy nor what she's capable of doing. And so far, she's always been in control. But last night, you saw something, a chink in her armor. You said she got rattled."

"Yes, she seemed off-balance, almost frightened."

Clem stepped into the living room. "Don't forget the most important thing. You won this round. She didn't get what she wanted."

Keri scrunched her eyebrows. "This doesn't feel like a victory," she said. "I'm even more scared she's gonna hurt Bailey."

"Bailey's in trouble for sure. But this lady seems desperate for the information she thinks you have. That might be what keeps Bailey safe."

"Yeah, Max said the same thing. So, what do we do? Just wait?"

"We don't have much choice. Ideally, we'd take the fight to these abductors.

"That sounds better than just sittin' around hoping that madwoman calls."

"No, too many unknowns for that strategy. Besides, we don't even know where she's hiding." Clem sat on the couch and looked at her sternly. "Listen, if the day ever comes that you have to face this person, or anyone else like her, remember the self-defense moves I taught you. They could save your life."

"I will."

"Keri, let the sheriff handle this."

Keri looked away, annoyed that no one seemed to understand how involving more people put Bailey at greater risk. She sighed. Part of her knew Clem was right.

"I know," she answered.

"Keri? I mean it."

"I'll call the sheriff."

"It's too dangerous. Whatever happens, don't go after this woman by yourself. She's liable to kill both you and Bailey next time." Clem's pupils aimed at her with a thousand-mile stare. In a stern and deliberate voice, he said, "Lord forbid this ever happens, but if you tangle with her and realize you're not gonna make it... then go out swinging. You hear? Don't ever give up. Don't ever let anyone break your spirit."

Clem stared at Keri to make sure she understood this point.

"I understand," Keri replied. "I hope it never comes to that."

"Makes two of us."

Clem sat back, seemingly satisfied with her pledge. "I wish we had better intel."

Suddenly, Keri's eyes grew wide. "Ahhh crap! I know where the photograph is. Doctor Kalmer kept it."

The phone vibrated on the wall, startling Keri.

She jumped up and answered. "Hello? Doctor Kalmer? ... Really? ... I'm on my way."

She hung up and stared at Clem, processing what she'd just heard. "That was Dr. Kalmer from Serenity. She said Thomas was asking for me. The doc wants me to visit."

Clem's face wrinkled. "You're going back?"

Keri nodded. "Yeah, he might have the information we need."

"And he might be part of it," Clem warned.

"That psycho is my only lead right now. Besides, there's lots of nurses and wards keeping me safe."

Clem seemed to relax and reluctantly gave his approval. "Listen for facts, locations, weaknesses, anything that will help us understand who we are deal-ing with."

"Will do." Keri grabbed her keys and headed for the truck.

Clem called after her. "Keri, keep your cool this time!"

CHAPTER 37

A Breakthrough

Will, the charge nurse, and Doctor Kalmer met Keri at the entrance of the Serenity Behavioral Rehab. After exchanging greetings, they began walking toward the visitation room.

"You look like hell," Doctor Kalmer stated.

"That's because I'm living in it," Keri answered.

"We've had a breakthrough," the doctor said. "I called you here because Thomas wants to talk with you again."

"What does he want to talk to me about?"

"He wouldn't say, but I believe the conversation will be useful for his continued recovery."

"Well, I wasn't that helpful last time," Keri said, wanting to add that she didn't give a damn about Thomas's recovery. His treatment plan wouldn't bring Tony back. However, Thomas might tell her something she needed to help Bailey.

"Oh, but your visit was more beneficial than you know," the doctor said.

"Really?" Keri asked, remembering how she tried to strangle him at their previous meeting.

"After y'all's altercation, Thomas began to face the core grief tormenting him—the loss of his mother."

Keri stared blankly ahead as they walked.

"You've heard of that event, I'm sure." The doctor spoke with an irritated tone. "Some local boys had too much to drink and thought it would be fun to scare an innocent woman. She fell and hit her head."

"Yes, I've heard the story," Keri said. "We've all lost people, Doctor."

Doctor Kalmer grabbed Keri's arm. "I didn't call you in here just for his sake. I think this may help you, too." The doctor pointed toward the visitation room before continuing. "Thomas is facing an awful injustice in his life and working hard to come to grips with a terrible loss." She drove the point home with her stare before continuing.

"I'm sorry, Doc, that was cold of me,"

"There are some things Thomas wants to say to you. What he says may be part of his previous pirate fantasies. Still, I think he is trying to let go of that and move forward. Letting go is something you need help with before your grief eats you alive."

Keri met the doctor's piercing eyes as if in a staring contest, then nodded her understanding. They resumed walking.

"I also insisted that the sheriff and myself be present during your visit," Doctor Kalmer continued. "Thomas agreed."

"Why did you invite Sheriff Cotton?" Keri asked.

"Because Thomas may be involved in Bailey's disappearance."

"I knew it!" Keri's cheeks turned crimson.

The doctor stopped them again. "Now we don't know anything for certain. However, I believe he's ready to tell us some secrets he's been holding tight. Do you think you can control yourself?"

Keri let out a sigh. "Yeah, I can."

"Good."

The doctor reached into her lab coat pocket and retrieved the photo of the mysterious stranger that Keri had taken.

Keri gasped. "I thought I lost that." She studied the picture again. "Mind if I borrow your magnifying glass?"

"The doctor raised a skeptical eyebrow. "Still looking for clues, are we?" She didn't wait for an answer but nodded to Will to retrieve the object.

Yes, I am, Keri wanted to say, but decided against that. "I just want to verify something."

They waited till Will returned with the magnifying glass.

Keri held the photo under the lens. "Just needed to see this again, to make sure I'm not dreaming."

"What is it, the tattoo?" the doctor asked.

"I need a minute with you and the sheriff before we see Thomas," Keri said.

When they reached the visitation room door, the doctor stepped inside and motioned for Sheriff Cotton to join them in the hallway.

The officer stepped through the doorway. If it had been any smaller, he would have had to duck or turn sideways to fit through.

"Keri," the sheriff said coolly. "How's your shoulder?"

"How did you…"

"The hospital contacted the office and reported the incident. Your friends also called me."

Even though she already knew that, Keri couldn't help feeling betrayed. They had all promised to keep the dealings with Jaquolette secret, at least for now. However, any feelings of aggravation were short-lived. She felt grateful and lucky to have such caring friends. Besides, she'd broken a few promises to them lately.

Keri felt the sheriff's stare like a white-hot searchlight. "I'm a bit rattled, but hangin' in there," she answered, averting her eyes.

Sheriff Cotton turned to the doctor to explain. "Last night, Keri was attacked at Saint Michael's Cemetery by the very person we've been looking for, the one who abducted Bailey."

"Oh, my Lord!" Doctor Kalmer said.

"Meeting with her was extremely dangerous. You should have told me about the threats," the sheriff said, reinforcing the doctor's reprimand.

"The lady left me no choice," Keri argued.

The doctor squinted. "We always have a choice, Keri. It concerns me that you're taking greater risks. I wonder if today's meeting is a good idea after all."

"Look! I had no other option but to meet with her!" Keri's voice raised a bit. She took a breath. After composing herself, she continued. "It won't happen again. I promise." Keri realized she'd made this pledge more than once already. *Maybe this time I'll find a way to keep my word.*

"Still, that's quite a trauma to be assaulted. We can talk with Thomas another time. It doesn't have to be today."

"No, please, let's go ahead. We all agree that Thomas knows more than he's telling us," Keri said. "Look at this."

She held the glass over the photo, magnifying the image on the underside of the lady's wrist.

"The good doctor here already showed me this," the sheriff said. "The image is the same insignia that Thomas had on the flag attached to his limo."

Keri glanced through the doorway where the patient waited. "Thomas said his former boss had the same tattoo."

"We ran a check on the name he gave," the officer said. "No such person exists in our databases."

The psychiatrist narrowed her eyes at Keri again, evaluating. "Could be someone he invented."

"We also talked with all the ink artists in town. No one has ever seen this design, so whoever this person is, she got that tat somewhere else."

"Very well," Doctor Kalmer said. "Let's go find out what's on Thomas's mind."

Keeping the photo, the sheriff turned and entered the room.

Doctor Kalmer stopped Keri at the entrance and said, "Just listen, and most importantly, don't lose your temper. Can you do that?"

"Yeah, I can do that."

Thomas sat at the same round table as the last visit. Another nursing assistant stood behind him. Sheriff Cotton also took a position near the table, holding his hat in hand. As they entered, Thomas rose in a gentlemanly gesture of greeting. The doctor dismissed the assistant, and the three sat down to chat while the sheriff remained nearby.

Thomas's hair had been trimmed and washed. Instead of hospital garb, he now wore a regular knit shirt and jeans. The contrast from their last meeting was remarkable.

Thomas looked at Keri with remorse in his eyes. "I'm sorry for the comment I made about your friends."

Keri sighed, feeling her temper rise. *Do you think sorry will cut it?*

"It was insensitive and rude," he added.

Keri swallowed the cutting remarks threatening to burst forth, pursed her lips, and nodded.

Thomas shifted his eyes as if searching for the next right words. "I told you. I've been played."

Keri turned to the doc. "How much more of this do I have to listen to?" she asked sharply.

"I know this is tough," Doctor Kalmer said. "Please continue if you can."

"Then who's behind this? And please don't tell me some mythical pirate who's been dead for three hundred years." Keri crossed her arms and focused on Thomas.

Thomas shook his head. "No, that's just her *persona*. Her real name is Angela, Angela Kali."

"Who is she?" the sheriff asked. Like a detective, he pulled a small paper pad from his pocket, clicked a pen he'd brought, and began to take notes.

"I guess one might say she's a real modern-day pirate. Angela is the one behind all of this."

"Right," Keri responded, tinged with sarcasm. "And I suppose you never faked an oil spill either, never manipulated a bogus real estate deal." Keri scoffed. *Why is the doctor listening to all of this? This man really does live in his own dream world.*

"I'll admit, I went along with her plans, the scare tactics, and even the real estate manipulation. But as I've said, I never told anyone to shoot at y'all. I couldn't understand why my men weren't following my orders. They were only supposed to threaten and scare, but not harm anyone."

"You didn't direct them to burn the Dauphin Island Marine Center?" the sheriff asked.

"No, certainly not. I admit, I wanted revenge against this town, but as I lost control of the situation, I realized nothing would bring my mom back, or save my dad, or reunite my family." Thomas looked at the law officer. "When you showed up, Sheriff, all I could think of was to find my grandfather's treasure chest. Then at least I'd have something to cherish, proof that we were here, and we mattered."

Tears puddled in Thomas's eyes, and he hung his head. Keri felt unexpected compassion for this broken man. Alongside her empathy, she also felt a volcano of frustration and anger. She looked at the doctor for reassurance. Doctor Kalmer's face creased in concern and perhaps puzzlement.

The sheriff slid the photo across the table to the patient. "Have you seen this woman before?"

Thomas glanced at the picture and answered, "Yes, that's her."

Keri's body grew tense. "Last time I asked you the same thing, you said you'd never seen her before."

Before Thomas could respond, the sheriff interjected. "How do you know her?"

Thomas breathed heavily, wiped his eyes, and answered, "She's my sister."

CHAPTER 38

Angela's Grief

"What the hell?" Keri replied, shaking her head from the shock. The idea that Thomas was related to the attacker disoriented Keri to the point that she could barely think.

The doctor and sheriff looked at one another, clearly not expecting this news.

"She's your sister," Sheriff Cotton repeated the statement.

"Well, my half-sister," Thomas replied. "We have the same father. Dad was a young sailor and met a girl while on shore leave in Virginia. The thing is, Dad didn't know he had a daughter till she was a teenager. Her biological mom abandoned her as a child, and she bounced around the foster care system for years before running away. She eventually tracked my dad down, and he took her into our family. He'd married my mom by that time. Mom was good to her and treated her like her own. Angela seemed like she was doing fine till mom got killed."

He looked away and swallowed hard as if seeing a painful distant memory. He took a minute to gather himself before continuing.

"After that horrible night, Angela lost it. Mom's death broke dad. The whole family fell apart. Grief hit us like a hurricane."

"That was a terrible accident," Keri said.

Thomas shot her an icy look and seemed more like his Martin-marauder persona for a moment.

"That was no accident," he said coolly. "Those local boys got drunk and killed her."

Keri regretted her choice of words but didn't apologize or explain what she meant.

Thomas took a few full breaths. The doctor nodded approvingly.

Managing his anger must be part of his recovery progress, Keri thought.

"So, Angela knew Tony?" Keri asked. The question might have seemed insensitive, given what Thomas had just shared, but Keri couldn't help it. She ached for any information about her beloved.

"Yes. My sister read about Tony's explorations in several journal articles he published. She posed as an investor to fund his work. She believed Tony was close to finding the *Generosidad*."

Keri uncrossed her arms and leaned her elbows on the table. "The *Gen Del Mar*?"

"Yes. She managed to get a meeting with Tony and convinced him she was a real financier. Angela is quite manipulative," Thomas stated. "She'd hoped to learn the location of the buried treasure. As far as I know, she never did."

"That explains how she had a picture of my fiancé," Keri said.

The patient nodded, and even seemed relieved to be confessing these details. "Tony quickly figured out that my sister wasn't a real investor, but by then she'd already laid the trap."

"He would never cooperate with someone like that," Keri said.

"Angela gave him no choice. She threatened to harm you."

It all made sense to Keri now, why her beloved had become withdrawn and secretive. He was protecting her. Tears pooled in her eyes, spilling down her cheeks.

"Did she kill him?" Keri asked.

The sheriff stopped writing. Everyone fixed their eyes on Thomas.

"I honestly don't know," Thomas answered. "But she might be capable of murder."

Keri felt a chill. The doctor scrunched her brow in a look of apprehension. The sheriff raised an eyebrow. No one said anything.

"My sister disappeared the same time Tony did," Thomas continued. "At first, I figured they both died in a freak accident like the papers reported about your fiancé. Or…" he paused, looking at Keri as if considering whether his next words would hurt her.

"Or they ran off together," Keri said.

"Yes. Everything made sense when you showed me that note the other day. I knew Angela was still alive. I also knew she had set me up to be the patsy."

"How do you mean?" the sheriff asked.

"After Angela… passed, Stanley gave me a letter from her. She told me she loved me and to keep fighting for justice for mom, that sort of thing. I was hurt and angry. This town had taken all my family from me."

"Who's Stanley?" Sheriff Cotton asked.

"Stanley was my right-hand man for many years. Bailey met him. Stanley encouraged me to follow through on my sister's master plan. He knew just what to say and when to say it. As it turns out, he was part of her deception."

"That's why you decided to wreck Lost Key with a fake oil spill and real estate fraud," Keri said, almost spitting the words at him.

"It was her plan, not mine. Angela became determined to make the town pay for our tragedy. She didn't care if the oil was real. It was my idea to use another substance," Thomas said.

"Well, your fake goop endangered hundreds of species, not to mention that it will take a while for the ecosystem to recover!" Keri felt Dr. Kalmer's hand on her forearm.

"I'm so sorry, for everything," Thomas offered.

"You're sorry?" Keri said, feeling her rush of anger. "You think sorry will—"

"I'm going to need that letter," the sheriff interrupted.

"I have it in my room."

Keri wasn't sure whether to believe Thomas. Yet, he seemed sincere, and his story made sense. It didn't sound like the delusional ramblings of a person with a mental health condition, but rather the account of an average, sane person, aware and remorseful for what he'd done.

Then Thomas sat back, his expression somber. "Like I said, she used me," he said with a hurt tone. "She uses everybody to get what she wants."

"What does your sister want?" the doctor asked.

"Money for one," Thomas answered. "She's after the loot and believes it's here, somewhere in Perdido Bay."

Keri thought of the proof in her pocket, the ancient medallion Tony had found. She kept it tucked away, her secret. However, Angela now had Tony's notes from half the journal that she had wrenched away from Keri.

"Money is one of the oldest motives. What's her other reason, revenge?" the sheriff asked.

"Yes, but it's deeper than that," Thomas said, his face turning pale as he spoke.

The doctor said, "There's an old proverb that says the child who is not embraced by the village will burn it down to feel its warmth. Perhaps Angela is suffering from that kind of pain."

Keri felt a shiver and shuffled in her seat. *She would have killed me.* Yet, Thomas's last comment puzzled her more than the doctor's explanation.

"You said her motives went deeper than revenge. What do you mean?" Keri asked.

Thomas paused as if summoning the courage to share a forbidden secret. Slowly he let his gaze fall upon each one of them. He carefully spoke with a spine-chilling tone that sounded like some ethereal spirit had taken possession of him.

"She wants to bring our dead mom back from the grave."

Keri gaped at Thomas, then looked at Dr. Kalmer, who leaned back, one hand covering her mouth. Keri had never seen the psychiatrist so unsettled. The sheriff stood like a marble statue. He seemed to be processing this news better than anyone.

"My sister is obsessed with death," Thomas continued. "Shortly after Mother died, she started using psychics to try to contact her. Then Angela researched every story she could find about people coming back from the dead, and especially those who claimed to be able to resurrect others' deceased loved ones. She traveled the world on this macabre venture, stealing what she needed to fund her dark quest."

"That explains her ghostly getup," Keri said.

Thomas fixed his eyes on Keri and scrunched his brow. "You've actually seen my sister, haven't you?" It was a statement more than a question.

A chill enveloped Keri, raising the hairs on her forearms. "Yes," she answered.

"Where'd she lure you? A graveyard?"

Keri inhaled sharply and nodded.

"Saint Michael's Cemetery," Thomas stated.

"How did you know that?" Keri asked.

"That's where Mom's buried."

Images of that dreadful encounter replayed in Keri's mind. She remembered another detail. The pirate lady had been standing in front of a grave marked with the name Morales. Someone had placed fresh flowers near the headstone.

"That's where I met her," Keri said. "At your mom's grave."

"Was she wearing Day of the Dead makeup?"

"Yes! She'd painted her face white, with dark circles around both eyes. Skeleton teeth outlined her mouth, and spiderweb lines covered her forehead. She looked terrifying."

"Day of the Dead is a celebration," Thomas said. "It's not supposed to be scary.

"Oh my," the doctor whispered. "Your sister may be suffering from Cotard's syndrome. It's a rare psychological condition where one believes they are a corpse, or that part of their body is dead."

"Angela never expressed anything like that, Doc," Thomas said. "But she did say the skeleton face paint helped her feel connected to the other side."

"Grief has taken her to a very dark place," the doctor stated. "It's normal to want to bring our loved ones back. But Angela seems to believe that's actually possible. What troubles me more is that Angela may see this as a justice issue."

"A justice issue?" the sheriff asked.

"Yes, the best revenge for death is life," the doctor stated. "But Angela may believe that her mom can't return to the living until the town pays retribution for what happened."

"That part fits," Thomas said.

"What's her idea of retribution?" Keri asked.

"Impossible to know without talking with her," the doctor said. "But whatever punishment she's intending, it won't be enough. It will never be enough."

"The death of our mother forever changed us," Thomas said solemnly, "but Angela has completely lost herself in sorrow. Part of me understands her pain. At first, I even went along with her crazy plans. Now, I realize how toxic her misery had become." Thomas looked at the sheriff with the sadness of accepting something he didn't want to believe. "She must be stopped."

"Agreed," the sheriff said. "I'll put out an all-points bulletin. Do you have any pictures of your sister?"

"Yes, but they're all at least three years old."

"We'll need those," the sheriff said, pocketing his small notepad and pen.

"I can give you something more valuable," Thomas said. Then he leaned forward and added, "I know where she might be hiding."

CHAPTER 39

Waiting

Keri stood on the deck of her houseboat the next afternoon, watching the gray-black canopy of the approaching storm. As the outer bands drew closer, the clouds had already begun moving in that eerie circular motion. The winds had picked up, and she knew it would soon increase dramatically along with blowing, stinging rain.

"Well, bad news for all you trick-or-treater's," Papa's perpetual radio blared. "Tropical storm Karl is expected to become a category one hurricane in the next several hours. Stay home, stay safe, and stay tuned right here at WJLQ for all your latest updates."

Gray sheets of rain streaked to the ground not far away. Inside the houseboat, a deputy sat attentively, waiting beside the monitoring equipment they had attached to her phone.

Keri heard the crunch of tires on the gravel dirt driveway as Sheriff Cotton pulled up in the department SUV. Clem approached from his house. Keri greeted them as the two men shook hands.

Sheriff Cotton got right down to business. "We confirmed that there is an Angela Morales, former last name of Kali," he said. "She was Thomas's half-sister. Didn't grow up here in Lost Key."

"No wonder Mark never mentioned her even though he was Thomas's best friend growing up," Keri stated.

"She broke out of a state mental ward in 1987, then fell off the radar," the sheriff continued. "No record of her anywhere. In most cases like this, the folks end up on the streets, addicted to drugs or worse."

Keri shook her head. "No, the woman I encountered was fit and strong. She's not an addict, nor homeless."

"It's unlikely that's who attacked you. We also must consider the source of our information. Thomas is suffering from mental delusions."

Keri couldn't argue that fact. Except that not only did Thomas's story seem believable, he also knew things about her encounter at the graveyard.

"No, it's the same woman," Keri said.

The sheriff raised one eyebrow. "Well, regardless of exactly who this mystery abductor is, we still need to catch her." Then he looked at her sternly. "Keri, do you have something you want to give me?"

She met the sheriff's glance and instinctively put her hand over the pocket which held the ancient coin. Tucking a thumb inside, she tried to act nonchalant.

The officer's eyes followed her sudden hand movement, like a poker player spotting a tell.

"No," Keri said, shaking her head.

The authorities already knew about one of the coins, she reasoned; that was enough for her. The one she carried in her pocket was private, Tony's gift to her.

Then, looking at her again, the sheriff said, "I understand that you still have half of Tony's journal."

Keri looked down and shuffled her feet. She pursed her lips and her stomach felt queasy.

"Do you really need that? It's the only thing I got to bargain with," she responded, letting her hand relax over her pocket.

"That's precisely why we need his notes. It's also evidence in a kidnapping case," the sheriff stated.

"Well, the kidnapper hasn't called," Keri said as she paced back and forth across her living room. She shot a glare at the deputy. "You said she'd call. Remember? That's what you said."

"Yes, ma'am. I remember," he answered solemnly.

"Try to be patient," Clem urged. "I know it's a hard ask, but hang in there."

"It's already been a week since Bailey was taken. Sheriff, you said the chances of finding her alive go way down after three or four days. I can't take it! If she's hurt my Bailey, I don't know what I'll do."

Clem placed his strong hand on her shoulder. "We'll find her."

"Not if we just sit here, waiting." She leaned her head back, letting out a sigh. Frustration grew. "What are we waiting for anyway? Thomas told us where she's hiding." She looked at Sheriff Cotton.

The sheriff took his hat off and held it in his hand. "Not really," he replied. "Thomas said she may be hiding on an abandoned oil rig."

"That's our only lead. You have to follow up."

"Of course, we will follow every lead, including this one." The sheriff's jaw clenched as he answered, but his tone remained even. "There's a lot of abandoned rigs out there. We don't know which one the kidnappers may be using. And," he motioned to the window, "there's a hurricane comin'."

Keri understood all this. The pirate lady had many options for a good hideout. But Keri's frustration and anger had to get out and go somewhere.

"Coast Guard is standing by, ready to go as soon as the storm breaks," the sheriff assured Keri. "Our police patrol boats are also searching the bay. They'll keep at it as long as the weather permits. And Matilda, your shrimper friend, has also volunteered her fleet. If the kidnappers are out there, we'll find them."

"How long will all that take? Days? Weeks?"

"Without a precise location, it's all we can do." The sheriff looked at the deputy. "And wait for them to call."

"I know you're doing everything you can. I'm just afraid it won't be enough." *It wasn't for Tony.*

"Stay positive. Never give up," Clem said.

Keri sighed again and retrieved the remaining half of Tony's journal from its hiding place in her bedroom. Holding the notebook close to her heart, she said, "This is precious to me. It's all I've got left of Tony."

The sheriff stepped closer. "We'll take care of it. I need my people to look it over. Who knows, we might even get a fingerprint from it."

Keri glanced down at the pages one last time. The diary had been torn at the drawing of herself that she'd lost on Snake Island. She liked that picture better than any photo of her. Of all the pages in Tony's journal, she wanted that one back the most. Keri clasped her necklace tight with one hand while handing the journal to the sheriff with the other. Her broken heart spilled out in tears just as the sprinkles from the storm began to fall.

Clem put an arm around her shoulder and led them inside. "We'll get through this," he said.

Keri shot a glance at the officer. "I need that back. That's a piece of Tony you have in your hand."

"I understand," the sheriff answered. "Hopefully, we'll find the other half, too."

"I need some air," she said.

Keri stepped outside and walked down to the lower deck. She considered jumping on her watercraft and conducting her own search, but the sheriff was right. Where would one even begin? What if they did call and she wasn't here? She sat down and put her head in her hands. A feeling of resignation came over her. *Oh, Bailey, I'm so sorry.*

Just then, she heard a splashing and the familiar whistles and clicks of bottlenose dolphins. Two of them bobbed in the water directly off the dock. Buddy was chirping at her, calling to her. Ben had something around his snout. He bobbed his head a few times, then, with a jerking motion, flicked the object onto the deck. It landed next to Keri.

"Hey guys, what are y'all doing here? Escaping the storm?" She grabbed the item and threw it back into the channel. Ben quickly retrieved it and tossed it back. This time it landed in Keri's lap.

"Sorry, Ben, but I don't feel like catch today." Keri stopped short of tossing the article back to her marine friends. The dolphins had brought her a leather bracelet with yellow beads woven together with blue thread. The ends had been tied together and reinforced with a light gray thread. The words 'friends forever' had been inscribed underneath.

She gasped. "This is Bailey's!" It was still tied in a circle, which suggested that this had not broken off by accident. Also, someone had added the gray thread. But why? She stood. *Of course! The strands had to be from Bailey's sweatshirt.* She remembered the last night Bailey had been at the houseboat and how she pulled on the loose strings. Keri had teased her about her shirt unraveling and that it would fall off one day. Mark said Bailey was still wearing the same gray pullover the day she disappeared. She held Bailey's friendship bracelet tightly in her hand realizing that only Bailey could have sent this.

"She's alive!" Keri exclaimed, looking at the dolphins.

They whistled and whirled in a playful gesture of understanding.

"You know where Bailey is, don't you?"

Ben and Buddy began to swim back and forth in front of the dock as if impatient.

Keri glanced back up at her houseboat. Clem stood at the door facing the deputy inside. She heard the muffled sounds of their conversation.

"I'll be right back," she told her ocean companions.

She walked back into the houseboat as casually as possible and discreetly grabbed the key to the B&B.

"Hey fellas, I'm beat. I'm just gonna lie down for a bit."

"Good idea," Clem said.

When she reached the bedroom door, she turned back to the three gentlemen and said, "Thanks for everything. I know you all are doing your best."

She closed the door and quickly donned a raincoat. The sheriff still held Tony's journal. No chance of taking that with her. She slid open the window and crawled out onto the narrow deck alongside her houseboat. She crouched as she passed the kitchen, keeping her head below the windows. Pausing at the corner of her main deck, she realized she'd have to sprint the rest of the way and would likely be spotted. Rain fell more steadily now and might give her cover, but they'd surely hear the engine of the B&B.

She darted toward the stairs to the lower deck, taking them in a single leap, and jumped onto the B&B. She looked at the dolphins again.

"Okay, take me to Bailey," Keri said as she turned the key and cranked the engine.

"Wait! Keri, stop!" Clem yelled, leaning over the deck railing.

She gave him an apologetic glance and mouthed the word *sorry*. She pulled back on the throttle and followed the dolphins into Perdido Bay, toward the Gulf of Mexico, and right into the path of Hurricane Karl.

CHAPTER 40

Into the Storm

What am I doing? Keri thought. The answer came immediately—*The only thing I can.* Keri glanced over her shoulder to check for anyone following. All clear. She scanned the surrounding brush on either side of the channel, wondering if Angela's minions were watching her even now. It seemed unlikely, given the spontaneity of this crazy decision, not to mention the poor weather conditions. Then again, this nemesis had always managed to be one step ahead.

Perdido Bay had grown choppy with the storm's approach. Droplets stung her face as the wind randomly whipped the rain. Ben and Buddy swam a few yards before her, leading the way.

Seriously! I'm following two dolphins into a hurricane. I've lost it.

Still, she kept going as if guided by a higher force. She had to do this. It didn't make sense by any scientific, deductive reasoning, but it felt right. Raging waves crashed against the B&B, almost toppling her several times. She knew the open Gulf would be a lot worse. *One problem at a time*, she advised herself.

Visibility had dropped so severely that she could hardly see the mouth of the Perdido Bay, now shrouded in a grayish fog. Surprisingly, blue lights flashed intermittently from the dense cloudiness as if concealing an alien spacecraft. At first, Keri thought it might be a shallow water warning buoy but quickly realized the hazy blinks emanated from a police boat.

This must be one of the patrols the sheriff mentioned.

She needed to hide. But where? The middle of the bay offered little cover. A fuzzy outline of grassy dunes and small brush appeared directly in front of her. Walker Island! The police boat approached from her left, so she diverted course to travel along the right side of the refuge. Hardly an island at all, this natural preserve sat on the Alabama side of Perdido Bay near the entrance to the Gulf. Tonight, it served as a different kind of refuge. The gnarly brush plus the storm might provide just enough cover to hide her. The patrol slowed. Keri could see the shadowy silhouettes of two men aboard. One switched on a large round circular light and aimed it along the shoreline. Keri cut her engine, drifted behind a section of thick brush, and waited. A bright beam bathed over her hiding spot but didn't stop. Then it swept back. The radio squawked. One of the officers picked up the small mic and answered. The howling wind muffled their conversation. The officer returned the mike to its holder and said something to his partner, who then turned off the searchlight. The driver pressed the throttle forward, and the boat sped inland. They hadn't spotted her.

Sheriff must have called and asked them to look for me.

Keri waited a few minutes before starting the B&B again. She navigated the short distance to the mouth of the bay. The weather intensified, turning Perdido Pass into a monstrous gray wall of wind and water.

"Ben! Buddy! Where are you?" she called. Only Karl answered.

After a minute, she saw a dolphin surface to her port side.

"Ben!"

Another bobbed behind him—Buddy.

"Good to see you guys. I can't do this without you."

But how will I be able to follow you in this mess?

Keri reached into her supply compartment, pulled out a glow stick, snapped it, and gave it a few shakes. The light wand illuminated a bright yellow. She tied a small rope in a circle on one end and pitched it to her marine guides. Ben stuck his snout through the loop, chirping with pride as he had done many times before when they played catch. Keri patted her sides with both hands, suddenly realizing she wasn't wearing a life preserver.

"Oh no!" she said.

She stood and flung open the storage compartment again but found it mostly empty.

Crap! I left my life vest back at the house! Slamming the seat shut, she yelled, "Damn it!"

Streaks of rain approached, flooding her with doubt. Ben and Buddy floated a few feet away, facing her as if awaiting instructions. Against her better judgment, and any sane scientific reasoning, Keri swept her arm forward.

"Let's go," she yelled, pointing to the Gulf.

Simultaneously, Ben and Buddy dived forward. Keri pulled the throttle, chasing the intermittent yellow light that surfaced as the dolphins swam. Keri gripped the handles tightly, leaned forward, and sped the B&B into the raging rain. Dolphins help humans and don't typically lead them into harm's way. It occurred that she was trusting these two not only with her life but with Bailey's, too. Somehow, she knew her trust was well-founded.

As predicted, the Gulf churned violently and more intensely than the bay. The waves doubled in size, cresting in white caps at the tops. The craft surged upward. In a few seconds, she was airborne, suddenly hanging inches above her seat. Then, the B&B hit the water hard, slamming her into the steering column. The impact almost knocked the breath out of her. She adjusted to a more secure position on the seat but was suddenly floating in air again as the craft crested another wave, this one from a different angle. The tiny craft landed again with a hard smack into an oncoming wave. Another wall of water hit her from the side, causing her right hand to slip free. A properly functioning watercraft would have slowed, but the throttle again stuck wide open. She regained her grip and stiffened her arms. The storm seemed more like a living sea monster than a meteorological phenomenon. It felt as if Hurricane Karl was aware of Keri's existence, and offended by her presence.

Keri leaned to the right, bracing for the impact from the oncoming swell when a side wave caught her unexpectedly from the left. With two mammoth water tentacles, Karl had snuck up on her and pushed her off the craft. Keri sailed through the air, detached and free-falling. She thumped with a slap and a painful pop in one ear before the Gulf swallowed her completely. The current rolled Keri like a rag doll as she somersaulted underwater. Keri looked left, right, then what she thought was up toward the surface, each direction equally dark. NOAA had taught Keri water survival techniques. She knew not to struggle but to allow herself to be carried with the undertow until she got oriented. However, Keri had inhaled some water before she went under, which now caused her to cough out what little air she'd drawn. Her need to breathe overrode her training. She kicked and flailed her arms and legs, attempting to find the surface. The net effect of such panicked movement got her nowhere. With no life preserver, she wouldn't float up fast, if at all, in these turbulent waters. Karl seemed intent on drowning her, using Keri's raincoat as another instrument to toy with her. She managed to shed the garment.

Her lungs burned with the need to inhale. Typically, she could hold her breath underwater for three to four minutes, but only after several full breaths and in a tranquil state of mind. The raging storm had denied her that preparation. She let out some air to relieve the pressure. Dizzy and light-headed, Keri flailed frantically, searching for the surface. *Where is it? I should have been there by now.* Still trying to sense direction, she realized she wasn't swimming anymore. Her arms had quit responding. A strange, almost blissful feeling enveloped her like the moment anesthesia took effect just before surgery.

It's okay," she thought, and exhaled her last bit of breath.

CHAPTER 41

Angela's Lair

What felt like two strong hands under each arm began dragging Keri down deeper, but she had no energy to resist. She wondered if she was even moving at all. As her scientific mind reasoned that the sensation of saving hands under her arms could be a hallucination induced by too much carbon dioxide building up in the lungs, Keri felt herself slipping into a warm sleepy state. She imagined Tony's arms pulling her, and she welcomed his warm embrace. Barely conscious, Keri unexpectedly felt the wind on her face and rain dousing her forehead. Dream or not, she gasped. Her lungs filled with air, and she coughed out some excess water that had snuck down her windpipe. The oxygen restored her strength. Fully alert, she began threading the tumultuous waters. Keri hadn't been pulled down as she had previously thought. Instead, someone had brought her to the surface. "Tony?" she said.

Just then she spotted her mysterious rescuer—not her beloved, but two smiling dolphins, bobbing and clicking a few feet away. "Thank you, guys!"

Buddy swam up beside her. She rubbed his head gratefully. "You saved me, Buddy. Y'all both did."

She grabbed Buddy's dorsal fin, and the dolphin towed Keri back to her watercraft. Somehow the B&B

still floated right side up, and for once it seemed the throttle hadn't stuck open. Managing to climb aboard, she lay on the steering column and composed herself.

"Thank you, thank you, thank you," she said to the dolphins and the universe.

That's when she noticed Ben no longer wore the yellow glow stick around his snout.

He must have lost it while saving me.

Her marine friends chirped and clicked, then resumed their course into the Gulf.

"Full speed ahead," Keri said as she steadied herself and followed.

After a few more rough waves, the wind subsided, and the swells decreased slightly. Keri realized the storm they'd just come through was only one of Karl's outer bands—finally, a break. *We still have time before the worst of it hits!*

They continued outward into deep waters, the dolphins swimming steadily. Keri checked the fuel gauge, something she should have done before chasing this crazy impulse. It read just below quarter full. That meant she had reached the point of no return with no oil rigs in view.

Even if I find Bailey, I don't know how we're gonna get back, she worried.

As the sun dipped below the watery horizon, the already-gray light grew dimmer, making the approaching hurricane more frightening and this whole trip way more dangerous. Without the aid of the glow stick, it became increasingly difficult to track Ben and Buddy. She squinted, having lost sight of her marine guides, then slowed, searching for any sign of a dorsal fin breaking the surface. There! Just up ahead, slightly off to the left, two dolphins splashed. She resumed her chase.

The wind gusted harder now. If Keri didn't find Angela's hideout soon, she'd be stuck on the B&B, at night, in the middle of a hurricane. Panic gripped her like an alarm growing louder. The only assurance she had was that the dolphins still swam forward.

Pretty thin, Keri.

Then, she spotted a dim, yellow glow way up ahead. The light remained stationary, meaning it couldn't come from a boat. As she drew closer, she could see the faint outline of four giant cylindrical pylons rising from the ocean, supporting a large flat platform. Atop the platform sat an industrial-looking structure. Several claw-like cranes arched over the water like menacing monster fingers. The dolphins had led her to an oil rig. In the brief glimpses provided by the lightning, Keri could tell that it stood tall and dark. No flames flared from the tall stacks. The drilling tower had been replaced with a lighthouse at one corner of the structure. It seemed abandoned except for the faint amber light emanating from several windows.

This has to be the place.

She slowed the B&B about a hundred yards from the platform where the dolphins had stopped, heads protruding from the water.

"Come here, guys," Keri called, clicking her tongue and patting her thigh.

The dolphins swam over. Keri retrieved Bailey's friendship bracelet from her pocket and gently placed it around Ben's snout. Then she removed her own and set it around Buddy's snout.

"Go find the shrimp lady! Go find shrimp!" she commanded.

The mammals immediately swam away, carrying two friendship bracelets. Keri watched as they faded out of sight.

I hope that works.

She nudged the throttle, easing her craft toward the spooky structure. A landing dock floated underneath, between the extensive cylindrical supports. Metal stairs led up to the platform. Two other small watercraft were moored to this dock. A flag flapped behind one of them. Keri felt a jolt of adrenaline when she saw the symbol— a skull with a sword underneath, a drop of blood dripping from the tip.

This is her lair! Keri thought, fear gripping her chest tighter.

Cautiously, she secured her craft to the opposite end of the floating dock. She depended now on the complete element of surprise. She hoped that the henchmen would never dream of anyone finding their hideout, much less boating right up to it. The wind blew harder, driving the rain sideways. Waves crashed over the dock, which twisted in all directions as if Karl were trying to rip it from the rest of the platform. Keri grabbed the stair railing to steady herself. She assessed the height as about two stories and at a steep incline. Her heart thumped louder than the storm. Thomas's warning echoed in her mind. "She could kill you." Images replayed of the skeleton lady trying to cut her. If they fought this time, there would be no place for Keri to run, and no friends would arrive just in the nick of time.

Maybe Cricket is on his way right now with his old beat-up boat, Keri said to herself.

She quickly dismissed that thought, surprised at the fantasies her brain could create under stress. Finally, the foolhardiness of this rescue attempt fully dawned on Keri. Usually, she was methodical in her approach to any project. This time, on the most important thing she'd ever attempted, she had acted hastily, out of sheer worry and panic, arriving unprepared. She didn't know the layout of this complex, how many opponents she would face, nor did she have any realistic escape plan. Clem and Max, her mentor and surrogate grandfather, would be furious. Even if she did find Bailey, where would they go? How would they get back? The B&B didn't have enough gas. If they eluded the pirates and managed to steal one of their craft, Hurricane Karl waited to devour them both.

"This is no time to second-guess yourself," Keri said as the wind laughed.

She swallowed hard to suppress the swirling mixture of guilt and fear. Clutching the railing of the stairs, she fixed her gaze upward and began the climb into Angela's lair.

CHAPTER 42

Finding Bailey

Keri gripped the railing and firmly planted her feet with each step on the ladder's rungs as the wind's intensity increased. Karl seemed determined to push her into the Gulf. She slowly peeked above the rig's main platform when she reached the apex. The wind howled more ferociously up here. She spotted a door off to her right. She crawled the rest of the way and crouched low against the gales. Suddenly a big gust swooshed, knocking her off balance. Instinctively, she dropped to the platform to make herself a smaller target against the bursts. The storm remained relentless, driving her toward the edge. She kicked her feet against the deck, arms grasping for any fixed object, but no objects presented themselves to stop her slippery slide. Her feet found no traction against the watery film covering the platform. Then her feet kicked only air as she reached the edge. Holding both arms outstretched as far as she could, she pressed her palms hard against the metal ground.

"Ahhhh," she yelled, the storm absorbing her voice.

As quickly as it came, the wind died down. Keri stopped just short of going over the side, her lower legs dangling mid-air.

Scrambling, she pulled herself up on deck, then lay on her back, catching her breath. *Whew, that was close!*

Adrenaline surged through her, and she got up and hurried toward the door.

Oh, please don't be locked!

The handle turned, and the door flung open just as a fresh gust blew again and clanged hard against the outer wall. Keri pulled, trying to close it, but the wind pressed it open.

"What the hell was that?" she heard a voice ask from down the hallway.

Quickly, she crouched behind a pile of crates just inside. Peeking through the narrow space between the boxes, she saw a man approaching. His footsteps echoed against the hard flooring. A large silhouette passed her limited field of vision. She listened and heard nothing but the wind. The man must have stopped at the entrance, assessing the situation.

Hinges squeaked, then a hard slam told her the man had shut the door. It sounded as if he'd locked it, too. Silence followed. Keri felt sure he could hear her heart pounding. She slowed her breathing as best she could.

The man's shadowy figure passed by Keri's narrow tunnel of vision between the crates.

First things first, she told herself. *Find Bailey, then a place to hide till the storm passes.*

The Coast Guard would start searching as soon as the weather permitted. With any luck, they might hold out till help arrived.

Bailey, where are you?

Slowly, she peeked around the corner. A faint glow of light spilled from a halfway-open door down on the left. The light bathed a spot on the floor and dimly lit the rest of the otherwise dark passage. As she crept closer, she heard muffled voices inside the room. Pausing in the shadows near the entrance, she pressed her back against the wall and squatted. Silverware clinked and scraped against plates.

"How long we gonna keep this girl around anyway?" a man asked with a husky voice.

"I'm surprised the boss hasn't already dumped her in the ocean, especially after what happened in the graveyard," another man's voice replied, harsh sounding but not raspy.

"There must be a reason. Boss's holding out for something."

"She better deliver on what she's promised," the harsh voice said. "This job's already taken too long."

"Ah, what are you worried about?" the gruff voice replied. "Boss's always taken care of us. She promised this one would be the biggest bounty yet. Besides, what else you got to do? Deliver newspapers?"

"It just seems like there's something else going on with her other than just finding treasure. Did you see her eyes? It's like she's… I don't know, going off the deep end or something."

"Don't let her hear you talk that way. She's libel to throw *you* overboard and into the deep."

A chair screeched against the metal floor; plates clinked.

"Well, time to feed the prisoner."

Keri's heart rate jumped as one of the men stepped out into the hallway carrying a plate of food. He abruptly turned left, heading away from her.

How did he not see me?

Keri watched, motionless, trying to stay invisible. The hallway offered no hiding places, no crates to provide cover this time. She'd be done if he glanced in her direction or caught sight of her in his peripheral vision. She pressed against the wall and imagined herself melding into it. Her eyes tracked the shadowy movements of the man as he walked down the dimly lit hall.

Lightning flashed just as the man stopped at the far end. He reached into his pocket, withdrew a ring of keys, selected one, opened the lock, and stepped inside.

Keri heard the second man push his chair back from the table, followed by water running. Quickly, she stole a look around the corner. He was washing dishes, his back toward the door. She dashed by, hurrying down the hall.

She paused for the briefest moment at the second room's entrance and glanced inside. Instantly, she spotted Bailey sitting on the floor in a corner, knees pulled into her chest. Bailey gasped in surprise at the sight of her friend. Keri had never seen such fear in Bailey's eyes before.

My Bailey is alive! Keri thought. *She's in bad shape, but she's alive. And she saw me.*

"What are you looking at?" the man asked Bailey bluntly. Keri raced into the adjacent room and slid under a desk. Gruff voice walked into the hall and stopped in front of the room where she hid. Then, he returned to Bailey.

"Here," the man said. "Eat something. You're going to need your strength."

The plate rattled on the floor as he laid it down carelessly. The henchman closed the door and locked it. His footsteps trailed down the hall and faded to silence.

Keri slid over to the vent in the wall connecting the two rooms. Keri could see Bailey's pixelated image sitting just on the other side. The checkered metal grill appeared to be twelve inches square. Carved into the lower corner of the wall and not connected to any ducts, its purpose seemed to be for airflow between the two rooms.

"Bailey," she whispered.

Bailey hurried over and put her hands on the grate.

"I can't believe you're here," Bailey said as she put both hands on the vent and leaned close. "I thought I imagined you." She began to cry.

"I'm real, girlfriend. You okay?"

It looked like Bailey shook her head. "No, I'm not," came her broken reply.

Keri grabbed the vent in both hands, anger fueling her courage. Mustering all her confidence, she said, "I'm gonna get you outta here."

CHAPTER 43

No Escape

"I see you got my message," Bailey said after finally composing herself.

"Yep, Ben slung your friendship bracelet right into my lap. That was brilliant, Bailey girl."

"It was a Hail Mary. They appeared outside my window. One had a scar on his head, I figured that must be Buddy. I remembered how they retrieved yellow things. So, I took a chance they'd know what to do with my bracelet and bring it to you. I can't believe it worked." Bailey sounded more than exhausted, almost defeated.

"Hey, listen to me," Keri commanded. "We're leaving this place."

Bailey kept quiet momentarily, then asked, "Who came with you?"

"Umm… no one," Keri answered.

Bailey sat back. "You're by yourself?"

"Yes, I got sick of waiting. When Ben lobbed me your bracelet, I just took off. I knew those dolphins would lead me to you."

"You came in the middle of a storm, too," Bailey said softly and began to cry again.

"Hey, hold it together, just a little longer."

"I love you too, girlfriend. But you shouldn't have come like this."

"Like hell! I had to come. I'm not leaving you in the hands of some lunatic. I don't care whose sister she is."

"What?"

"Jaquolette, the pirate lady who kidnapped you? Her real name is Angela and get this—she's Thomas's half-sister."

Bailey gasped. "Wow. I didn't see that one coming."

"Thomas gave us an idea of where she might be keeping you. The sheriff and the coast guard will search for us as soon as the storm breaks. Matilda even volunteered as well."

"So, they don't know exactly where to look?"

"No. We'll have to hide here till the storm passes and the authorities find us."

"I've overheard them talking," Bailey said "I think they might move me tomorrow."

If that were true, Bailey and the kidnappers would be long gone before the cavalry arrived. It also meant they only had a few hours to make their getaway. The odds weighed heavily against them successfully escaping. Keri's shoulders slumped.

"Closer to morning, we'll bust you outta that room and find a good hiding place till help arrives," Keri said, mustering all the hope she could fake.

"Okay," Bailey said softly. Her tone sounded placating, like she knew something and had said 'okay' for Keri's benefit.

"What?" Keri asked. "What is it?"

"Just a vision."

"You don't just have visions. You have premonitions. What are you seeing?"

Bailey paused before answering as if gathering her thoughts. "We're underwater, struggling, drowning… then a light is pulling us into another place, another world."

For a moment, neither said anything. Keri felt a chill. She leaned back against the wall. To her, Bailey's vision could only mean one thing. They weren't going to make it. They would both meet their end in a watery grave.

The wind howled, and the rain pelted the old rig. Lightning flashed, and thunder crackled. Two best friends were caught in a haunted house where the goons and ghosts were real and from which there was no escape.

All of a sudden, she heard Clem's voice in her ear. *Never give up.*

Drawing strength from her mentor's words, Keri leaned toward the grate and said, "We're not done yet."

"Okay," Bailey responded meekly.

"Hold on, girlfriend. A lot of people are working to find us. Mark would swim here if he knew where to look."

Bailey sparked at the mention of her boyfriend. "How is he?"

"Worried sick, like the rest of us," Keri answered.

"I'd hoped to see him again."

The resignation in Bailey's voice alarmed Keri. She had to be strong now, for both of them.

"You will. But first, we gotta get away from this freak show."

Keri didn't know how to pick a lock, and stealing the keys wasn't an option. Bailey would have to pass through this vent. Keri pulled at the grate. One corner opened about a quarter-inch. Saltwater had rusted the screw and weakened the connection. The other corners, however, held fast.

Keri rummaged through the desk. She had to search slowly, cautiously opening the metal drawers so they didn't squeak too loudly. She found a long, thin, rusted knife and inserted it at the loose corner of the grill. It gave another inch but yielded no more. She slid it along the top to the other side and tried to pry apart the opposite end. Her flimsy tool bent, then broke in half. She stuck her fingers behind the loosened corner, pressed her feet against the wall, and pulled as hard as she could. The gap widened a few inches farther but nowhere near enough for Bailey to crawl through. Keri tugged again till her grip slipped, and she shot backward, pain piercing her fingers.

"Damn it!" she said. "I'm gonna need a Phillips head or a crowbar."

Bailey nodded but said nothing, her face an abnormal blank expression.

"Hey!" Keri said. "Look at me."

They held each other's gaze through the checkered bars between them. Keri wanted to hug her friend so badly that if she'd had a sledgehammer, she'd have knocked the wall down, noise be damned.

"I'm gonna find something to get this grate off, and then we hide for a while."

Keri thought she saw Bailey nod, but she couldn't tell. "Hey, you hear me?"

"Yeah, I heard you," Bailey answered softly.

Keri didn't want to leave her friend captive for one second, but she had no choice. She crept to the door and peered down the hallway toward the kitchen. She figured she'd find something there that could get the job done, but ruled out that option when she saw the light still on and heard muffled voices coming from inside. Turning the opposite way, Keri headed down the dark hallway to unknown corridors.

Most rooms appeared to be unused offices since the operation had shut down. Keri didn't bother searching these rooms; she figured she wouldn't find anything more useful than in the previous office she'd just left.

There's gotta be a place where they store the tools.

Illuminated by intermittent flashes of lightning, she walked as quietly as she could down the winding halls. Turning left, she paused, waiting for another bright burst from Karl, then proceeded a few yards farther till her path dead-ended into another hallway. A dim glow radiated from a room about midway down on the left. The faint yellow light flickered, unlike the steady beam of a standard bulb. She approached the shimmering yellow stealthily and stopped just outside and to the left of the door.

Keri ventured a glance into the room. Seeing no other person, she entered. The illumination came from several candles spread across a table draped in a black cloth. Three sugar skulls had been carefully arranged, along with numerous photos.

An ofrenda! Keri thought.

She stepped closer, taking in the memorial at a glance. Many pictures showed a brown-skinned woman with soft, beautiful features and dark hair. In one photo, the woman smiled; in another, she had her arms around two children on either side, a boy and a girl, presumably hers. The boy looked familiar, but she couldn't place him. Then Keri noticed a picture of Tony leaning against one of the skulls. His journal lay next to it, at least the first half of it.

"Oh, my God!" she said aloud as her heart fluttered at the sight of him. Tony looked handsome and confident. Keri had never seen this photo before. Someone else had taken the picture of him with his head turned toward the camera, not posed, but as if caught by surprise. Like whoever took it had called his name and then clicked the shutter. A folded piece of paper lay to the right. She quickly unfolded it to see the sketch of her with the handwritten note from Tony across the top. *So, we didn't lose this back on Snake Island after all.* Keri stuffed the paper in her back pocket as she rapidly took in the rest of the scene. Newspaper clippings adorned the walls. Their origins varied and spanned several different countries, but all of them told stories about people returning from the grave. Some even featured gurus touting their ability to speak with the dead and even cross over to the next life. Scattered on a table beneath the clippings lay several books about the afterlife, the physics of resurrection, and ancient cultures and their beliefs about death and sacrifice.

Wow, this lady's out there, Keri thought.

Then, the flames of the candles flickered as if a breeze had bent them in half, but there were no windows, and the tiny fires returned to attention just as quickly. Keri felt a chill and an intense sensation that she was no longer alone. Turning, she saw a woman standing in the doorway. Keri recognized the long, thick, red hair and athletic figure. Unnerving confidence radiated from her. Add some macabre makeup, and this could only be one person.

"Angela!"

CHAPTER 44

The Invitation

Keri stood, knees quivering slightly. Her heart thumped so hard she thought it might burst from her chest. She expected the pirate lady to go into a sudden rage and finish the attack she had started at the graveyard. Instead, the marauder remained motionless, her fingers wrapped around the knife handle she wore on her hip. She hadn't drawn the dagger but stared at Keri with piercing dark eyes, like a beast hiding behind tinted windows. Keri couldn't see the creature inside.

"How do you know my name?" Angela said sharply.

"Sheriff Cotton, he found out who you are," Keri answered.

"How many more are with you?"

"No one else, just me."

Angela withdrew the knife, pinned Keri against the wall, and held the blade at her throat.

Keri let out a scream.

"Don't lie to me!" Angela yelled. "I'll end you right here!"

A slight tickling sensation descended the left side of Keri's throat. She'd been cut. One swipe would end her life.

"It's just me, I promise," Keri managed to say while staying still as possible for fear the edge of the blade would sink deeper.

The attacker held fast, clearly not satisfied with the explanation.

"I couldn't wait on you to call anymore," Keri continued. "I had to do something. All anyone knew was that you were on an oil rig somewhere. I took a chance. I had to find Bailey."

Tears spilled freely from Keri as the pirate studied her. Then Angela's forehead wrinkled. She stepped back and sheathed her weapon.

Keri sank to the floor and sobbed.

"So, you've been talking with my brother," Angela said in a detached, even voice—as if rage were a thing she could put in her pocket and pull out when needed.

"He's worried about you," Keri answered.

Angela scoffed. "He's worried about what I'll do, as all of you should be."

Then she squatted in front of Keri, elbows on her knees. She seemed agile, like a panther ready to strike at any moment. Keri felt heavy and slow next to her.

"You're crazier than I thought," the pirate said with a hint of admiration. "You surprised me, showing up here in the middle of a hurricane."

"Please, let Bailey go. Take me instead," Keri offered.

Sacrificing herself for Bailey wasn't the original plan. Hell, she didn't have any plan. But somehow, this new idea made sense. She'd save her friend and be with Tony on the other side of this painful world. Besides, Keri saw no other options. Whether following intuition or methodical reasoning, there seemed no escape. A sliver of hope remained that she could reason with her captor. Otherwise, Bailey's vision would be their fate.

Angela glowered at Keri again as if considering the proposal, then stood and said, "Loyalty is a trait I prize. Too bad yours is misplaced. Under different circumstances, I might have made you a member of my crew."

"Okay, make me a member of your crew," Keri asked.

The pirate scoffed. "You can't even follow my simple command to tell no one else."

"I'll follow your orders. I swear," Keri pleaded. She felt like a spectator in her body, as if watching someone else make the offer.

Angela seemed distracted now. "I've got to move this operation. The Coast Guard will come soon. If they're not here already." She squinted at Keri when she said the last part.

Keri felt her last shred of hope evaporate. The pirate enemy, who thought one step ahead, seemed unreachable. Perhaps there was no rational being behind those piercing eyes, as if whoever Angela used to be had disappeared long ago, replaced by a fierce creature driven by revenge. Keri and Bailey seemed destined for the blue light in Bailey's vision.

"Angela," Keri said softly, "this won't bring your mom back."

The candle flames reflected in her antagonist's black pupils and made them look ablaze. Angela's nostrils flared. "How do you know…" she began, then her expression softened. "Thomas." She tapped her fingers on the handle of her knife. "So, my dear brother has betrayed me. I'll deal with him in good time."

"This won't bring her back," Keri stated again.

"Yes, it will!" Angela fired. Then she squatted again in front of Keri. In a whispery voice, she said, "One day, when I was a little girl, a tiny bird flew into the window at our house accidentally killing itself. I rushed outside and cradled its lifeless body. I prayed. I poured my love into this delicate creature and suddenly its wings flapped to life, and it flew away."

Keri shivered. "You're crazy."

"No, I'm gifted. I can move back and forth between this world and the next. If conditions are just right, I can bring someone back from the beyond." Angela's expression turned deadpan, like she was more disappointed than offended that Keri didn't believe her.

Oh my God, the doc was right, Keri thought.

"It's glorious, Keri." Angela smiled as she spoke. She seemed almost blissful. "The other side is so… beautiful and peaceful."

Memories flashed in Keri's mind of her own near-death experience. She felt the warmth of the ocean water as it had engulfed her, the peaceful rest beckoning her.

The pirate tilted her head to one side, studying Keri. "You've wondered, haven't you?" Angela asked.

"What?"

"You've felt death's call."

Tears welled in Keri's eyes again.

Then, Angela looked at her as one would a dear friend. "I recognize your pain," she said softly. "I can see it in your eyes. I've been there. You don't have to suffer."

"Stop it, please," Keri said. As if it wasn't enough to physically overpower her, the pirate lady also seemed intent on breaking her spirit.

"It's real, Keri. The other side is everything you're dreaming it to be."

"Stop, please." This time Keri's voice broke as she felt any resolve slipping away.

"Maybe you have the gift just like me," Angela continued. "We didn't imagine seeing Tony the other night."

Keri gasped. "You saw him!"

"Of course, you know I did. You can be with Tony again. I'll teach you how to cross over."

Part of Keri wanted, even needed, to believe everything her abductor said. She longed for Tony's touch, to hold him, to feel his embrace again.

"Did you kill him?" Keri asked.

Angela sat on the floor, leaning on one arm, the other propped on one knee. "No, I didn't kill Tony. But I was with him the night he died."

Keri took a few breaths and then asked, "What happened?"

The pirate stared blankly, watching a reel only she could see. "A storm came suddenly. It capsized the boat. I tried, but I couldn't save him. I almost drowned that night, too. Somehow, I survived. I awoke on the beach the next morning. Ever since then, I've been able to cross over." She brought her eyes back to Keri. "I could never harm Tony, such a brilliant, lovely man."

Keri closed her eyes and dipped her head, stabbed by Angela's comment. She mustered the courage to ask the question that had haunted her for several years. "How far did the attraction go?" She braced herself for the answer.

Angela gave a small smile but didn't reply.

"How far?" Keri shouted.

The marauder glanced down at Keri's necklace and the ring she wore. She scrunched her forehead as if puzzled.

"Did you sleep with him?" Keri repeated, her voice breaking.

"No," Angela finally answered. "He loved you."

Keri didn't know whether this twisted lady told the truth, but the answer was precisely what she wanted to hear: Tony had remained faithful, and he hadn't succumbed to the wiles of this woman. Angela could have taken this opportunity and tormented her even more. It had to be true, Keri reasoned.

"He misses you," Angela said with absolute certainty.

Keri gasped and cried. *I miss him too.*

"I can take you to him," Angela said casually, as if the other world were an amusement park, and she had a season's pass.

Keri's heart outweighed her logical brain. She found herself entertaining the idea that, crazy or not, this woman might actually be able to transverse the bridge from this life to the next and back. Keri wondered if she, too, might have the gift. That would explain the allure of the ocean's gray void. Maybe that's why she got interrupted whenever she got too close to the point of no return. Perhaps God had another plan in mind—Angela.

Keri had met her angel, her escort to the other side. The answer she could never find sat right in front of her. A warm, peaceful sensation enveloped her. Fear left her body, replaced by a comforting certainty that she was in the hands of a higher power. How else could she have made it to the rig during a dangerous storm?

The scientist in her screamed in protest at these wild conclusions. Thomas had admitted that his sister had played on his pain perfectly. Angela was mostly likely up to the same antics right now. Even so, Keri's heart and mind agreed on one thing. She needed to get out of this room and back to Bailey. If playing into these delusions accomplished that, then so be it.

"Okay," Keri said. "Show me how to get to Tony."

CHAPTER 45

Walking the Plank

Angela pulled a small portable radio from her belt, pressed the side button, and said, "Bring her to the lighthouse. Now."

"Right away, boss," came the cackling reply.

She looked down at Keri as if the latter were a defeated prey or an adorable new pet. Keri couldn't tell which.

Angela stretched her hand and said, "Come on, get up. I have something to show you."

Keri accepted the assist and, with considerable effort, stood. "Where are we going?"

Angela gripped Keri by one arm and led her down the hallway. "It will become clear in a moment."

They headed in the opposite direction Keri had come from, further into the maze. In a junction at the end of the hallway, the pirate's accomplices stood on either side of Bailey, escorting her by the arms.

"What did she tell you?" Bailey asked.

Keri gave her best friend a questioning look. "What do you mean?"

"Don't listen to her, Keri," said Bailey, her voice shaky.

"Hey, I thought you were gonna let Bailey go," Keri said.

Angela scoffed. "I never said that." Then she motioned to her men. "Take them upstairs."

One crewman released his hold on Bailey and took Keri by the arm instead, clasping so tight it almost cut off the circulation.

"Oww! You're hurting me!" Keri protested, but the man's grip proved too strong. As if jolting her from a trance, the pain in her arm brought clarity. Angela had no intention of connecting with her. Keri couldn't trust any promise this lunatic made, no matter how sweet it sounded. *I can't believe I entertained the idea that she could bring Tony back.*

"I'm so sorry," Keri said, reaching for her best friend.

"It's not your fault," Bailey managed to say, clasping Keri's hand.

"Shut up!" the one holding Keri said with his gravelly voice as he jerked her away from Bailey.

The henchmen forced them down the dark hallway, turning left, then right before entering a round room with a spiral staircase—the lighthouse at the corner of the rig. Angela began to ascend.

"Climb," the underling commanded as he pushed Keri toward the stairs. She took one heavy step upward, then another, followed by her guard, Bailey, and the second goon.

She thought of Bailey's vision and the blue light leading to whatever life exists after this one. Clem's words echoed distantly in her mind. *Don't let her break your spirit.*

Too late for that, she thought. Tears flooded her eyes again as she realized she would never see Clem again. She'd eaten her last meal at the Tropical Palm. Who would look after the marine life she'd come to love? Bailey was all she had left, and, it seemed, only for a few minutes more.

The wind screeched as they reached the opening and climbed into the octagonal room. Lightning bolts darted in jagged random directions, the bright flashes strobing. Water burst in from an open door at one section. Keri couldn't tell if there had ever been a door there or not. The archway led to a slender platform jutting about six feet outward. Rust had eaten holes into the bottom, and pieces of the railing were missing. What once must have been an observation post, tonight looked more like a pirate's plank.

A bright flash followed by a loud boom of thunder startled the two friends, but not Angela. She didn't flinch.

The kidnapper walked over to Bailey. "You represent the best of Lost Key. You're the chosen sacrifice."

"What? I didn't do anything," Bailey protested.

"It's not what you did but what you are about to do that matters. You're going to help right a wrong."

"What are you talking about?" Bailey asked desperately.

"A ritual as old as time, one in which our entire civilization is founded—sacrifice. Ancient cultures practiced human sacrifice to appease their gods. Isn't our own culture based on the great sacrifice to atone for our sins? To reconnect humanity with God?"

"You're twisted!" Bailey said.

"The point is that sacrifice isn't about death, but a key to open the door between this life and the next."

"God doesn't want us to kill anyone!" Bailey shouted.

Angela remained undeterred. "The good folks of Lost Key let some of their own get away with murder. Now they must atone for that horrible act. Your sacrifice will allow Mom to come back to me."

"You're insane!" Keri yelled, struggling unsuccessfully to break free.

The marauder ignored the insult and continued to instruct Bailey. "The portal will appear as bluish light," she said with a placid, indifferent voice. "You'll know it when you see it. All you have to do is step through."

Bailey looked at Keri, her face awash with horror. Sinister forces beyond their control now pushed them toward Bailey's vision.

Angela looked at the wall clock with broken glass and stationary hands. The thing hadn't worked for who knows how long. "It's almost midnight," she said, signaling the minion holding Bailey. "Time's up."

Bailey kicked and screamed as the hired hand dragged her toward the opening, but her resistance proved useless. Keri's heart raced faster than the wind. She had known this moment might come, but nothing could have prepared her to watch.

"Wait!" Keri yelled. "Please, take me instead."

"Don't worry," Angela said, like a psycho consoling her victim with her demented plan. "She's going to a far better place. As for you, I'll keep my promise. Soon you'll be with Tony again."

"No! Not like this."

The pirate shrugged. Keri's mind swirled, looking for any way out of this situation. Then, behind the platform, just outside the window, she saw Tony. Surrounded by the same aura as in the graveyard, he floated in the wind. Then he smiled. Real or imagined, a warm feeling passed through her, followed by a moment of peaceful silence, as if they shared a liminal space away from pirates and out of the reach of hurricanes.

Tony spoke in almost a whisper, but somehow, she could hear him.

"Never give up," he said. The exact advice Clem had given her on the houseboat.

Angela watched Keri with curiosity, peered out the window, and then turned back to her. "What are you looking at?"

Keri kept her eyes fixed on her beloved as his apparition faded. She saw Angela's mouth moving in her peripheral vision, and the pirate seemed to be speaking to her, but Keri couldn't hear what she said.

Tony's ghost faded, and a loud rattling replaced the silence as Hurricane Karl tried to shatter the fragile glass. Bailey stood at the precipice of the small platform. The henchmen pushed her through the opening, exposing her to the storm's fury.

"What about our deal? The journal for Bailey's life?" Keri pleaded.

The pirate stared at Keri, then brought her eyes again to the ring she wore around her neck. Angela stepped closer and took Keri's necklace in her hand and yanked it from her neck.

"Well, how romantic. A string of numbers engraved on the inside. Wonder what they mean?"

Keri shrugged.

Angela grinned. "The remaining coordinates, perhaps."

Keri's startled reaction gave her away.

"Now I don't need the journal anymore."

"Wait!" Keri yelled. "I've already found the gold."

Angela glared at Keri. "You're lying," she scowled.

"I can prove it," Keri said desperately. "Just reach in my right pocket."

With his boss's approval, the man holding Keri retrieved the gold medallion Tony had given her and flipped it to Angela. She studied it carefully, clearly surprised by this new development. She stepped closer.

"Where did you get this?" she demanded.

"Tony gave it to me."

"So, he did find the treasure after all," she murmured.

"Yes, and he told me where it's buried. I've moved it to a safer location."

The pirate-lady scowled again. Bailey tried to come back inside, but the goon blocked the doorway and shoved her back. Bailey screamed, thoroughly drenched now.

"Get her off there," Keri cried out as panic jolted her body.

"Tell me where the gold is, or your friend will die," Angela demanded.

With every scrap of courage she had left, Keri looked directly into the villain's eyes and said, "NO! Let us go, and I'll show you."

She hoped Thomas had told her the truth and that his sister was equally motivated by money and not just a twisted understanding of the Day of the Dead.

Angela turned the coin over, then yelled to her stooge, "Bring her in."

Just then, a strong gust of wind hit Bailey. She slid to the right and clutched the railing, which broke off under the strain.

"Nooooo!" Keri screamed. She could hardly breathe now. Another bolt flashed, revealing a vacant platform. Bailey was gone.

CHAPTER 46

Go Out Swinging

"You two, go see if you can find her," the pirate ordered. "I've got this one."

The underlings hurried down the stairs as Angela loomed over Keri, now slumped on the floor in a daze.

Keri stared vacantly out the door, her gaze fixed on the spot where Bailey had stood just a moment before. *How could things go so wrong? I screwed up this time.* Tears spilled freely. *Please be alive.* Though unlikely that Bailey survived, Keri couldn't accept the reality in front of her.

The wind grew quiet again. Keri felt herself slipping into that quiet realm beyond hurricanes and the reach of tragic losses.

She felt a nudge on her left shoulder as Angela pushed her with one foot. The effect snapped Keri out of her numbed state.

Keri looked up at her nemesis and lusted for revenge, a feeling she welcomed over the endless torture of unresolved grief. Her body, however, felt like a lead-filled bag. She didn't think about her survival now, but wondered how to take the pirate lady with her. She imagined Angela going over the railing instead of Bailey.

Let's see you come back from that dead, red.

"So, where's your portal? Where?" Keri spat in a cold, stern voice.

The pirate shot her a warning glance.

"Where's your mom? I don't see her."

Angela leaned down and glared. "Shut up!"

"You can't cross over or bring anyone back. You're just a sick psycho!"

Angela lifted Keri to a standing position like a rag doll about to be shredded by a rabid beast. The only thing holding Keri upright now was the force with which her attacker had pinned her against the window.

"Tell me what I want to know, or you will join her."

Strangely, Keri felt numb. The threat seemed more like an invitation. Maybe Tony was there too. "Promises, promises," Keri taunted.

The pirate gave her doll a violent shake. "Answer me!"

Keri didn't comply. Her attacker spun her around and slammed her against the glass. Though Keri's face hit hard enough to leave a bloodstain on the window, she barely felt the force of the impact.

The marauder yelled something, but she might as well have been miles away. Keri had returned to that quiet space again. This time she saw a faint blue glow on the water's surface. Or was it just below? She couldn't tell from here. She blinked, thinking the light might be a last desperate vision in the moments before certain death, or an illusion from the blow to her head. Its glow remained clear and beckoning. A tranquility replaced the feelings of resignation. Courage surged in her with force more powerful than the tropical storm raging outside. The window moved away from her slightly, then her face slammed into it again, leaving a fresh bloodstain behind. Keri felt like she was in a movie theater with a front-row seat, watching this happen to someone else. Surprisingly, she felt no pain.

Then Keri heard Clem's voice, crisp and clear as if they were visiting on her houseboat.

"Go out swinging," he said.

As if channeling her Navy SEAL protector, she stepped back between her attacker's legs and twisted her body, freeing her arm. Pulling hard against her enemy's leg, she leaned backward with all her might. She not only broke free, but the motion toppled them off balance. As they fell, Keri turned, delivering an elbow with all her strength directly to the woman's face, just as Clem had taught her. Angela landed hard on her back, the breath knocked from her. Keri heard the satisfying thud of her attacker's head connecting with the floor and saw blood splash from her nose.

"I'm not going anywhere!" Keri said. With considerable effort, she rose to her feet. This time, she looked down on Angela.

Dazed, Keri rushed onto the platform. A gust from Karl nearly blew her overboard. Shards of rain beat against her with stinging pricks. She grabbed onto the remaining railing to keep from falling into the sea. Thankfully, it held. She scanned the waters for any sign of Bailey but spotted none. She hoped against all odds that Bailey had somehow survived the fall. Even so, one could tread water only so long in a storm like this. The swells must be ten or twenty feet.

Hang on, my friend.

Keri turned to make her way back inside, only to find Angela rushing toward her. Rage blazed in the pirate's eyes as she attacked. Keri had dreaded this moment. There was no place to hide and no friends to save her, just the two of them in a final standoff.

Instinctively, Keri twisted her body, hoping to use Angela's own momentum to deflect the attack. The maneuver worked, mostly. The pirate landed hard, her back hitting the remaining railing. The supports buckled under the impact but held firm. Angela grimaced in pain and fell to a half-sitting position.

Keri felt a sharp pain in her lower left side that drove her to one knee. She noticed the blood-stained knife in the pirate's hand and realized Angela had stabbed her. Keri looked down at a growing blood stain on her shirt. Pulling the fabric aside, she saw her vital life fluid spilling from the cut. Keri put her hand over the wound. The blade had penetrated the outer edge of her side but, as far as Keri could tell, hadn't punctured any vital organs.

Slowly, Angela managed to get back on her feet. Still brandishing her knife, she stood tall despite the fierce wind and pelting rain, as if she'd now partnered with the hurricane and had become part of Karl's plan to finish her off. Keri tried to stand, to at least face her attacker on her feet, then doubled over in pain. Angela smiled slightly.

Keri considered retreating inside, but in her current condition, Angela would overtake her in a few steps, long before she could reach the stairwell. Keri thought of rolling over the side. That would be easy since most of the railing had disappeared when Bailey fell. She wouldn't survive this one, but at least she'd go out on her terms. Then, Clem's voice echoed again. *Go out swinging.* Her path became clear.

I'm gonna take you with me, Keri concluded. She'd only have one chance. Keep her eyes fixed on the knife, trying to avoid a fatal blow. When Angela attacked, she'd pull them both into the raging sea.

Keri leveled a defiant glare at the pirate. Still on one knee, she glared and said, "Bring it! You crazy bitch!"

Angela looked confused, but that quickly changed to fury. She stepped forward, moving in for the kill. Then Keri heard a creaking sound followed by a pop, and suddenly both were weightless. The platform had given way.

CHAPTER 47

The Portal

Keri slammed into the Gulf. The right side of her head and right shoulder hit first. Her legs followed at a greater angle, causing her right foot to impact with a slap. Pain shot up her leg, and she yelped, releasing precious oxygen bubbles. Like before, when she had been knocked off the B&B, the current tossed and rolled her. Only this time, she kept her sense of which way was up. She quickly swam to the surface. She gasped a desperate breath, and the pain in her lungs subsided as the fresh air filled them.

"Bailey!" she yelled, but the howl of the hurricane drowned her cry. She took a deep breath and dived. The wound in her side protested with every stroke of her arms. She saw no sign of her best friend or the woman who had just tried to kill them.

"Bailey!" she yelled again, forgetting she was underwater.

She surfaced and cried out, "Come on! Give me a break!"

Diving again, she frantically searched in the dark, churning waters, but no Bailey.

Keri felt on the verge of uncontrollable tears, but it would do no one any good if she lost control right now. She treaded the swells, composing herself as best as she could. She wouldn't be able to save Bailey, assuming her friend was still alive, if she didn't attend to her own safety.

The rig stood about twenty-five yards off to her left, holding its ground against the storm. Under normal circumstances, Keri could easily swim that far. The conflicting currents would make that the equivalent effort of fifty yards at least. Then she had to be careful that a wave didn't smash her into one of the pylons. Her injury, however, made swimming next to impossible. Even if she reached the rig, another threat lurked beneath the surface. Oil rigs often acted like artificial reefs attracting smaller fish, which lured the bigger ones looking for food. She'd heard more than one account of sharks even feeding off the organic waste these operations dumped into the ocean. Now she was the wounded, bleeding prey. Keri would have to fight Karl and avoid the sharks to get to safety. Then, how safe would she be in a pirate's hideout?

What choice do I have? Get back to the rig, she told herself. *Then hide till help arrives.*

The dock underneath the platform rocked and bobbed as the waves tossed it like a toy. Amazingly, the B&B hung on, still attached where she'd moored it. While a comforting sight, the craft wasn't any help without fuel.

Surely these pirates had stashed some gas somewhere. Otherwise, they'd be stuck out here too.

Then she noticed the other two watercraft were gone. Either the storm had blown them away, or the goons were searching for Bailey or their boss. Her stomach twisted tighter at the thought of Bailey in these waters. She pushed the feeling down, focusing on her immediate survival.

A wave crashed over her head, dousing her. She swam toward the dock, aiming for a path between the concrete towers. The pain slowed her down, but she kicked and pulled as hard as she could till her arms and legs ached, forcing her to pause and catch her breath. She could hardly tell if she had made any progress.

Then she saw a large object cresting a swell. She recognized the watercraft from before, one of Angela's flunkies straddling the seat. The momentum of the wave had catapulted his craft into the air. From her vantage point, he looked like an incoming missile whose trajectory would land him on top of her. There was no time to paddle out of the way. Instead, she took a breath and dove to avoid being crushed. She heard the slapping, booming sound of the craft smashing into the ocean, then a louder thump as the hull made contact with her head. The impact scraped her so hard she felt a sharp pain, followed by numbness on one side of her ribs. All went dark.

She dreamed she was swimming, struggling to reach the surface. Her lungs ached for air. Just then, her right shoulder and the right side of her face felt cooler. The pinpricks of hard-driving rain awakened her. She had floated back to the surface. Head throbbing and dazed, she struggled to get her bearings.

She saw her attacker floating about ten or fifteen yards away, now joined by a second henchman riding the other watercraft. They seemed to be talking to one another, but she couldn't understand what they were saying. Both shined flashlights along the surface, and a bright light suddenly blinded her eyes.

"There she is!" one of the men shouted. The two watercraft turned, heading right toward her. She wouldn't survive another blow, and she couldn't out-swim them.

Exhaustion overwhelmed Keri. She didn't have any fight left. She listened for Clem's encouraging voice but only heard the howling, indifferent wind. She looked for a vision of Tony but instead saw the henchman leaning forward on his watercraft, aiming to run her over.

Keri leaned back, trying to make herself a less visible target. Glancing up, she saw not even one twinkling star. Darkness had fully enveloped her. Even Mother Nature seemed to be working for her demise. As the craft got closer, she pulled her knees to her chest, closed her eyes, and took a full breath.

The impact of the hull stung her feet and shot pain up to her knees. Even so, as soon as it hit, she pushed off with both legs as hard as she could. Agony tore through her body. It was all she could do not to scream underwater. At first, she wondered if she had broken her legs or further torn the wound in her side. Finally, the torment eased. The deeper she descended, the warmer the water seemed and the more peaceful she felt inside.

The roar of Hurricane Karl had faded. A serene melancholy came over her as she surrendered to the depths. For Keri, this wasn't suicide but simply the final act of embracing her fate. She would cross over from this world to the next, just as Bailey had pre-dicted, but on her terms, not the victim of demented thugs nor dinner for the mindless predators of the sea. Her lungs began to ache. She didn't paddle for the surface this time.

Slowly, she sank, eyes closed, enveloped by the Gulf. The tension eased in her shoulders. Memories flashed of searching for treasure with her father, laughing and splashing in the bioluminescence of the sea. She saw Tony's smile, which had won her heart at first glance. The ache in her lungs increased. She let some air escape and heard the bubbly sound as they floated away. The violent storm was gone now—no waves crashing on her, no blowing rain stinging her face. For the first time in a very long time, she noticed the longing in her gut had eased, and her sense of grief had lessened. A new world awaited, a new life beyond this one. All she had to do was breathe it in and embrace this undiscovered country. She felt Bailey, her father, Tony, and all her loved ones waiting on the other side. If loved ones came to visit on the Day of the Dead, why couldn't it work both ways? Maybe she would see them? Only this would be a one-way trip.

The instinct to breathe in became overwhelming. Not much longer now. Keri opened her eyes and prepared to inhale, to let the water take the pressure off her lungs and soul forever. Then, through the liquid darkness, she saw a faint blue glow. She almost gasped but held her breath.

Is this the portal that people see when their end time arrives? Maybe an angel had opened a secret window. Strangely, the light didn't have the otherworldly glow she expected. Instead, it seemed more defined, the edges sharper. The wavy silhouettes of several small fish swam across her field of vision, also not something she associated with a portal to heaven. The bluish glow had to come from a real object on this side of life.

She swam toward the mysterious blue glow, her heart swelling with hope, and a reserved strength coursing through her body.

Slowly, she released the remaining air in her lungs to keep from passing out. She pulled and kicked. When she reached the ocean floor, the light grew brighter and seemed to emanate from a small opening in a reef. The hole was large enough for a person to fit through it. She hesitated outside. *What if that hole goes nowhere? And worse, what kind of creature might live in that hole?* There was no time; she couldn't hold her breath any longer. Keri swam inside.

Once through the opening, the light brightened. Feet planted on the sandy bottom, Keri stood. Her head and shoulders emerged into a chamber of air. She inhaled, desperately gulping the oxygen. Aside from a slightly stale smell, she could breathe. She took a few more precious breaths. Just to her left, a steel ladder led up to a platform. The rungs showed the corrosive effects of the saltwater but still held firm. When she looked up, her heart somersaulted.

"Bailey!"

CHAPTER 48

Another World

Keri clambered up onto a grated platform. "You're alive!" she exclaimed, hugging Bailey.

"You're really here." Bailey's voice broke as she spoke. "I thought I was dead." Her hands shook. She squeezed Keri's shoulders as if making sure this was not a dream.

Keri winced and grabbed her wounded side.

"Oh my God! You're hurt!" Bailey exclaimed and pulled Keri's shirt to get a better look.

"Angela got me during our fight," Keri grunted.

"That looks like a knife wound."

"Yep."

"Here, sit down," Bailey helped Keri to a nearby square metal container.

Keri groaned as she sat on the hard surface, the pain worsening.

Bailey began searching the room. "There's got to be a first aid kit around here somewhere."

"How did you get here?" Keri asked.

Bailey stared blankly momentarily, then continued looking for a med kit. "I don't know. I can't remember anything after hitting the water. I felt like I was dreaming, being pulled somewhere. I woke up leaning against that lower railing in this chamber with a terrible head-ache." She looked at Keri. "They must have brought me here."

"What? Who brought you here?"

"Who do you think? Her men," Bailey answered, slightly annoyed. "There's no escape! Haven't you fig-ured that out yet?"

"Those goons didn't bring you here," Keri said. "They're still looking for you on the surface."

Bailey scrunched her brow, puzzled. "I don't under-stand. Are you sure?"

"They just tried to run me over. Yeah, I'm sure."

"Then how did I end up here?"

Keri shrugged.

"No, someone dragged me here," Bailey said. "I felt two arms grab under my shoulders." She paused, then continued, "You think it was Ben and Buddy?"

"No," Keri answered. "I sent them for help."

"Another Hail Mary."

Keri nodded.

"Ah ha!" Bailey exclaimed as she pulled a rectan-gular orange case from underneath a pile of old stuff. "Here it is." Though faded and dirty, it still displayed a white cross on the top. She sat next to Keri and opened it. "We're in luck!"

"So, how did you find me here?" Bailey asked as she tore open a pack of bandages.

"After you fell, Angela sent her minions to search for you. She began roughing me up, forcing me to tell her where the gold was buried. We struggled. I broke free."

"You used that self-defense move Clem taught you." Bailey poured peroxide on the wound.

"Oww," Keri said.

"Sorry."

"It's okay." Keri took a breath and then continued. "So, I ran to the spot where you had gone over, desperate to see if you were alright. She came after me. The platform gave way and sent us both plunging into the Gulf. When I couldn't find you…" Keri's voice choked with tears.

"I feel ya," Bailey said, tearing a piece of medical tape into a small strip. "You need stitches, but this should work as a temporary fix."

Bailey carefully applied the tape across the puncture. Then she positioned some clean gauze over the sealed wound.

"Hold here," Bailey instructed.

Keri held the bandage while Bailey taped it in place.

"I saw the blue glow, just like in your vision," Keri said. "I swam toward it. I figured worse case," then she paused. "I figured, worse case, I'd meet you and Tony on the other side." Her tone had changed to nearly a whisper.

They exchanged a long soulful look between them.

Bailey hugged Keri. "I love you too, my friend."

"I love you back." Keri looked down at the patchwork. "Good job, Doctor."

"Hopefully, that will stop the bleeding till we can get you to a hospital," Bailey said.

"I thought I was a goner. The light did lead to another world, and thankfully not the afterlife."

"I flicked this switch over there," Bailey said. "And this bay lit up."

"Your timing is miraculous," Keri commented. "Amazing that the batteries still have any juice. Assuming that's the power source."

"What is this place?" Bailey asked. "It looks old."

"Seems to be part of an underwater station, though you'd never know it from the outside. It looked like some kind of reef." Keri wasn't certain whether that was intentional, or mother nature slowly absorbing this structure over time.

Remnants of dive equipment lined the walls—air tanks, old masks, a set of fins, even a wet suit top.

"How come this ain't flooded?" Bailey asked.

"This structure is somehow still pressurized. That's what creates this bubble that's allowing us to breathe. What are the other rooms like?" Keri asked.

"I don't know. There's a door over there," Bailey said, pointing. "I was trying to open it when you showed up."

Keri attempted to stand, but a sharp stabbing pain from her wound compelled her to sit back down quickly. "Whoa," she said, catching her breath.

"Maybe you should sit tight. I'll go exploring," Bailey said.

Keri nodded her agreement.

Bailey walked to the valve lever that seemed to operate a heavy door. She pulled it downward. Nothing, no movement.

"It's jammed," Bailey said.

Keri grabbed her side, rocked forward, and pushed with her free hand. Searing discomfort shot up her left side as she stood. She gasped and leaned against the wall.

Bailey rushed to her friend's side. "Hey, take it easy!"

The stinging ache in Keri's laceration lessened. "Just give me a minute. We need to get through that door."

Together they pulled on the handle.

The latch remained locked despite their best efforts.

"Neither of us is at a hundred percent," Bailey said.

Keri surveyed the room. "We need some leverage. Look for something to pry this open."

Bailey found a steel pipe lying nearby. They placed it between the handle and the door.

"Wait," Bailey said. "What if the other room is flooded, and that's why we can't open it?"

Keri considered that momentarily, then said, "Well, there's only one way to find out."

The women strained against the steel lever, pulling with all their strength. A grating sound, and the door handle moved from horizontal to perpendicular. The hatch slid sideways a few inches with a loud clang and hiss of air, but no water.

Keri bent over and breathed in deeply.

"Hey, you alright?" Bailey asked.

Keri looked at her friend. "Not really," she said. "But I'll make do." Taking another breath, Keri scooted into the small opening and pushed while Bailey pulled. The door opened all the way. They stepped into a galley with a sink. Keri steadied herself against a rectangular table attached to a wall on her left, just under a porthole. A small desk nook sat on their right—loose papers covered the top, along with dated computers and old electronic equipment.

"This is an underwater research lab," Keri said. "At least it used to be." She carefully sat on the bench next to the table.

High shelves near the ceiling still held some packaged, ready-to-eat food. Bailey grabbed an unopened can of nuts and brushed the debris from the lid.

"I'm surprised it's so dusty down here," Bailey said as she tore open the seal.

"The dust is most likely paint particles," Keri replied.

Bailey grabbed a handful of nuts and passed the can to her friend. Keri crunched on the salty snack, surprised they had any crispness. The expiration date had passed a long time before.

Bailey sat heavily in a chair beside the desk and leaned on her elbows, shoulders slumping. She seemed completely exhausted and on the verge of tears. "I can't believe we escaped," she said.

Keri couldn't reason how they had managed to survive and somehow end up still breathing in another world at the bottom of the Gulf. "Well, we're not home free, but at least we're not on the rig anymore."

"Thank God for this place, whatever it is."

"Amen to that. Where's a good blender when you need one?"

Bailey smiled. "Make mine a double."

Keri stopped eating when she saw a faded picture attached to the cabinet.

"What is it?" Bailey asked.

Keri took the photo and stared at it. She blinked and shook her head. "It's me!"

CHAPTER 49

Going Blue

The faded image captured Keri as a kid building sandcastles with her father. She showed the photograph to Bailey.

"That's my dad and me at Johnson's Beach. I must have been five or six."

"What's a picture of you and your father doing here?"

Keri looked puzzled and dazed. She scanned the room for any other connection with her father. Glancing back at the doorway they had just entered, she saw the words 'Going Blue' painted in indigo letters on the wall above the opening. She gasped.

"Going Blue! Isn't that what your dad used to say?" Bailey asked.

"Yes, he did," Keri answered. Curiosity overrode the pain from her wound as she stood and stepped toward the words.

Keri suddenly yearned to see her father again, even as she felt comforted. It seemed that her dad had saved her life just now with something he had created years ago.

"My dad built this place."

"What? Wow!" Bailey said. "So, this is what he meant by 'going blue.' "

Choked with emotion, Keri smiled and nodded.

"He was going to bring you here?" Bailey asked.

"Maybe he did," Keri whispered. She felt her father's presence, looking after them. *You still have my back.*

Composing herself, Keri continued. "Dad helped design the early underwater sea labs, even the Aquarius." She could tell that Bailey had never heard of that project. Why would she have? "He promised to take me to one, but we never got to it before he died." She sighed. "I think this was the one he'd intended to show me."

Keri felt five years old again as she marveled at her father's work. From sandcastles to sea labs. She pointed to another large door just past the gallery. "Wanna see what's behind door number two?"

The two friends pulled a similar lever and again heard a loud clink of metal as the hatch unlocked. This one opened more easily. They stepped into a bunk room that could sleep four, two bunk beds stacked on each side. An oversize porthole capped off the room. It formed a large bubble seat, providing a broad underwater view like a giant aquarium. Keri flipped a switch near the large window, turning on an outside floodlight. Visibility was near zero, and not just from the darkness. Karl was kicking up a lot of debris.

It must be breathtaking when there's no storm.

Most bolt fittings had rusted, and water dripped around several seals. Then she noticed the pillow on the top left bunk bulging as if covering something. Keri looked underneath and found a water-tight cylinder. She opened one end. Several pens, a compass, and some loose notes spilled into her hand, along with the ends of several rolled-up documents protruding from the tube. Keri emptied the contents onto one of the lower mattresses. Unfurling the papers, she discovered meticulously, professionally drawn maps of the Perdido Key area. Notes had been scribbled in the margins and other places.

Keri inhaled sharply. "This is Tony's handwriting!"

"Tony was here?"

"I don't know, but that's his writing."

"Look, there's something else in the container," Bailey said, pulling out a laminated sheet of old-looking paper.

Keri unrolled it and laid it atop the stack. "This can't be."

"Looks like a map."

"Yes, it's a map—a very old one. If this is what I think it is, we have found it!"

"Found what?"

"Max said an older map, more antique than the one hanging in the diner, contains missing information that would lead right to the lost shipwreck, the *Generosidad*! I believe this is that map!"

"This is extraordinary!" Bailey exclaimed. "You sure it's real?"

"Oh, it's genuine, alright. It has to be," Keri said. "Why else would Tony hide it here?" Tears glistened as she looked at Bailey, who nodded her understanding. Keri had found something far more valuable than lost gold. These things represented a link to Tony.

"So, what's next?"

Keri began packing the items back into the protective case. "We wait for Karl to pass, then we get out of here and find this treasure!"

"Sounds good, but I'll settle for just getting out of here."

"Absolutely," Keri said as she slung the case over her shoulder. "We'll gather the…"

They heard a loud smack and clinking sound.

"What was that?" Bailey asked.

Keri pointed to the bubble window in the bunk room. "Look! Something hit the glass!"

Water seeped from an impact point just off the center. Three large fractures spread in jagged directions, with random smaller ones stretching from the main branches.

"The cracks are growing!" Bailey said.

"The window isn't gonna hold much longer. We gotta get out of here."

They heard a crinkling sound followed by pop as water pressure forced a small opening at the point where the debris had struck. The trickle of water quickly became a steady stream, then a strong gush as more of the glass gave way. The water rose to over ankle-deep in seconds as the ocean spilled into the chamber.

"Come on," Keri yelled. "We need to seal this room."

They stepped back into the galley and together shut the door, closing off the bunk room just as a loud bang shook the entire structure. Ocean water had spilled over the lower rim and covered the galley floor already rising above the tops of their feet.

"The window must have fully collapsed," Keri stated.

An air vent under the porthole shot off its rusted screws as the ocean poured through like ten fire hoses.

Both women slipped as the rushing water knocked them off their feet. Keri scrambled to her knees in the rising tide. Bailey had managed to stand up.

"You okay?" Keri asked.

"Yeah," Bailey answered.

Keri noticed the water had also crested the lip of the big door.

"We have to leave, and fast!" Keri yelled.

They waded back to the diving bay. "I saw some scuba gear; maybe it still works."

They sloshed around, checking the tanks along the wall. One had rusted out completely, and the others had no air left. The water reached waist level now.

"Damn it!" Keri yelled. "Is the whole universe against us?"

"Look for a life jacket!" Bailey shouted.

Keri took a breath and dipped down, the saltwater stinging her eyes. She found nothing that would support them on the open water.

Surfacing, she said, "I don't see anything that will float."

"I found one," Bailey yelled, holding a faded orange vest.

A quarter of it was missing, like something had ripped the padding away. The rest felt squishy to the touch.

"It'll have to do," Keri said. "We gotta swim for the surface. Take a few deep breaths and don't forget to—"

Her sentence was cut off by a loud pop and sizzling sounds, followed by various electric sparks, then darkness as the hurricane flooded their habitat.

The sudden rush of water filled every inch of space and knocked them against the far wall. Keri held her eyes wide open against the sting of the saltwater but could see nothing in the darkness. Caught by surprise, she hadn't completed her preparation, and already her lungs ached. She frantically searched for Bailey, paddling till something bumped her leg. Keri reached but found only water. Then she felt a hand grab her arm. The edge of a life vest brushed her side.

Bailey!

Her friend was alive and moving, but neither would be if they didn't get out quickly.

Lord, help us.

Just then, a faint blue glow filled the room. Keri saw Bailey looking back at her. The light emanated from outside the entrance of the diving bay. Keri wondered if it could be from another diver, which seemed highly unlikely.

Probably some form of bioluminescence.

Whatever the cause, the light lit the way out. Bailey swam through first. Keri followed closely.

Once outside, a blue glow surrounded them, the light emanating from bioluminescent plankton. Keri wanted to scoop a handful and take it with her. Strange to have such fleeting thoughts when you're fighting for your life. Then she saw the life vest floating in front of her. Bailey had dropped it, paddling in a frenzied swim for the surface. *She must be desperate for air.* Keri grabbed the preserver, hooked it on her shoulder, and headed after her friend. She guessed their depth at thirty-five feet, maybe a little more, which meant they should be able to swim to the surface with no decompression stops.

Suddenly, Bailey stopped paddling. Her arms and legs jerked and twitched oddly for a few seconds, then went limp. Motionless, she began to sink.

"Noooo!" Bubbles encapsulated Keri's scream.

She frantically swam to Bailey, hooked one arm around her friend, and pulled with the other toward the surface. Keri felt her chest might explode if she didn't take a breath. She fought against her instinct to inhale, and the searing pain from her wound, and kept swimming. Feeling light-headed, her limbs increasingly heavy, Keri kept her eyes focused on the dim light of the surface. The edges of her vision grew dark, and the periphery seemed to be collapsing as if she were swimming through a tunnel. She closed her eyes, unable to hold them open as Bailey slipped from her grasp. The night sea had been replaced with the image of a bright sunny day. She recognized the location. *How did I get to Johnson's Beach?* Keri saw her dad kneeling near the water a little ways in the distance. His face beamed when he spotted her as if he'd seen an angel. He waved her over and then began filling a plastic bucket with sand. Keri smiled and took a deep breath.

CHAPTER 50

Trust the Light

Fresh air filled Keri's lungs, and energy surged through her body. She opened her eyes to find herself no longer on the sandy beaches of home with Dad, but in the watery clutches of Karl. She concluded that the good half of the life jacket must have floated her to the surface. *But how? That old thing couldn't support both of us.*

"Bailey! Where are you?" she yelled into the wind, but no answer and no sign of Bailey.

Leaving the vest topside, Keri inhaled sharply and dove. The bioluminescence still provided some faint light, enough for her to see the shadowy outline of her friend floating about ten feet below. She swam down and pulled Bailey to the surface.

"Come on, girlfriend. Don't you die on me now!"

She laid Bailey on her back and placed the preserver underneath for whatever buoyancy it could provide. A wave splashed over them. Keri had never attempted resuscitation while still in the water, and certainly not while bobbing helplessly in a hurricane, but she had no choice. She put two fingers on her friend's neck. Bailey still had a pulse, but that wouldn't last long if she didn't start breathing soon. Keri took a breath and maneuvered herself underneath. She wrapped both arms around Bailey's upper abdomen, clasped her hands together, and pulled inward several times, trying to expel the water from Bailey's lungs. When she surfaced, Bailey still wasn't breathing.

"Come on!" Keri yelled.

Pulling Bailey's chin down to open her mouth, Keri tilted her friend's head back and gave Bailey several breaths. Then, submerging again, she repeated the abdomen compressions. Bailey's body jerked to life. Keri heard coughing and surfaced.

"Oh, thank God!" Keri exclaimed.

Bailey began to tread water on her own. "What happened?"

"You scared the hell out of me, that's what happened," Keri exclaimed, then hugged her friend. "I almost lost you, girl."

She gave Bailey the life vest. "Here, you take this for a while."

Bailey coughed a few times but seemed alert, her breathing becoming easier.

Keri spotted the oil platform about a hundred yards farther away.

"Crap! The current is pushing us away from the rig," she said.

No watercraft were tied to the dock. That meant Angela's henchmen were still looking for her, and they had either taken her ride, or the hurricane had trashed it.

That's just great. Keri slapped the water. Then she slowed her arms and legs to conserve energy.

Keri pointed toward the structure. "We gotta swim for it."

A wave crashed over Bailey, temporarily submerging her below the surface. She popped up and shook her head, whipping her hair away from her face. "I'll try."

"Swim on your back, keep your face toward the sky," Keri directed, doing her best to be strong for both of them.

They paddled and kicked as the turbulent sea splashed and batted them, and the rain beat down. After their arms and legs reached an unbearable ache, they took a break to assess their progress. They had drifted farther away.

Bailey had fallen about ten yards behind, and seemed to be struggling.

"Hey! Stay with me," Keri said.

Bailey shook her head. "I'm just so tired."

Keri swam over. "Lean back." She got behind Bailey's head, hooking one arm under her shoulders like a lifeguard pulling someone ashore. Ignoring the stabs of pain from her knife wound, she swam with one arm and kicked both feet, trying to reach the dock again. When her arm ached to exhaustion, she let go of Bailey, and they both floated as best they could manage.

"The current is too strong," Keri said.

Bailey lifted the vest slightly out of the water. "This thing doesn't work anymore."

The preserver looked heavy, as if it had become a sponge absorbing the ocean instead of repelling it. Long past its expiration date, the safety device had lost its ability to keep anyone afloat. Now it would just drag them under. Bailey let go of the jacket, and it sank.

"Where's the rescue team when you need them?" Keri asked.

"The who?"

"Last time I faced this pirate, Mark, Cricket, and Max came to my rescue at the last minute. They'd all be here now if they knew where to find us. Clem too."

Bailey looked around, then at Keri. "We're not gonna make it, are we?"

"I don't know."

"Yes, you do."

Keri didn't say anything at first. Her friend was right. They were both fresh out of ideas and running out of energy. Keri thought she might last longer than Bailey. Despite being stabbed, she was a stronger swimmer, and she wasn't recovering from drowning. However, she couldn't keep them afloat nor bear to watch Bailey succumb to their fate, which seemed all but assured.

"What's that?" Bailey yelled. Panic filled her eyes.

Keri turned and saw a gray dorsal fin swimming erratically toward them. The fin moved past, then circled back.

"Is that your dolphin friend?" Bailey asked.

"It's a shark," Keri said. "It's a damn shark."

The women paddled backward while keeping the predator in their sights. Their efforts didn't matter. They couldn't gain any distance. Exhausted, they had to stop swimming and tread water. The gray fin of the beast still accompanied them, visible between the waves, then a second one emerged.

"Behind you!" Bailey yelled. "It's another one."

Keri's heart thumped in fear to see this one was even larger than the first.

"I can't believe this!" Bailey cried.

"There are probably more," Keri said. "Sharks gather around oil rigs." She touched her wound. "And I'm bleeding."

The marine biologist knew that shark attacks were not that common. Humans weren't naturally on their diet. But with blood in the water, they might not figure that out till it was too late. Keri tried to ignore the thought of their jagged razor-sharp teeth biting into her side.

A bright blinding light suddenly fixed on them, obscuring any vision of who might be shining it. The beam rose and fell with the waves, becoming visible again with each crest.

"Someone found us! We're rescued." Bailey began waving her arms. "Hey! Over here!"

Keri pulled her friend's arm down. "Stop waving. It's them. They were looking for me when I swam down to you at the lab."

The glare was moving closer.

"They're gonna try and run us over," Keri said.

"Let's just surrender. It's better than being eaten by some mindless fish."

Keri shook her head. "They're not here to bring us back."

"NO! No, no, no!" Bailey protested and cried.

Tears spilled from Keri's eyes. "I'm so sorry."

"It's not your fault. I hate that you're caught up in this."

"When they took you, they snatched both of us."

The blazing orb of light approached, and the sharks circled as the two young women floated helplessly in the ocean like Karl's playthings. The hurricane, the predators, and the pirates had cut off all avenues of escape.

"You're right," Keri said. "We're not gonna make it."

"You've given me an incredible gift," Bailey said, her voice cracking. "I'll die knowing I was loved."

"I do love you, my friend," Keri said in a broken voice.

"I love you too… friends forever."

"Absolutely."

A blue glow appeared below about ten or fifteen feet down. Keri felt a warm melancholy. Strange, but the turbulent water once again seemed peaceful and welcoming. They had done everything they could and fought hard with all their strength. They still had one final choice.

Keri pulled Bailey close and said, "Look, see the glow in the water?" She glanced down at the bioluminescence and then looked lovingly into Bailey's eyes. "Let's go blue."

Bailey's face contorted in an expression of angst. "You don't mean… I don't want to die."

"Me neither," Keri said, shaking her head. "I'm saying, let's follow the light."

Bailey's eyes darted frantically. She seemed scared and confused.

"It's been guiding us, Bailey. I don't know how or why. But it seems our only option is to trust it."

"Are we just supposed to hold our breath till we're rescued?"

"I can't explain it. This can't be a coincidence. Let's trust the light."

Bailey nodded her approval, as if she understood at some intuitive level. They both took a breath and pushed themselves underwater. Holding hands, they let out a steady stream of air and slowly descended, then hugged each other tightly as they floated in the mysterious glow. Keri took some comfort that if this were the end, the last sensation she would feel on this side of life was the love of her friend.

As she opened her eyes one final time, the grip of a thousand hands suddenly surrounded them both, pulling their bodies sideways and upward. The two friends tried to swim but were so completely encapsulated they could hardly move. They broke the surface and continued their climb, floating in the air now. Pelted by the rain, Keri realized they had been caught in a large fishing net attached to a long mast. No longer blinded by the glare, they could see the familiar face of a dear friend standing tall on the deck.

"Matilda!" Keri yelled. Relief flooded through her as tears of joy spilled down her cheeks.

"Gotcha!" the shrimp boat captain whooped, loud and celebrating. The other crewman cheered as well.

"Oh, thank you, God!" Bailey gasped, and she, too, broke down.

"You got that right," Keri echoed.

The crew carefully maneuvered the net as the boat pitched and swayed. After several attempts, they gently lowered them to the deck, bringing the precious cargo safely aboard. Keri and Bailey sat up, stunned by their good fortune.

Matilda walked over, towering, hands on her hips, wild red hair flying in all directions. She leaned down with a look that would make a hurricane turn the other way.

"Now, where's that damn pirate?"

CHAPTER 51

Day of the Dead

"Well, we dodged a close one there," Keri's continuously playing radio announced. "The eye of Karl has moved well inland and the storm has been officially downgraded to tropical wave. For those celebrating the Day of the Dead, this evening will be mild and beautiful, a perfect time for remembering your loved ones."

Keri lounged on the deck of her houseboat and stared at Tony's shrine. Bailey and Clem had helped her set it up, and she had invited them to join her for remembrances. The small table of candles, photos, and sugar skulls didn't compare to the more festive celebrations this day, but they had spent most of the day at the hospital being treated for their wounds and questioned by the police. Finally discharged and exhausted, Keri just wanted a quiet evening with a couple of dear friends. She reached for the engagement ring she usually wore around her neck, but it was gone. She still had trouble reconciling herself to the fact that the pirate had taken the necklace from her, a personal, sacred reminder of Tony now stolen.

"I'm still mad at you," Clem said.

Keri looked away from his reprimanding stare. She glanced at Bailey sitting in the lounge next to her.

"I'm also damn proud of you," he added.

Feeling a flood of relief, Keri looked at her mentor.

"That was the bravest thing I've ever seen," the veteran proclaimed, half smiling.

"She saved my life," Bailey added.

Keri still couldn't believe their good fortune. "I really thought it was the end," she said solemnly.

"Your Hail Mary worked," Bailey said. "Those dolphins led Matilda right to us."

"Maybe one of them will find my necklace," Keri said. "Or that container we found with Tony's notes inside."

"The most important thing is that y'all are alive," the veteran stated.

Both women nodded.

"That's for sure," Bailey added.

"Please don't put yourselves in harm's way like that again. I'm a tough ol' Navy SEAL, and I've survived unspeakable horrors, but losing you two… that would break me."

Keri leaned up and said, "Don't worry, we won't. I promise."

Clem frowned. "Mmm-hmmm. I've heard that before."

Keri caught Bailey grinning at Clem as though they shared a secret.

"What's going on?" Keri asked.

"Come on. We'll show you," Clem answered. He stood and motioned toward the dock.

Keri saw the surprise immediately—a brand new watercraft. Slightly larger than her old one, it had a dolphin painted along one side and the name Ben underneath it.

"Wow!" Keri exclaimed as she ran to the craft and hopped on board. A second dolphin and the name Buddy adorned the other side, and on the back, below the seat, the letters B&B.

Keri couldn't stop smiling. "A new B&B! I don't know what to say. How did you guys do this?"

"Oh, it wasn't just us," Clem answered. "The whole town pitched in."

"We were going to give it to you to celebrate your new promotion at the university, but considering our recent adventure, now seemed the best time," Bailey said.

"What?" A warm feeling filled Keri's being. The notion that so many cared surprised and moved her. "But—"

"Oh, don't go analyzing," Bailey interrupted. "You're loved, girlfriend. Just accept it."

"Wow," Keri whispered.

"Slide back. I'm gonna take you for a ride this time," Bailey said with a wink at Clem.

Keri had long passed the point of just being tired. She felt she could sleep for a week. "Oh, I'm not up for a ride tonight. How about tomorrow?"

"Come on, I think you'll enjoy this."

Reluctantly, Keri scooted back, and Bailey jumped on board. The craft eased forward, smoothly and powerfully, as they headed toward Perdido Bay.

"So, where we goin'?" Keri asked.

"You'll see."

As they passed the no-wake zone, Bailey opened up the throttle. The new B&B rode noticeably faster than her old watercraft, and the waves didn't seem as rough.

The sun had already retired for the night. Keri figured that the day's last glow would fade in a few minutes.

"It's gonna be dark in a few. Where are you taking me?"

"Be patient. You'll see. But first, you have to close your eyes."

"Why?"

"Just close 'em, please," Bailey said.

Keri closed her eyes as they glided along. A few minutes later, Bailey eased up on the throttle and cut off the engine.

"No peeking," she said.

Keri heard a zipper being pulled open and Bailey fumbling about inside the bag, then the click of a lighter.

"Okay, you can open your eyes now."

Keri saw her friend holding a flat blue candle.

"For Tony," Bailey said, handing the candle to Keri. "And for you. You're not alone."

Keri's heart swelled with love. "Not as long as I have you, my friend."

She took the candle and placed it gently in the water.

"You have so much more," Bailey whispered.

As she watched the flame float away, Keri noticed they had stopped near her lighthouse. A tiny flicker of light appeared in front of her house along the shore, then two more along either side, then two more and again. A line of dancing flames spread in both directions and all along her deck. There must have been a hundred or more people holding candles. Then, a blue running light glowed from a boat on the left and another on the right. Like the candles, boat lights spread in a wide semi-circle on either side of them. Keri's mouth fell open, and tears flowed down her cheeks as the love and light of her community surrounded her.

The water began to glow blue between them and the shore, evoking gasps and murmurs from those gathered for this vigil. The glow lingered and could not have been timelier.

"Do you see him?" Keri said, abruptly standing. "Tony!"

"I see the blue sea sparkles," Bailey answered.

Tony seemed to be standing on the water, surrounded by an aqua-green aura. His vapory image smiled and gazed at Keri like he used to look at her with pure adoration. Despite the tears, Keri kept her eyes locked on this extraordinary vision.

He did come back. Your loved ones really do visit you on the Day of the Dead.

Her heart hurt to see him, but she wouldn't trade this for the world. Tony put both hands on his heart, brought them to his lips, and gently blew her a kiss. Keri returned the kiss as her tears continued to flow. Slowly, he sank into the glowing water as if he were part of the bioluminescence, and the blue light faded.

Keri and Bailey sat in silence, surrounded by the candlelight of the community.

"You okay?" Bailey asked.

"Never better," Keri answered.

She raised her arms high and tilted her head back. "Yessss!" she yelled and then laughed. "Ha ha, yessss!"

Cheers erupted from the crowd as they raised their candles high. Boat horns blasted, and their lights blinked.

"Where did all these people come from?" Keri asked.

"We're a tight-knit community."

Suddenly, hundreds of tiny indigo-colored lights came aglow, attached to Keri's deck and windows. It looked like someone had gone overboard decorating for Christmas, only instead of red and green, they preferred shades of cobalt and azure. Finally, a bright blue beam shined from Keri's lighthouse. It began to move, spreading its radiance in a circular motion.

"Ha! They fixed it!" Bailey exclaimed.

Keri put a hand over her heart. "How did they know?"

"Maybe you should ask her," Bailey said, pointing toward a woman in the crowd.

Keri recognized the soft cheekbones and welcoming expression of Tony's mom. When she saw Keri, she took two steps into the bay, holding her arms outstretched.

Keri jumped off the B&B and sloshed toward this strong, gentle soul, who almost had become her mother-in-law. They embraced, and both cried.

"I'm so sorry," Keri said. "I should've come to see you sooner."

"You're here now, my dear," the loving voice said, and she squeezed Keri tighter. She looked Keri in the eye and said sternly, "You're family. We're always here for you."

The rest of Tony's family joined in the hug, followed by Mark and Cricket. Max winked at her, and Mary blew her a kiss. Keri's mom stood beside Bailey, reveling in the moment before one of Tony's family members pulled them into the group hug.

Keri finally had an answer to the ache that had haunted her for the past three years. How do you live with the unacceptable? *Not by yourself.* She felt the pain of Tony's absence anew, but she didn't feel empty inside for the first time since he had disappeared. Though she would grieve Tony and miss him for the rest of her life, she would no longer be shackled in a prison of isolation. The love of all these people, and a goodbye kiss from Tony, had broken those chains and set her free.

Maybe we did cross through a portal. She felt as if she stood at the precipice of a new life she could have never imagined.

Bailey leaned toward Keri and said, "This is quite a shindig you got goin' on here."

"Yeah," Keri replied, looking over the gathering, which had now become a full-blown party. She wanted to soak up every detail of this night.

"This is going blue."

CHAPTER 52

Time's Up

Matilda's boat bounced along the waves, moving steadily into the Gulf of Mexico. The larger craft crested the swells more smoothly than Keri's new B&B or Cricket's skiff. Keri felt grateful for her friend's help. The midday sun perched high and bright, warming the air enough that a light jacket kept Keri cozy. She loved being on the water during sunny days like this, when you could see where the sky met the ocean, marking the edge of the world in a gray line. She inhaled the crisp and clear air, wishing for more fun reasons for this outing. Two long wooden arms extended from each side of the shrimp boat. Nets had been tightly rolled and secured for their journey. Keri could still feel their roped webbing wrapped around her from when her captain-friend had rescued her and Bailey.

"We're not supposed to be doing this," Keri said.

Clem looked up, unmoved by her comment. Max shrugged his shoulders.

Cricket smiled as if he liked doing things he wasn't supposed to do.

"So, you think the map with Tony's notes is still inside the sea lab?" Max asked.

"It's gotta be," Keri answered. "I had the cylinder slung over my shoulder when the window busted. Water must have knocked it off."

"How do we know the police ain't already got it?" Cricket asked.

"Sheriff Cotton told me the divers aren't going out till tomorrow. They're focused on processing all the evidence on the rig. Since no one thinks Angela knew about Dad's lab, it's not their priority."

"I doubt we'll get close," Clem stated. "The Coast Guard probably has a patrol boat guarding the place."

Matilda appeared in the doorway that led to the bridge. "How y'all doing?"

"Doin' fine, Captain," Cricket said.

The others gestured their agreement.

"Remember, we're just out here shrimping," Matilda ordered. "So y'all better look like you're fishin' or part of my crew." She put her hands on her hips like an exclamation point.

"Best fishin' I know is around a shrimp boat," Cricket said.

"I'll help out with the crew," Max added.

Clem told Keri, "You and I'll get in the water before anyone knows we're on board. You up for that?"

Keri met his stare with her resolve. "You bet I am."

Matilda leaned toward the group. "That means either you'll have a long swim, or I'll be dragging y'all behind the boat."

"Precisely," Clem answered. "Swimming or hitch-hiking, we gotta be underwater and outta sight before we reach the rig."

"Easy for you to say, Navy SEAL," Keri teased.

"Don't worry, you got this," he replied.

Keri felt the confidence of her mentor, which boosted her own.

"Seems like Bailey oughta be here," Cricket said.

"She wanted to come," Keri replied. "Mark and I convinced her to sit this one out. He's planned a fun and safe day for her."

Clem nodded his approval and said, "Good for them."

"I'm worried about her. She doesn't seem quite like the old Bailey," Keri said.

"She's been through a life-and-death trauma," Max stated. "You both have."

Keri took a moment to make eye contact with each one. "I appreciate everyone coming out today."

"Of course," Max said. "We'd have come with you before if you'd told us what you were doing."

"I know, and I'm sorry about running off alone. I was just in a strange place mentally."

"But you're not gonna do that anymore, are you, hon?" Matilda said, her tone both reprimanding and pleading. The sun's glow behind her head made it look like her red hair had caught fire.

"Clem already made me promise I won't," Keri answered. She held the fierce captain's scrutiny. "You have my word, Matilda."

Matilda seemed satisfied with that answer. Then she looked up and frowned. "Uh oh, a patrol spotted us."

Though still a ways off, they could make out a police patrol boat heading toward them.

"Change course. Head straight for that boat and lower the nets!" Matilda barked, pointing in the direction of the oncoming craft. Then she turned to her passengers, "Get ready," she said before stepping through the door and taking the helm.

"Why are we heading straight for them?" Keri asked.

"That'll give you two cover to dive off the back," Max answered.

Clem unzipped a large duffel bag he'd brought on board, retrieving two sets of masks with snorkels attached to one side and two pairs of fins. He handed one pair of each to Keri. Then he draped a black rubber vest around her neck. Two small hoses protruded from each side, attached to a cylinder device with a mouthpiece.

"What in the world ya got there?" Cricket asked.

"It's a rebreather," Clem said. "We used them in the SEALs. They're lighter than normal scuba tanks and emit virtually no bubbles."

"Cool," Cricket said.

"Yep, it sure is," the SEAL replied.

Keri slipped the apparatus over her head and adjusted the straps. Then she bit gently on the mouthpiece and breathed. She looked at Clem and nodded.

"Breathe slow and steady. We got about six hours of air, and the sea lab is not that deep, so we should be fine."

"Look alive, people," Matilda said, poking her head through the door.

Cricket grabbed a fishing pole and quickly baited the hook. When the boat slowed to trolling speed, he cast off the back.

Clem pulled back a tarp near the side, revealing a black oval-shaped device with a propeller at one end.

"This is an underwater scooter. It'll save us some swimming, but I'm not sure if the battery is strong enough to get us back. Just hold on to this handle here on the left."

"Got it," Keri said.

She and Clem finished donning the dive gear and gently lowered themselves into the water off the back platform. Clem motioned for Keri to follow him, and they swam directly underneath the boat, careful to avoid the large nets now deployed.

The metal hull of the patrol boat drifted alongside Matilda's and shut off its engines. Keri could hear the muffled conversation. She breathed effortlessly using the special gear, and just as Clem had said, she saw no bubbles.

The two large motors on the police boat growled to life, and propellers whirred, churning the water and pushing the craft away.

Clem gave Keri a thumbs up, motioned for her to grab a handle on the scooter, and flipped a switch. The propeller spun and pulled them forward.

Wow, this sure beats paddling, Keri thought, remembering the onerous ordeal she and Bailey had just faced. Keri estimated she could see fifty feet or more, especially with no saltwater stinging her eyes this time. The familiar serenity of the ocean returned, but it no longer beckoned her like it had. She didn't want to inhale the water or jet off to the horizon. The absence of those strange compulsions told her that something had changed for the better. She couldn't quite pinpoint any single cause for this progress. The sight of Tony had quenched her pain. Feeling the love of her community had filled her heart. Of course, by successfully rescuing Bailey, she felt like she had saved her own soul. Maybe her peace resulted from all of these things. The fact that she wasn't out here alone, nor trying to be, proved that something had shifted.

Roughly fifteen minutes later, they arrived at the remnants of the sea lab. The underwater station sat deep enough to not be seen from the surface, even on a clear day, like today. Keri could make out the grayish structure covered in barnacles about twenty feet below them. A variety of small fish swam all around it. Keri could see sizable chunks of rubble scattered nearby. She figured they must be old parts of the rig that had collapsed. These nearby fragments could provide more camouflage against radar detection. Anyone searching might conclude the grayish structure was just another piece of the old drilling machinery.

Clem pointed the scooter down. When they reached their destination, he slowly circled the structure. They stopped at a large opening at one end. A few jagged shards of glass protruded around the space—remnants of the bubble window that had collapsed. Keri's stomach tightened as memories of her harrowing experience deluged her.

Clem gave Keri an 'okay' hand signal.

She replied with a thumbs-up.

He detached a long, heavy-duty flashlight from the scooter, then let their small transport gently sink to the bottom. Clem took the lead, clearing away the broken glass as they entered.

Debris floated aimlessly; the rushing water had scattered everything not tied down. They searched from stem to stern but found no sign of the cylinder that carried Tony's notes—no sign of any maps. Keri spotted the picture of her and her father from when she was a girl and tucked it securely in her wet suit.

I suppose it could be outside, perhaps nearby, Keri thought. But that theory didn't seem plausible since the water had pushed everything toward the other end of the lab.

She felt a tap on her shoulder. Clem held his light on the wall and pointed toward it. Her eyes followed the beam till she saw the writing on the metal hull. The scribbles hadn't been there before when she and Bailey were trapped. A small open can of the special underwater paint lay to one side, along with a brush still coated in red. Someone had brought the can in from the dive bay area. Keri blinked and shook her head, trying to process the mysterious graffiti. She inhaled sharply, realizing the message could only be for her eyes. Heart pounding, Keri stared at the words: *Time's up!*

The End

Acknowledgments

It takes a village to write a book, and I could not have completed this one without the support and help of many friends, family, and colleagues. This series began as a fun exploration of writing. As much as books can be love letters, this is a continuing one for my wife, Sherri. She is the inspiration for Bailey and the whole story. Though the characters have taken on a life of their own and would argue their uniqueness and independence, several have been inspired by her life journey. Sherri, without you, these stories wouldn't exist.

I would also like to thank:

Linden Gross, my writing Jedi master. So often, I just wanted to be done. You were steadfast in your encouragement and showing me the actual finish line and all that goes into a well-written book. You continue to push me toward my best writing. Also, Keri Barnum, Lieve Maas, and your whole team are top-shelf. You truly provide a one-stop writing shop. I don't know that I'm a fully trained Jedi yet, but I'm learning more of the ways of the force.

Corie Guzman-Thornton. Your creative journey inspires me to keep writing. Your stunning paintings capture the feel of the Lost Key Mystery series and have made the most beautiful book covers I've ever seen.

My nephew Hunter Hutcheson. We are not only kin but kindred creative spirits. Our weekly calls are sustenance for my creative soul. Producing *Excuse Me Santa* with you is one of the epic experiences of my life. I look forward to more stories and films together!

Kristen Law-Sagafi, my friend and writing sojourner. I'm grateful for your continued encouragement. Your exceptional feedback on the story has helped make these books as much fun as "drinking fizzy cherry soda."

My "Chimps," Alan, Debby, and Sallie. You are my tribe as I transition from the wonderland of executive to the magical world of writer/film producer. I'm grateful for your friendship and collegiality. Y'all keep me connected to my spiritual home.

Kari Mac-Buck, my real-life cousin. You brought inspiration for *Going Blue*'s main character, Keri, and introduced a new one. Matilda would have never found her way to Lost Key without you.

Alexis M. Janosik, a marine biologist from the University of West Florida, whose office is miles of protected gulf coast seashore, you get all the credit for "sea sparkles," a much more delightful description for bioluminescence than the one I originally came up with.

Ron Davidson, you are my spiritual brother and fellow traveler on this life trek. You are a treasure, my friend.

TJ, Cecil, and my Gulf Coast friends for enchanting me with many fun tales of Pensacola's local legends and mysteries of America's "First City."

To the treasure-hunters and enthusiasts of lost gold and pirate adventures. Check out their fun website at treasurenet.com.

The many friends and family who were not surprised at all by this encore career of writing and filmmaking.

Helen Attridge, our friend and life coach, for helping me step through the portal and sit in the captain's chair of my own starship.

Mom and Dad, you made this whole dream possible in so many ways. My love of stories began somewhere in the Storyville of my childhood.

Finally, thank you to Pensacola, a city full of character, a storied history, and haunted by ghosts. Thank you to Perdido (Lost) Key. Though I have taken author liberties with some of the geography and the institutions there, Perdido (Lost) Key is a real place that protects its seashores, loves its sea turtles, and is brimming with that Gulf Coast vibe.

www.ingramcontent.com/pod-product-compliance
Lightning Source LLC
Chambersburg PA
CBHW030529190726
48283CB00006B/1826